BEAUTIFUL STRANGERS

When Cait joins a singles' week in Oxford and realises that there are far more women than men, she resigns herself to the concerts, museum visits and punting with a heavy heart, until a spur-of-the moment decision leads her and fellow party member Ralph to discover a completely different side to the city. Cait falls hopelessly in lust with a younger man, and Ralph ends up pursued by both the police and violent drug-dealers. Searching for Cait and Ralph, Daniel also finds himself caught up in Oxford's exotic parallel universe, with strange consequences that lead him to an idyllic north Wales smallholding...

BEAUTIFUL STRANGERS

BEAUTIFUL STRANGERS

by

Julie Highmore

Magna Large Print Books
Long Preston, North Yorkshire,
BD23 4ND, England.

British Library Cataloguing in Publication Data.

Highmore, Julie
    Beautiful strangers.

    A catalogue record of this book is
    available from the British Library

    ISBN   978-0-7505-2901-3

First published in Great Britain 2007 by Headline Review
an imprint of Headline Publishing Group

Copyright © 2007 Julie Highmore

Cover illustration © Rachel Ross by arrangement with
Headline Publishing Group

The right of Julie Highmore to be identified as the author of this
work has been asserted by her in accordance with the
Copyright, Designs and Patents Act, 1988

Published in Large Print 2008 by arrangement with
Headline Publishing Group Ltd.

Magna Large Print is an imprint of Library Magna Books Ltd.

Printed and bound in Great Britain by
T.J. (International) Ltd., Cornwall, PL28 8RW

For Sue

ONE

Caitlin The porter ticks me off a list and hands me a leaflet and a key. He calls me 'Miss' a lot, then says something about turning right and a staircase two and a room five. I must look blank because he asks his colleague, a younger guy, to help me with my case. We pass Virginia creeper and stone-framed gothic windows, then walk along a shady cloister before turning into a dark hole of an entrance. I can't believe I'm actually staying in this place. When we reach my room, right at the top, I wonder if I should tip, or if that would be seen as crass in an Oxford college.

The leaflet invites me to 'the Hall' at 4 p.m. for 'Afternoon Tea and Introductions'. It sounds a bit formal, but I suppose that's the idea. Since it's only three, I close the curtains, lie on the single bed and stare at the slope of the barley-white ceiling. It had been a disrupted journey from Bangor – cancelled train, long wait for another – and all on a scorching July day. I want to shower but I also want to sleep. Come to think of it, where's the shared bathroom? I should have asked.

This evening we have open-air Shakespeare, which sounded fun and romantic on paper, but now feels like an exhausting obligation. I hope everyone's as knackered as I am. We're all over forty-five, so there's a chance they will be. My eyes close and I think of sitting through an entire play on an uncomfortable chair, possibly in an increasingly nippy evening. *Love's Labour's Lost.* The story of our lives, I'd guess. Why else would we be here?

When I come to, I take in the wardrobe, chest, bed, mirror, wash basin, desk and chair. My room is neat but unexciting. There's lots of corporate dark blue – the chair seat, the bedspread, the curtains – and no indication that students have lived here. I don't know what I was expecting. Tattered books, a quill used by Oscar Wilde. Or just Blu-Tack and the odd sock.

I get up and go in search of the bathroom, looking for other signs of life en route, but finding none. I wonder if I'm the only person in this slightly creepy building, or worse still, the only person on this singles' week.

I'm not. There are about a dozen of us, I discover, once in the Hall. It's an impressive room smelling of polish and housing long tables and paintings galore of men in gowns. A woman labelled 'Gemma' and a man labelled 'Ben', both young and fair-haired, ask us to stand in a circle and throw a ball to one another.

'When you catch it, tell us your name and something about yourself,' says Gemma. There's a bit of dialect there – *taow* us your name – which could be local. It's disappointing that no grown-ups have come to meet us – where's the Val I've been emailing? – but quite nice to be looking at Ben's flawless face in the sea of old ones.

There are seven women and four men. Quite predictable, I suppose, for a week promising concerts, museum visits and a walk around the Botanic Garden. Maybe if abseiling down the Bodleian were on offer, there'd be me and ten men.

'Hi, I'm Pauline,' says the first person to catch the ball. She's short and plump with a lovely face. 'I'm a dental hygienist and in my spare time I enjoy doing sudokus. I live in Tonbridge with my two dogs. One's called Jack and the other's Russell, so I expect you can work out what breed they are.'

'Alsatian?' asks a portly dark-skinned man. Perhaps Indian. Pauline and others laugh tentatively, not sure if he's being serious, then the ball's lobbed my way.

'I'm Caitlin,' I tell them, 'from North Wales, where I work at home making children's clothes.' I don't mention the organic smallholding, the stall at the farmers'

13

market, or that I've left my son, Frankie, in charge of the goats, chickens and vegetables – because what else would I have to talk about all week? I throw the ball to a slim and dapper man in his sixties, who manages to let it slip through his fingers. It bounces between his feet, then under a table. There are more nervous laughs and I say, 'Sorry,' quite unnecessarily.

Young Ben retrieves it, bending effortlessly and showing us all his nice rear. He hands the ball to the dapper man, who introduces himself as Ronald, a retired accountant and widower. Ronald then throws to fifty-something northerner Barry, who's a boat builder, divorced and the father of two. Barry is very overweight. As I look around the circle, I notice that overweight is rather the norm – Ronald, myself and a tall and attractive dark-haired, brown-eyed man excepted. I used to long for curves, but curves can grow out of control and you end up like the matronly Sheila, telling us she works in local government and enjoys spending time with her grandchildren.

My heart's grown heavy and I want to go home. How stupid of me to forget I'm not a group person, and that I find Shakespeare taxing and museums boring. They'll probably take us punting and I get nauseous in boats. Why did I come? How has this happened? After mentioning the ad to Frankie, he did rather go on and on about what 'a laugh' it would be. Obviously I saw 'Parties!' in his eyes, while he urged – begged me, really – to have a week away. 'Get out of the sticks and soak up some culture,' he kept saying. 'Meet new people. I'll take care of everything. I do it all anyway.' That's absolutely not true. Frankie just doesn't see the work I put in when he's at school, asleep, in the pub.

I sigh, a bit too loudly perhaps, for half the circle turns my way. Putting on a smile, I run my eyes around the faces. I don't need new people, I tell Frankie in my head, or a laugh. I want my handful of close friends in Wales. I want the chickens, the goats and the dog I know will be missing me.

'I don't suppose you'll remember all the names,' says Gemma when the game's over, 'so there's labels on the table.' She points and we make our way there. I find my name tag, pin it on and talk about what a beautiful room it is with Pauline (of Jack and Russell).

'Oh, look,' she says, when the others have wandered off, her eyes on the one remaining label. 'Do you remember a Ralph?'

'No, I don't.' But then I did switch off after a while. I look around and see everyone's wearing their tags. Maybe Ralph's had train problems too. Or wisely changed his mind.

When Gemma starts herding us towards a table laden with food and drink, I manoeuvre

15

myself away from Pauline and am one of the first to pile a plate with sandwiches and accept a cup of tea. Taking them to the table we've been allocated, I go to the far end, so I'm not squashed between two large bodies. I casually look for the nice brown-eyed American, Daniel, who'd said he was a visiting academic at UCL, and wanted to see 'Ux-furred' before going home to New England for the vacation. New England – how romantic that sounds compared to England. But then I see him take a seat at the other end of the table, between two busty, very made-up women, and instantly go off him.

When everyone's settled, no one has taken the seat next to or opposite mine. This is slightly embarrassing, but also, listening to them nattering, something of a relief. I don't feel like swapping personal details right now, so keep my head down and start on the sandwiches, wondering how Frankie's getting on. After a while, I take out my phone and write him a text message, saying I've arrived and that Oxford is pretty and the college ancient, and don't forget to walk Merlin.

It takes some time, and I'm about to sign off with a 'love Mum' when someone says, 'Do you mind if I sit here?'

I look up and read 'Ralph'. Above the name tag is a friendly open face. Below the tag, a slim body. He's wearing shorts and is tall enough for me to see his knees over the table.

16

He has rosy cheeks and short wavy hair and looks like a large Enid Blyton character.

'Yes,' I say. 'Or do I mean no?'

He sits anyway and offers me a hand. 'Name's Ralph.'

'Caitlin,' I say, although we can both read.

'Well, Cait. Did you get held up?'

'Er, no. I just couldn't face the introductions bit. Did they make you stand in a circle and say something about yourselves?'

I laugh. 'We threw a ball.'

Ralph nods knowingly – how many of these weeks has he been on? – and lifts a piece of bread. 'Cucumber,' he says. 'Of course.' He takes a small notebook out of his shorts and, with a tiny pencil, writes something. 'So, Cait,' he says, popping the book back, 'what's someone as interesting-looking as you doing on ... well, let's call a spade a spade ... a lonely hearts weekend?'

'I could ask the same of you.'

'Actually...' he says, leaning towards me. I see now that it's broken veins making him ruddy. A drinker? '...I'm researching. Hoping to start similar cultural breaks in Lincoln. You know, for older singles. Er, but don't tell anyone.'

I wonder why he's confiding in me and want to suggest he lower his voice.

'Although I might make it for the over-fifties,' he says. 'I mean, look at you, Cait. You could be that guy's granddaughter.'

17

He's nodding towards Ronald.

'Very funny. I'm forty-five. And you?'

'Ye-ah, something like that.' He laughs and pops a tiny sandwich in his mouth, then when he's finished says, 'So, I take it you're from Wales? Welsh name, slight Welsh accent. Plus you've got that black-haired, brown-eyed, pale-skinned Celtic Welsh look.'

'I have?'

'Mm. North, South or middle of Wales?'

'North.'

'Ah, my very favourite bit.' He sips his tea for a while, then says, 'These introductions. Anything juicy? Like "My hobby is cross-dressing"?'

'More like cross stitch,' I say in a whisper, encouraging him to pipe down.

He laughs loudly, then writes something in his book again. 'I'm a mature student,' he tells me while he scribbles. 'Doing a degree in tourism and recreation. I worked in a bank for yonks and fancied a career change. How about you?'

I tell him about Cait's Kiddie Clobber, and how I get most of my orders through my website. And about the smallholding. 'Very small,' I add, then briefly mention Frankie.

'Were you married?' Ralph asks.

'Once.'

'Are you leaving those? I'll eat them.'

'Help yourself.' I push the plate towards

him and ask if he's ever been married. He nods and puts another sandwich in his mouth.

Ralph then falls quiet, giving us both a breather, and I watch Sheila and Ronald exchange photos of grandchildren, and hear Pauline telling the Indian chap, whose name I can't quite read, about cosmetic dentistry. 'Veneers, that's all they want now.'

'Shakespeare tonight,' Ralph says, and I turn back. *'Love's Labour's Lost.* Do you know it?'

'No, I don't. Can't say I'm really looking forward to it.'

'Oh, it's a great play. Saw it in Lincoln. Complicated plot, but then it's more about language than plot.'

'You're not selling it to me.'

Ralph laughs again. He seems a happy soul. 'What's different – well, this is what it said in the programme – is that in the final scene they don't all pair off and announce their engagements. Oops, probably ruined it for you now. Actually, I'm a bit of a writer myself. Well, planning to be. Got a terrific idea for a novel.'

'Oh?'

'A sort of gritty urban thriller. Drugs, murder.'

'Wow.'

'I'll tell you all about it some time.'

'Great,' I say, not meaning it. Another tiny

sandwich goes in his mouth and he's quiet again.

'Bonding, bleaching, veneers,' Pauline's telling the man I can now see is 'Hamid'. 'You'd think they were renovating a chest of drawers. Good old-fashioned flossing and a bit of bicarb, that's what I tell them.' Hamid, beaming away at her, appears to have perfect teeth.

After an early and surprisingly good silver-service dinner in the hall and a chance to 'freshen up', we all meet by the porter's lodge and set off for Worcester College with Ben, under a gradually darkening sky. Before I know it, Ralph's by my side and talking about Lincoln – the castle, the Bishop's Palace, the only Roman arch in Britain still used by traffic. I tell him I went once as a child and remember the cathedral looming enormously above me.

'Did you know,' he says, 'that until the spire collapsed in 1549, the tower of Lincoln Cathedral was thought to be the world's tallest structure?'

I can see Ralph's going to be good at his new project. He knows his stuff and has a natural enthusiasm. 'I'm not surprised,' I say. I tell him how we could see Lincoln Cathedral from miles away when we were driving there, the surrounding countryside being so flat.

'And Lincoln being on a hill,' he adds. 'This is a very fiddly route we're taking.'

'Yes.' I've noticed too. We're going down a little cobbled lane, which isn't easy in Faith sandals. Suddenly, in my spindly heels and gorgeous new wrap-round dress, I feel over-dressed for three hours on a bench.

'I expect Ben's avoiding the city centre on a Saturday evening.'

'Ah.' I'm trying to keep up with the group, who in turn are leaping ahead, despite their weights and ages, in an attempt to keep up with Ben.

'Packed with foreign students, apparently.' Ralph turns and looks at me, hobbling along. 'Listen, Caitie...'

'Cait.'

'We don't have to go, you know.'

'What do you mean?'

'I know we've paid, but I've seen the play and you'd rather have teeth pulled.'

True.

'We could give them the slip? Go and explore the city?'

Bunk off! All of a sudden, I feel ... well, lighter. I laugh and say, 'Why not?' Then, when the others take a left at the end of the lane, we turn right. We instantly speed up – easy, now we're off the cobbles – and dart into the first shop doorway.

Ralph, panting, looks again at his map. 'I think we're in George Street.'

After a while I poke my head out and see our party turning right and out of sight, feeling perversely miffed that they haven't checked to see we're still with them. 'Well,' I say, 'now what?'

Ralph suggests a pub. 'Maybe we'll find one with live music. It is Saturday night, after all.'

I hesitate before agreeing, wondering what I've done and whether I should make a dash for Worcester College, after all. How rash of me to have put myself in this stranger's hands, and in a city I don't know. It occurs to me that he might not even be the real 'Ralph'. That he's some psychotic gate-crasher no one's checked out properly. Uppermost in my mind, though, is that if I lose him, I'll never find my way back to the college.

'OK,' I say, convincing myself no psycho would wear pale lemon shorts and flip-flops. 'Sounds good.'

Joe I leave the Italian Job, relieved to be out of the oppressive heat and in slightly less oppressive heat. Looking at the sky, I wonder if it's going to rain at last. I walk down the High Street, along the Cowley Road and halfway up Divinity. Once home, I head upstairs to the laptop to pick up messages. I almost call out, 'Hi, Dad!' as I pass the front room, but the chances of getting a response are about zero. My father's working on a paper and therefore out of touch, emerging from his downstairs study only to pee, snack or sleep. Although sometimes he even sleeps in there.

I don't mind Dad's obsessive spells, as it means I can more or less do as I like in the house. Not that I can't anyway, seeing as I've done the place up for the two of us. But having your old man around is limiting, even if he spends a lot of time on Planet Maths. In fact, the reason I'm home again, aged almost thirty, is partly to protect my hopeless father from himself – make sure he eats, occasionally sees daylight. Because when Julian Sollars gets his head down, nothing else exists for him. It's how great theoretical work is produced, he once explained. I sometimes wish I'd inherited my father's brain, but then I probably wouldn't have a successful café or a flair for photography. But to be honest, the main reason I'm home again, aged thirty, is that it's cheap, comfortable and convenient.

I shower and dress, grab cash, phone and keys, and leave again. Having grown up in east Oxford, I can walk into just about any pub and find someone I know. I start with the Duke, where Ozzie and Tim are playing pool. I have a drink and watch them for a while, thinking there must be better ways of spending a Saturday night. Of course, if I sold my share of the café I could have a whole different life – leave Oxford, go abroad even – but first I'd have to get excited at the prospect.

I ask Oz and Tim if they're going to the Drome later, and agree to meet them there. It's ages since I've been to the Drome – a vast and basic nightclub that was once compulsory but which we've more or less grown out of. Tonight there's a has-been seventies band playing, but they're being supported by Sam's new outfit, Dysexlia. Sam's had lots of crap Oxford bands, but we've heard this one's good.

I have a drink with Tasha and her friends in the Oak Tree, then wander into St Clements to casually check out the new cocktail place. I know I'm bar-hopping in the hope of seeing Charlotte, who hasn't spoken to me for two weeks. I'd told her, yet again and in a jokey way, not to keep coming to the café for free meals. Well, not that jokey. It had been pissing Carlo off no end, especially the times she turned up with a friend. Charlotte didn't seem to be getting the message, though, and I was only prepared to put money in the till for her so many times, so I spelled it out one evening. Now she won't answer emails, texts or her phone. I can't face going to her bitchy shared house – call me timid – I'd rather just bump into her.

I thought I might find her sipping cocktails, as it's Charlotte's kind of thing, so casually glance in the window as I pass the bar. The place is surprisingly full, considering all the students – the people with money, oddly enough – have left. I turn, walk back and check the place out again. Should I go in? What if she's with a bloke?

I'm hesitating by the door, when it suddenly flies open and a middle-aged couple practically fall on the pavement, red in the face and in hysterics. The man straightens himself, looks up and down St Clements, hands on hips and says, 'Excuse, me. Are you a local?'

'Er, yeah.'

'Great. We were wondering where we might find some live music? In the mood for a bit of a bop.' The guy sort of gyrates, right there in the street, and in long yellow shorts too. The woman pulls a face and says, 'Ralph, *please.*'

I'm guessing they've had a few. 'Not much happening,' I tell them, 'although there'll be lots of music tomorrow at the Cowley Road carnival. But they have got–' I stop to snigger – 'the Space Hoppers at the Drome tonight.'

'No!' says the man. 'Not *the* Space Hoppers?' He starts singing a song that goes something like, 'Bouncy, bouncy, rock and roll. Bouncy, bouncy, you're my doll.'

'Was that their Eurovision song?' asks the woman, and I suddenly feel faint. I'm paying money to see a Eurovision act?

'I had all their LPs,' says the man, and he begins to list them.

'The Space Hoppers will be on around ten,' I say, interrupting him. I give them directions, keen to get away in case Charlotte finds me with someone singing a bouncy song. 'My friend's band, Dysexlia, are supporting.'

'Don't you mean Dyslexia?' asks the man.

The woman rolls her eyes and says, 'Duh, Ralph,' then he suddenly gets it and smacks his forehead and almost falls into the road.

Completely pissed, I decide. I check the time on my phone. 'They'll be on stage by now,' I say. 'Better run. See you guys later, maybe.'

'If you're going there now, you could show us the way,' suggests the man.

Yeah right, and be lumbered with them all evening. 'I would,' I call out, walking backwards, 'but I really need to pop home first. Just keep going up the Cowley Road. On the right. You can't miss it.'

The Space Hoppers are no doubt so uncool, they've become cool. Whatever it is, the place is rammed. It's a weird mix. There's the dozen or so people I've known forever – Sam's friends, basically – and hordes and hordes of kids, of course. But there are quite a few middle-aged people too, many of them doing some kind of pogo thing. Not like the punks' pogoing, more like bouncing on a space hopper, knees bent.

I can't bring myself to dance to the Space Hoppers, although just about everyone is, including the drunk couple I'd met earlier. The bloke's making a total arse of himself, jumping around and waving his arms in the air, but the woman's just sort of swaying. She's quite pretty, in the semi-darkness, anyway. Nice figure-hugging dress and good legs. And she can dance. Her husband, or whatever, has no idea.

I scan the place for Charlotte again. She knows Sam, through me, so might have come along to see his band. But then, if she thought I'd be there, maybe not. I can't see her, so begin searching the room for someone gorgeous to hit on. Trouble is, all the pretty ones are so young. On top of that, how could anyone dancing to the Space Hoppers be remotely attractive?

I go and buy another beer, get into a shouting conversation with Tim, then stand for a while at the back of the crowd, checking out the women again, but in a half-hearted way. As my eyes go from girl to girl – too young, known her for years, too young – I feel my shoulder suddenly grabbed. I swing round and see it's the woman.

'Ralph's collapsed!' she shouts. 'Could you

27

help? I'm sorry but you're the only familiar face.'

I notice now the space forming around the slumped Ralph. What a dickhead. *'Please?'* the woman begs in my ear.

With the help of a bouncer, I get Ralph outside and prop him against a lamp post. I'm hoping fresh air will sober the guy up, but he's too far gone for that. If anything, he's worse.

'Oh God,' the woman says, 'if only we'd gone to Worcester.'

I wish they'd gone to Worcester too, as I try over and over to get Ralph upright. And to really make my day, it's pissing down.

The woman says, 'I don't know what to do, or how to get back.'

I'm watching every passing car for an empty taxi. 'Where to?'

'Um. Well, it's a college. Um ... oh dear, I can't remember the name. It was the cocktails. I tried to tell Ralph, but he kept insisting we have another. Anyway, we're on this organised week, staying in one of the colleges. It's ... let me think ... it's in the city centre, and it's got a big wooden entrance, and a quad and a big hall and a chapel. Does that ring any bells?'

I laugh, despite the fact these two are ruining my evening. 'There are about forty colleges like that, all in the city centre.'

'Oh, sorry. How stupid of me.'

Now I feel bad. 'You weren't to know,' I say. Tourists in town often ask me to direct them to the university. 'You're in it,' I tell them.

We're all getting wetter and the woman's dark hair is sticking to her face and forehead. She says, 'Perhaps Ralph will... Ralph, what's the name of our college? Ralph? Oh God, he's nodding off again. Is it possible to sleep standing up ... er ... I'm sorry, I don't know your name.'

I groan and give up on the taxi search. If they can't come up with an address, what's the point? 'Joe,' I tell her.

'I'm Caitlin. Cait. Look, this is really good of you. Um ... I don't suppose you live nearby, do you? You said something earlier about popping home? I mean, if we could just get him indoors and give him a coffee, then he might...' She stops and wraps her arms around her middle. 'Oh dear. Feel sick.'

I swear under my breath. No way am I having these two come home with me. Not finding Charlotte, or, better still, a new girlfriend, and watching a dire band are bad enough for a Saturday night. 'Has he got a wallet?' I ask the woman. Cait.

'Good thinking.' She pats the guy's pockets, then pulls a leather wallet from his girly shorts. 'Perhaps we'll find the address in here.'

We don't, so I start looking for a cab again.

The taxi driver helps haul Ralph towards our thousand-pound sofa. Cait thanks him ten times and at the front door I double-tip.

'I'm not sure we'll get coffee into Ralph,' says Cait, when I return. 'Maybe he just needs to sleep it off.'

Since I've given up on my night out, I say, 'Can I make you one?'

'Thanks. Perhaps it'll help me remember ... C. It, definitely began with a ... or maybe it was P. Oh, I don't know.'

While I go the whole hog and get the cappuccino machine going, I suggest looking in the phone book. But when I hand it to her, opened on the right page, she says, 'Oh crikey, the words are swimming. Sorry.'

I don't feel like reading the list of colleges out loud, and it might be pointless. Since she's pissed, they'll only go to the wrong one, then end up back here. 'Do you know the name of the company organising the week? We could do a search online.'

'Er, I'm not sure it's got one. Or maybe it has and I've forgotten. It's just a woman called Val.'

'Or have you got a mobile? Maybe they're trying to get in touch with you. There'd be a number we could call back.'

'Uh-uh. Left it in my room. We were going to a play, you see. Shakespeare. Silly to take it, I thought.'

I nod, unsurprised. Some people – older people – are so useless with their mobiles. 'Oh, I don't like to have it switched on,' Mum says when I can't get hold of her. Then there's Dad and predictive text. How can someone who understands cosmic strings not get it? Cait doesn't look that old, though. 'Anyway, it could be a bit late to call them now.'

'True.'

'What about your husband?' I ask, nodding towards our open-plan room off the kitchen. 'Has he got a mobile?'

She smiles, which makes her face light up and look quite different. 'Not my husband. In fact, we've only just met. It's a singles' week, you see. Ralph did have his phone with him, but then when we got to the Drome it was missing.'

I sigh and promise myself I'll never help tourists again, not unless they're customers. 'Didn't you say you've got a son? Would he know the college? Call him if you like.'

'Hey, good idea.'

I hand her the mobile I *always* have on me. 'Sugar?'

'No thanks.' She closes the directory and taps in her number, then after a while says, 'No. Not home.'

'Has he got a mobile?'

'Yes, but I don't know the number. It's in my er...'

'Mobile?' I shake my head. No one my age would go out without their phone. It would be like leaving your shoes behind. I tell her this and she laughs again.

'And how old *are* you, Joe?'

I'd never be able to ask her age. Late thirties, I'd guess. 'Thirty,' I tell her. 'Almost.'

'My son's seventeen,' she says, and then she's off. Telling me about Frankie, who wants to study business and economics and become something in the City and be paid huge bonuses, even though he's been brought up to appreciate nature and a simple life. I'm not all that interested in Frankie, but I sit at the large bare table in my urban-chic, high-spec kitchen and listen anyway. Basically, because I'm a polite person, but also because I've got nothing better to do this Saturday night. Which is a bit puzzling for someone not that bad looking with money in the bank.

She began her business making children's clothes, Cait's now telling me, after her husband ran off with a good friend, also married. Cait and Rob, the woman's bereft husband, then started an affair, which didn't last long but was 'rather comforting'. I stare at the table – way too much information – then Cait asks where my parents live.

'Well, my father lives here. It's his house, was the family home ages ago. And Mum was just around the corner till I was eighteen. I used to go between the two as a kid, but then she married an arsehole and I more or less stayed with Dad all the time. Mum's in Ireland now.'

'Brothers and sisters?'

'No.'

'You're like my Frankie.'

I don't think I'm a bit like her Frankie, being thirteen years older, an entrepreneur and something of an artist. 'I am?'

'An only child.'

'Oh, right.'

'It's not such a bad thing. I had two sisters and the rivalry was–' She stops and stares because Dad has wandered into the kitchen in only underpants. He's got a pen in one hand, and in the other a mug, which he fills with milk from the fridge before turning and saying, 'Excellent,' through his glasses and his long mangled fringe. 'Well, back to er...' He then plods off with his funny walk, mumbling and scratching a buttock with the pen.

'Dad,' I explain.

'Oh dear.'

'No, he's all right really. Just ... you know, clever.'

'Ah.'

We go quiet for a while and drink our coffees. She's gradually getting a bit more colour, although not that much. She's quite pale, which sort of goes well with the straight, black, shoulder-length hair. If she

33

wasn't drunk, I'd find her quite attractive.

'Hey,' I say, when an idea hits me. 'What about your emails?'

'What about them?'

'Well, you could check them on my computer. I expect you emailed the woman running this singles' week? The name of the college would have been mentioned, surely?'

'Er...'

'You'll be able to access your emails from my computer, won't you? Everyone can these days.'

'I can't remember my password.'

'No?'

'No,' she says quite adamantly. 'Always using different ones, you see.'

I don't know why, but I'm not sure I believe her. 'Do you want to stay the night?' I ask.

She looks at me and smiles and her cheeks colour up some more. 'If it's not too much trouble,' she says.

TWO

Caitlin I come round to the sound of, 'Cait, are you awake? *Cait?*'

'I am now,' I tell Ralph, who's poking his head round my bedroom door. Well, not my

34

bedroom. I stretch my arms and yawn and try to make out what the noise is.

'Where the blazes are we?' he asks. 'And what's going on out there? Sounds like fun.' He points at the open sash window, through which I now make out bongos and those annoying little trumpet things.

I try to think, but need coffee. My mouth's dry, my head hurts and it's very warm. After sending Ralph to the kitchen, I sit up in the double bed and look around the room, not that there's much to look at. Just me, a bed, a sleek chest of drawers, a mirror and white walls. The curtains are also white, the floor is wooden – new boards, I notice. The more I look, the more I see how beautifully finished everything is. The sunken lights and the chrome switch with dimmer buttons. The slim cast-iron radiator hung on the wall. I have a memory now of a fabulous kitchen. It's a lovely house and a lovely bedroom. Lovelier than my room in Peterchurch College. I picture the room – policemen going through my things in their missing persons' case – then Ralph arrives back with two mugs and hands me mine.

'Found a pot already made. And I met the strangest guy.' He parks himself on my bed and looks more alert and ready to seize the day than he should.

When the coffee's woken me up, I explain about him passing out and me not knowing which college we're staying in. This isn't entirely true. I did forget the name of the college at first. Once we were installed in the house of the devastatingly gorgeous Joe, it came back to me, but I'd chosen to forget it again.

'I remember now,' I tell Ralph, 'but last night... God, those cocktails. We tried your wallet for the name. No luck.'

'Maybe if you'd looked in here...?' He's pulling his little notebook from his shirt pocket.

'Damn. Anyway, Joe – he's the guy we got directions from, remember?'

'Er ... no.'

'Tall, lovely brown sort of floppy hair. *Very* good-looking.'

Ralph shakes his head.

'Broad shoulders? Amazing blue eyes?'

'Nope. Don't recall him.'

I fill Ralph in on the cocktails, the Space Hoppers and how kind Joe was. 'The strange man you came across is probably his father.'

'He was eating sardines from a tin and asked if I'd strim the lawn edges today.'

'Right.'

'He wasn't wearing much.'

'No.'

I finish my coffee and ask Ralph to leave the room while I dress. I wonder if it would be OK to have a shower. Outside, the bongos seem to be gathering and multiplying. Joe had said something about a carnival, but it all feels a bit dark and threatening, and I quite want to be having a full English breakfast in a quiet college with people who have grandchildren. I see from my watch, though, that we've well and truly missed breakfast and should, in fact, be gazing at old pottery by now.

Downstairs there's a note from Joe telling us he's had to go and take photos, but to help ourselves to breakfast. This is something of a relief, really. I'd lied about forgetting my email password, and I think he'd known it. What a sad old slapper he must think I am. I hadn't actually phoned Frankie, either. Just dialled my friend Jude's number, knowing she's away for the weekend.

Joe's kitchen feels too terrifyingly pristine to use, so Ralph and I leave the house and make our way towards the bongos, the trumpets and the arresting smell of Indian food. When we turn into the main road, it's like landing in the middle of the Rio Carnival, and not just because of the intense heat.

'Wow!' Ralph cries, and he's instantly dancing and clapping, as people of all shades pass by in spectacular costumes. One woman is a giant butterfly. There's a juggler on stilts and small armies of children in outfits that must have taken every spare moment for a year to create. The sun is making all the gold and silver even shinier, the colours even stronger. People are playing assorted instruments as they parade past, while others sing or dance. Some sing, dance and play instruments all at the same time.

Ralph, beside me on the sidelines, is doing a cross between salsa and the hippy-hippy shake. He keeps shouting, 'Whoooah,' a lot, and I wonder if now's the time to slip away and catch up with the Peterchurch lot. After I've eaten, perhaps.

While Ralph does his wacky dance, I find a nearby café. I sit on a stool in the window, eating a croissant, drinking good coffee, reading a Sunday paper and occasionally looking up at Ralph. He spots me one time and I wave, then finally he joins me with his own breakfast.

'Terrific, eh?' he says. He eats quickly, perhaps anxious not to miss anything, then points at a large stage. 'Caribbean steel band,' he says. 'Fancy?'

When I look over the road, I can't see the band for people, but I do spot lovely Joe taking photos. 'Yes,' I say. 'Definitely.' But once we've woven our way across the road and Ralph's begun his strange contortions again, Joe's nowhere to be seen. Probably for the best, I decide.

I sit on a wall and people watch. There's quite a mix, not just ethnically. Lots of kids who could be students, and quite a few ageing hippies, many in couples. What I don't see are people who look like tourists. From all the, 'Hi, how are you?' and 'Haven't seen you for ages. Still at Oxfam?' going on around me, I get the impression everyone's local.

When I turn back to Ralph, he's gone. I stand and scan the crowd, then eventually see him on the stage of all places, bashing away on a steel drum. It occurs to me then, and not for the first time, that he might be a bit of a plonker.

Daniel I stare at the hieroglyphics but my mind is on Caitlin. Where the hell is she? And that guy? Ralph, I learned his name is. No one else seems bothered by their non-appearance, least of all Val, the weekend's chief organiser. There'd been no, response from either room, apparently. Keys had been fetched, doors opened.

'Oh, it's happened before, Daniel,' Val had whispered earlier, when I cornered her by the Japanese ceramics. She has a charming cut-glass accent and wears her thick grey hair tucked up in that messy but classy way only the British manage. 'Romance strikes early and the lovebirds hotfoot it to the nearest hotel.' She smiled sweetly and raised her eyebrows at me. 'Our single beds aren't made for canoodling. I imagine you have much bigger ones in the States.'

'Possibly,' I said, trying not to think of Caitlin canoodling with lanky Ralph. The moment I laid eyes on her in the hall, I knew she was the one I wanted to get to know. When she told us about the children's clothes, it conjured up such a pretty picture. Lovely Caitlin at an old treadle machine, surrounded by vases of wild flowers and Welsh mountains. But then, as I'd been making my way toward her at the table, the woman from Cheltenham invited me to sit between herself and the woman from Suffolk. What could I do? They were perfectly lovely people, if a tad loud and low-cut, but I wanted to be talking to Caitlin.

Over tea, however, I'd gleaned a good deal about the pitfalls of internet dating. Never use an old photograph, I was told. Apparently, it isn't worth the devastated look on your date's face when you meet. 'Well, obviously that wouldn't happen to a chap like Daniel,' one corrected the other. 'Not when you're a cross between George Clooney and Al Pacino.' It sounded like an odd hybrid to me, but I thanked them and carried on half-listening to their dating woes, whilst also keeping an eye on Caitlin and the guy who'd gone and sat himself opposite her. He was tall and OK-looking, and had quickly gotten into conversation with her. I was kicking myself, obviously. Just that tiny event – the woman from Cheltenham saying, 'There's a seat here, Daniel' – may have derailed a beautiful relationship before it began.

I wondered, as I consumed my afternoon tea, how common an activity this is. Just when I've come to think of Britain as a progressive, egalitarian twenty-first-century nation, I arrive in Oxford to find toffs still eat cucumber sandwiches at four.

I move on to the next set of hieroglyphics and make like I'm engrossed. Barry and I are the only spare males now – Pauline and Hamid, and Sheila and Ronald having more or less paired off – and with Barry being so very rotund, I'm having to avoid being monopolised by the internet daters. Sticking to our frail, elegant and adorable leader, Val, and constantly engaging her in conversation, flirting even, seems to be working well for now. Val must be mid-seventies, and if that makes me look suspiciously like a fag, all the better.

We eat lunch at a café beside the old castle and prison, at small tables that seat only four. I manage to dodge the interneters and find myself with Val and the two round blonde women who are hard to tell apart. Val is fussing with her cellphone, while the blondes talk about the places they'd love to visit in America if it wasn't for the gun crime. I tell them I've never once been shot,

41

but can see from their faces they think it's only a matter of time.

We finish up our lattes and paninis, etc., and whilst the rest of the group head for the Visitors' Centre, I hang back, then make a quick right, taking the path up the grass-covered Castle Mound I've been watching others climb. At the top I stand and admire the view and take one or two photographs. There are the famous dreaming spires, of course, and dotted here and there are the tops of more modern buildings, many unattractive. But the new business school that greets you at the railroad station, with its own green geometric version of a spire, is imposing and stunning in the skyline.

After turning full circle a couple times more in the welcome breeze, I put my camera away and lie on the grass, as others have. A nearby tree provides a little dappled shade and, with hands beneath my head, I decide to give the group twenty minutes for their tour before going down to meet them. I close my eyes and contemplate the afternoon's activities. A walk around the Botanic Garden, then the Natural History Museum, then free time, then dinner. This evening we're to attend a concert in some place called the Holywell, which I pray, after last night's damp experience, has a roof.

There's no sign of our party, but then I did

doze for longer than intended. I hover by the Visitors' Centre exit, although the woman at the desk has assured me they'd be through with their tour by now. After five minutes I give up and leave the castle complex, walking in the direction of the city centre, where, without the map we were each issued, I hope someone will direct me to the Botanic Garden. On my third attempt, I find a local person, who says, 'End of the High Street, on the right. Bit of a trek,' and is gone.

'Thanks,' I call out, then set off in the direction indicated, now realising just how easy it is to lose this group. It makes me believe that Caitlin and her pal are probably OK, although I do think the cops should be informed if they're not back this evening. As we all know from *Morse*, there's a murder a day in this beautiful city.

The High Street is impressive and I take my time strolling down (or possibly up) it, marvelling at the historic buildings and cobbled side streets – things that never fail to thrill Americans, no matter how many European cities we visit. At Magdalen College I see a sign saying 'Open to Visitors', and after peering into its enticingly shady entrance, I hand over money to go see the rest.

'Look out for the deer,' I'm told by the porter. My experience of late-middle-aged British ticket salesmen is that they are often jokers of the subtle, ironic, here-comes-aforeigner kind. I therefore don't expect to see any deer – right here in the middle of town? – until I do, in fact, happen upon them. And they're quite lovely.

The grounds too are fabulous, as is the college, which is much larger than Peterchurch. Having gone most of the way around, I stop for a lazy cold drink in the café. It has a terrace where you can sit and laugh heartily at folk setting off ineptly in long cumbersome punts. Some are even dressed up for the occasion in pale floating garments, and have bottles of champagne poking from baskets. This is too perfectly *Brideshead* not to photograph, and so I do.

Later, I go back and take shots of the deer and then a tranquil quad, before I'm back on the sidewalk again, still looking out for the Botanic Garden. It's past three, however, and I guess the others could be well on their way to the Natural History Museum. But maybe not. I'd imagine the day's activities, together with the heat and humidity, have slowed everyone down. Not least poor Val.

Once over the bridge that crosses the river and the champagne-drinking punters, I come to a pretty roundabout with three roads leading off. Having been told it's a bit of a trek, I head for the road directly opposite, assuming that's the continuation of the High Street. Once there, however, I feel as though I've stepped through Oxford's secret wardrobe door into a whole other land. This is especially so when a large black guy, naked but for a short tasseled skirt, takes my hand and starts dancing with me.

Joe I see Charlotte. She looks great in her tiny top and long skirt. I'd forgotten how skinny she is. She and a friend are dancing to the band on the main stage and I can't resist taking a photo of her, and then another. I'm taking a third when she maybe senses something and turns my way. I swing round, pretending to photograph the band, but it's too late. With the camera still covering my face, I can see with a sideways glance that Charlotte's coming my way. Shit.

'Is it digital?' she asks, pointing at the camera.

'Um, yeah.' I'm taking it in turns with the digital and my old Canon.

'Can I see my photo?'

'OK.' I press the review button, get the last picture of Charlotte up and hand the camera over. 'There are three. Just press this.' Our fingers touch and quickly bounce off each other.

'Hey,' she says, 'not bad. Would you email them to me?'

'Yeah, of course.' Why can't I ask how she is? What she's been up to. Why she hasn't been in touch.

'Thanks,' she says. 'Listen, better get back

to Rachel.'

'Right. I'll, er, send you the pictures.'

'Cheers. See you.'

'Yeah.' I watch her walk away, and wish I hadn't taken the day off work. A deep gloom descends. Women are cold, scary creatures and I'm not sure I like them any more. Sometimes I think being gay might be easier. I need a drink, I decide – something I've avoided till now, wanting to get some decent pictures. After packing the cameras away and throwing one last glance at Charlotte, I make for where I think Oz and Tim might be, in the garden of the Duke.

Yet another band is playing. They have a girl singer with a wailing, high-pitched voice that begins annoying me immediately. Why does everything annoy me these days? Charlotte, I suppose. Selfish, immature Charlotte. But then maybe that's what you get with a twenty-two-year-old. She probably thinks I'm old and boring, and she might have a point. It's the café that's the problem. Such a tie. I mean, I could hardly go jetting off to India for two months, as she'd wanted me to do.

I walk through the Duke and into the garden, and although there are familiar faces, I don't see anyone I want to talk to. In fact, more and more, in amongst the manic, hey-let's-have-fun scenes of the Cowley Road Carnival and Festival, all I want is to be alone.

I leave the pub and buy a six-pack in the nearest Asian store, then work my way through the crowds and the entertainers and hot food along the pavements, not really aiming for anywhere but not wanting to go home either. In the end, I turn into the churchyard.

In front of the church are stalls, games and a few people milling around, but I go behind, to where there are just trees, grass and gravestones. It's cool and quiet and peaceful, but best of all dark, making it a good place to go through the pictures, deleting the crap ones. Maybe I'll delete Charlotte too. If only I could get rid of her altogether. Just press a button, say at the back of my neck, and have all images and thoughts disappear – *whoosh*. Someone should work on that.

I find a tree to sit under. Ignoring the sign forbidding alcohol, I open a can and drink half in one go, have a rest, then drink the other half. All the while I stare at the best photo of my ex-girlfriend, finger poised on the delete button. But I don't delete it, or the other two. Instead, I open a second can and look through all the shots I've taken of the carnival. A couple aren't worth keeping, a lot really aren't bad, and a few are truly brilliant.

While I'm clicking through them again, this time zapping the ones I don't like, something catches my eye in the distance. I lower the camera and see it's last night's house guest, Cait. She's got her back and arms pressed flat against the church wall. Every now and then she takes a quick look round the corner, then shoots her head back again. I laugh, maybe for the first time today. I don't know if it's the beer or what, but when I could easily stay hidden in the greenery and the shade of the tree, I put a hand up and wave at her.

Daniel I lose my large black dancing partner and decide to explore the mayhem ahead. A pungent waft of marijuana hits me, then it's the aroma of hot vegan tortilla wraps, then incense, then sizzling Bengali dishes.

But it's not only my sense of smell being overly stimulated, for music of all kinds fills my ears and rattles my ribcage as I amble along – some from sound systems, some live, all of it loud. Then there's the colour and the frenetic activity – people dancing, juggling, or just walking in their bright clothes and painted bodies. I know I should turn back and go look at dinosaur bones but I can't help being drawn further into this parallel-universe Oxford. I take photographs, just to prove I didn't dream it and to show my mother and sister back home.

At one point, I wander down a side street,

where tiny nineteenth-century houses either sprout directly from the sidewalk, or have a yard the size of a small couch out front. Many of these mini-yards contain garbage bins and sacks, and one does happen to have a small couch in it. I photograph these row houses, imagining the original inhabitants living without electricity or an inside bathroom, unaware that their small hovel will one day command £395,000 – the truly shocking figure I'd just seen in a real-estate window.

Back in the fray, I sit on a wall watching an African band perform on stage. There are two women and five men, the women in fabulous clothes and headgear. Their music is infectious and people are dancing enthusiastically. I almost join in, but remember I'm not much of a dancer and just tap a foot.

'They're Sudanese,' says the girl I've just asked. 'Like me.' She has big brown eyes and a lovely smile. I photograph her, then turn around on the wall and capture some of the characters passing by in the street. Many you can barely see beneath their costumes, others wear very little.

I keep shooting. There's an oriental woman who's a pineapple. Click. Beside her are children dressed as what could be kiwi fruit, or small mangos perhaps. Click, click. A tall white man has joined the group of kids now and is dancing in their midst. He's waving his arms and wiggling his ass, and appears to be disrupting their choreographed steps somewhat. It's almost amusing, so I hold the camera and take a picture, but then lower it again when I realise I recognise him.

'Ralph?' I shout, and incredibly he hears me.

He dances my way and says, 'Hi. Do I know you?' He's perspiring heavily, but then we all are.

'I'm in your Peterchurch group.'

'Ah.'

'Where's Caitlin?' I ask, because that's all I really want to know.

'Not sure.' His arms still swirl above his head. 'Last saw her heading towards the church.' He points a wavy hand and I nod a thank you, and then he wiggles off in his long baggy shorts to join a group of passing panpipe players.

Well, I think. At least she's alive.

I meander through the crowds until I reach the only church in sight. People are selling things on tables, kids are playing games, families are waiting in line for drinks that can't possibly be cold in this heat. I check inside the church too, but don't see Caitlin, and so I head back along the road toward a sign I'd noticed earlier. It had sounded fun and different, and I see, when I get there, that it begins in five minutes. I pay my money and enter a large tent, experiencing a degree of surprise as to where I've found myself. Had I been asked to make a list of what I'd expect to be doing on my cultural week in Oxford, a Senegalese drum workshop would have been way down there.

Caitlin I'm certain Ralph won't find me here, especially as I'm hiding myself behind Joe's broad back for the time being. Joe's been telling me all about the churchyard restoration and what the place used to be like. Full of winos at one time. He says he sometimes comes here to take photographs, when he's not at work in the Italian café he half owns. The churchyard is always changing, apparently. The trees, the light, the visitors. Joe's far more talkative than he was last night.

'I think you can come out now,' he says. 'Here, have a lager.'

'Thanks.' I move away from the fine shoulders and hair I've been admiring – long, but not that long, lots of different hues, shiny, casual but beautifully cut – and settle myself on the grass beside him. The can is lovely and cool, and I open it quickly and gulp some down. 'Thirsty,' I explain, breathless.

By the time I'm halfway through, I feel so much better than I have all day. It could be the hair of the dog lifting my spirits, or it could be shaking off the embarrassing Ralph. It could also be sitting beside a stunning young man in a tight black T-shirt.

'I feel so grubby,' I tell him. 'Yesterday's clothes. I had a shower at your house, hope that was OK?'

Joe shrugs. 'You don't look grubby, you look great.'

I laugh, embarrassed. 'I love your house, by the way.'

'Yeah? I talked Dad into letting me modernise the place, with a bit of help. It used to be a seventies museum, all beige hessian walls and chipped cork floors. Half-dead spider plants everywhere.' He laughs and shakes his head and has another swig.

'Well, it's fabulous now,' I tell him, 'especially the wet room.'

'Thanks, but I'm sure your cottage is nice too?'

'Not really. It might be if I wasn't so busy and didn't share it with a seventeen-year-old.'

Joe puts his can down and lifts his camera, about to photograph me, it appears. I quickly put my hands to my face, slopping lager in the process. 'Damn,' I say, rubbing at my chest just as the flash goes off. 'No, don't!' Aware too that my cotton dress has slipped up my thighs, I straighten my legs out and pull the material kneewards, but not before he snaps again.

Joe takes one more shot. 'You must have been really young when you had your son. What, twenty?'

'Um, yeah, something like that.' I laugh girlishly, as though to prove it.

'Have another lager,' Joe insists, handing me one.

I thank him again, knowing this was not what I'd paid hundreds of pounds to do in Oxford. Although, thinking about it, I might have done.

'Why are you hiding from Ralph?' he asks.

'How long have you got, Joe?'

He smiles, then reaches across and moves lager-soaked hair from my cheek with the tip of a finger.

I ignore this gesture, although it sends a shiver through me, and tell him about Ralph leaping on stage with a Caribbean steel band, dancing, then being escorted off when he knocked a drum over. And about Ralph trying to juggle with fire and almost setting light to his hair. 'It's quite badly singed.'

Joe laughs again and opens himself a new can. He seems to have got through a few. 'Have you remembered the name of your college?'

'Mm, Peterchurch.'

'And have you told them you're safe?'

I find his concern quite touching, and it shows a maturity neither Ralph nor I have, it seems. 'Er, no. Perhaps we should have done. We just thought we'd get back in time for dinner, since the group will be out and about all day.' I lean back on my hands and stare up at the pattern of leaves and branches, the sun barely twinkling through them. 'It's so hot and noisy out there and so cool and peaceful in here.'

'Quiet as a graveyard.'

'Perhaps that's why we're the only ones in it.'

'Er, we're not,' says Joe.

That's when I hear Ralph's booming voice. 'There you are, Cait!' He strides towards us in feathered headwear, but then manages to trip up, perhaps on a gravestone, and go flying.

While he's down and I'm rolling my eyes, Joe leans towards me and kisses my face, somewhere between cheek and mouth. 'You're very pretty,' he says, and I tell him not to be so daft.

'No, you are,' he says, kissing the other side.

After dinner, in the quad, I receive a ticking-off from Val, who does indeed run the show and is older than I expected.

'A night on the tiles is acceptable, but I became terribly worried when we returned earlier and you two *still* weren't in your rooms.'

I'd tumbled into the Hall just as dinner got going, minus Ralph, who'd stopped on the way for a full body paint. 'I'm really sorry,' I say again.

'And on top of that,' sighs Val, 'I've mislaid our lovely American.'

'Daniel?'

'Mm. Charming man and so very concerned about you. It did occur to me that he went looking for you.'

'I doubt it. We've never even spoken.'

'You know...' says Val with a dreamy smile, 'sometimes words aren't necessary.'

'Yes,' I agree, remembering some of those times.

We've all taken our coffees outside, since it's such a lovely evening, and after Val leaves to have a chat with Pauline and Hamid, I sit on the stone steps to the Hall and wonder how, after a man-drought of almost three years, I've suddenly acquired two admirers in a day. Three, if you count Ralph, which I don't. I take the small mirror from my bag and examine my face. It's fairly in proportion and because of the heat my colour's quite good, but I haven't turned into Catherine Zeta Jones overnight. I can only guess it's to do with vibes and signals I'm emitting.

And that's without trying. Unlike some. The two tarty women, whose names I forget, have resorted to cornering one of the college gardeners – a stooped man who must be past retirement. He's giving them a tour of his work, a hand in the crook of his back. Meanwhile, the round and homely blonde women, whose names I don't know either, are laughing uproariously at every-thing Big Barry says.

I sigh, thinking fondly of Joe's drunken kisses. He's going to be so embarrassed later, but at least he made a forty-five-year-old women feel eighteen, which really doesn't happen enough. I close my eyes against the warm orangey glow of the evening sun and picture the floppy brown hair, the playful blue eyes, the flat stomach, the long legs. Joe isn't what you'd call muscular, but he is solid. Last night I'd seen him as a boy – a quite beautiful one – but today in the churchyard, with my clearer head and his close proximity, he was definitely a man. 'You're very pretty,' he'd said. I smile to myself. 'You're very pretty.'

'I am?' asks someone casting a shadow over me.

'Sorry?' My eyes open and I see Barry looming.

'You said I'm very pretty.' He gives a chesty laugh. 'Not sure I've ever been called that.'

With some heavy breathing, he lowers him-self uneasily on to the step beside me and rests his cup and saucer on his tummy. 'Lovely evening for it,' he says, and I stop my-self asking 'What?' in case he's being smutty. Perhaps that's how he's had the blondes in stitches.

'What did you think to Pitt Rivers?' he asks.

'Sorry?'

'You know, the museum within the museum.'

'I wasn't there.'

'You weren't? Oh, it were magic. Dead dark and atmospheric. Where was you, then?'

After the mild euphoria over Joe, I'm now feeling deflated by Barry's remarks. Perhaps, after all, there's nothing as invisible as a middle-aged woman. I tell Barry I was shopping. Then, noticing how late it is, I excuse myself and go for a shower.

'See you at the porter's lodge at half-past!' he calls after me.

I've got twenty minutes. Just enough time.

In the shower the silliest thing happens. I imagine having sex with Joe. It all takes place rather slowly and sensually, and involves a certain amount of detail, and by the time I'm through and back in my room, not quite recovered, I see that it's a quarter to eight. With wet hair and no make-up, I fly to the porter's lodge. But I'm too late. The concert starts at eight and it's now five to.

'Where's the Holywell Music Room?' I ask, and the porter directs me. But it's quite a long walk and I take two wrong turns, so when I reach the sweet little building it's twenty-five past and the doors are firmly closed. Obviously, it would be rude to go in now. And once in, I'd have to look for my group, then keep saying, 'Excuse me, excuse me,' to people's knees, and no doubt get

57

tutted at. No. I've missed the boat and will have to find another way of passing the evening. Alone. In a strange city. Where I know no one. Except Joe.

My stomach, churns and I sit on the low wall outside the concert room, partly because I've come over funny, but also to look at the map I'd forgotten was in the bottom of my bag. I find Holywell Street and see that it's parallel to High Street, which will eventually lead me back to Cowley Road and the festival. And, who knows, maybe Joe.

I take some deep breaths and rummage for mascara and lipstick. It's a beautiful street, I notice, as I sit doing my face. The houses are assorted shapes and sizes, and centuries old – sixteenth, seventeenth? Some have shutters, many are painted in pastels. It's an idyllic setting on a balmy evening, and I blame my sudden yearning for excitement on Joe. Those soft kisses, those nice words, the things we did when I was showering...

But what if he'd just been having a laugh in the churchyard? Or perhaps I'm right that it was a brief alcohol-fuelled moment of madness in a surreal, vaguely romantic setting. Dare I go back and risk rejection and disappointment, or should I savour the kisses and the 'You're very pretty' and take them with me into old age?

I decide to go and find him. I refold the map, slip it in my bag, stand and straighten my skirt, and step purposefully but nervously eastwards. *Yes*, my head's telling me. You'll soon be fifty, sixty. Go for it now, while you're still presentable.

But then I hear, 'Caitlin! Caitlin!' and turn to see Val at the door of the concert hall, beckoning me over. 'Quickly,' she says, now walking towards me with an outstretched arm. 'They're between pieces.'

Daniel Since the Senegalese drum workshop, one thing has led to another and now, at nine in the evening, I find myself at a table in someone's funky house discussing fair trade, carbon emissions and Islamophobia. Not the most comfortable of subjects for a US citizen. However, I believe I've established my credentials with this mixed bunch of wine-drinking, dope-toking, green and left-leaning types, who range from mere teens to a woman called Olive, who's in her sixties, keeps touching me, and talks a lot about her days at Greenham. In fact, I'm being more critical of my home country than is exotic Persian-by-birth Faiza, who spent a year studying in the States and has far more scorn for China.

A joint comes my way again, I partake twice and pass it on. I agree with Faiza that China is a problem, but add, 'We can hardly blame developing countries for wanting to do what we in the West have been doing for decades, centuries even...' Someone places a hand on my knee and squeezes. I'm hoping it's Faiza but think it's Olive. '...making rapid technological and economic progress at the expense of the environment.'

'That's a rather patronising attitude,' says Faiza, putting me in my place, then going on to quote more statistics.

I shift my leg and lose the hand, then notice my glass is full again. On a large grubby cushion someone plays a flute, and at the far end of the long basement kitchen a guy with brown and grey waist-length hair is cooking up a stew. It smells garlicky and good, and I'm hoping some will soon come my way, since I've been on liquids only for a little longer than is good for me. The lunch beside the castle feels like days, not to mention a whole different lifetime, ago.

I picture my singles' party, sitting sedately and soberly through their concert – a small baroque ensemble – and feel kind of glad I'm where I am. So far today I've drummed therapeutically, listened to Sudanese, Cypriot and Jamaican bands, and been introduced to four local pubs. This is all because I struck up a conversation with Zac, my neighbour in the drumming tent.

Following the workshop, Zac gave me a tour of the Cowley Road, pointing out the impressive new mosque, the music and poetry venues, the assorted delis, including a Russian one, his favourite Japanese restaurant, the best place to buy local hand-crafted gifts, and where to drop in should I need benefits advice. By the time we hit the pubs, Zac was introducing me to others as though I were an old friend.

Several times he said he really ought to find a cash machine, but I was told by the others that, even if he did, it would be of little use. Zac, it seems, is persistently penniless. At the final pub, I bought him yet another drink, deciding that would be my last act of generosity. Then, for some reason – food, I think – a bunch of us drifted back to this narrow but tall Victorian house and made our way to the basement, where Olive is now lambasting Islam for its treatment of women and Faiza is agreeing with someone at last.

Occasional thoughts that my other group might be missing me are quickly scotched when I recall Val's lack of concern over Caitlin and Ralph. And besides, I'll be back in the fold tomorrow, when we're due to tour Christ Church, go punting, then follow a literary trail.

The last of these intrigues me in my mildly stoned and inebriated state. I imagine a trail of books, all laid out along the streets and cobbled lanes of central Oxford, and ... well, it just becomes *the* most hilarious idea. I giggle to myself, at some length, then tell the others, who, with no exceptions, start giggling too. Even the intense Faiza laughs, but then she's likely had more draws on the weed than any of us. When the stew finally arrives, there are so many cases of the munchies around the table that most of us eat straight from the pot, which is also incredibly funny.

There are more than the average number of musicians in our midst, and by two in the morning, when the playing begins petering out, I feel I've had enough entertainment for one day and get up to leave. Only getting up proves harder than expected and I promptly fall back on the floor of the living room, where I decide to stay. Other, admittedly younger, people are managing to sleep perfectly well on the carpet, and considering my college might be locked and impenetrable at this hour, spending the night here seems like a good plan. If Olive would just put the ukulele down, I'd be asleep in seconds.

I stretch out on the floor below Faiza, who's fortunate enough to have the couch, and at first try using my hands as a pillow. When this proves too awkward, I sit up and gently tug at one of the two cushions beneath Faiza's lovely sleeping head. Miraculously, I gain it without disturbing her. While Olive's playing gradually slows, I close my eyes and order myself to wake at seven exactly. Sometimes that works. I want to be out of this crowded room and back at college in time for the breakfast I've paid for. I want to see Christ Church, go punting and take a literary tour. I also want to talk to Caitlin before the week's through, but am beginning to give up hope on that front.

I believe the ukulele's finally stopped. Two people are snoring and the air is thick with dope. I wonder whose house I'm in, because no one ever told me. The long-haired guy, Barney, who cooked for us, would be my guess. If I dined in London with an acquaintance who owned a house this age and size, the talk would be of improvements, extensions and its doubling in value over the past month. But maybe Barney rents. In the dark, someone is bedding down a little too close to my crotch.

Olive, I believe.

THREE

Ralph I wake up in the back of a van next to Dog, who's breathing alcohol fumes in my face and taking up way too much room. On the other side of his substantial body I can just see Lenny. Lenny's snoring loudly, but probably not waking anyone but me up, on account of the fact that we're in what looks, through the open van doors, like an empty field. I prop myself up a bit and wonder why we just didn't sleep under the stars, only then I see a couple of sheep. I suppose they might have nudged us or done their business on us if we'd bedded down on the grass.

From the cab comes the noise of someone coughing in a horrible, phlegmy chesty way. The name Trev comes into my head. We were on our way to somewhere. To a party, that was it. In a place I hadn't heard of, like Bisto or something. Then ... what happened? Can't quite recall. Yesterday evening has a sort of spooky other-worldly swirlyness to it.

I badly need a wee, so sort of slide forward to the end of the van, trying not to wake Dog, because I've got the feeling he wouldn't be happy. When I've found a spot not too near the sheep, I relieve myself at surprising length, then suddenly find I've got company. It's Lenny, relieving himself right beside me, even though there was the whole field to choose from.

'Sleep all right, mate?' he asks.

I say, 'Very well, thanks,' as though we're having a chat in the campsite urinals, which I suppose we are. 'Are we still going to Bisto?' I ask.

He laughs at me and shakes his thing. 'Bister,' he says, 'only it's spelt B I C ... er, it's spelt different from how it sounds. And no, why would we be going there now? For a start, Dog and Trev's got to get to work.' It's funny, but I hadn't imagined them having proper jobs, what with all the tattoos and booze and druggy talk. 'Labouring,' he adds.

'Is that in Oxford?' I ask hopefully.

'Yeah, don't panic, mate. We wasn't gonna leave you halfway to fucking Bisto. Bisto! Good one.'

Now I remember Trev, the driver, stopping and being sick by the side of the road. Saying he couldn't effing drive any more, because he was seeing everything in triple and it was making him effing dizzy. Ha, not because he might kill us all, I remember thinking at the time.

We get back to Oxford in quite a speedy and haphazard way that involves a good deal of hooting, and a good deal of being flung around in the back, then Lenny and I are dropped off somewhere quite suburban and run-down. Lenny wants to know if I fancy a tour of the bits of the city no tourist ever sees. I say, 'I thought I'd already been there,' and he tells me I haven't seen nothing yet.

It's a bit late in the morning to rejoin my singles' party, and my novel-to-be could definitely do with some edgy and interesting setting details, so I tell him, 'OK, only I'd love a change of clothes.'

'No problem, mate,' says Lenny, patting me on the back. 'You're a bit taller than me but I can get you fitted out fucking brilliant back at my gaff. The missus'll sort your hair out too.' I rub at the singed patch and say, 'Cheers, mate,' because the 'mate' thing is catching. Once you get past the tattoos, the shaved head, the language and the multiple face piercings, Lenny's not a bad bloke, really.

Joe At half ten I send an email. 'Hi Dad, I'm going to do a big shop. Anything you need? Cheers. Joe. (PS. Hope the paper's going well.)' I click on 'Send' and try to imagine the route his message will take just to get downstairs.

Back in bed, I plug myself into music and hear a couple of tracks before the laptop shows I've got new mail. I get up and read 'Kindly buy ink cartridge?' He gives me the printer details and signs off 'Daddy'.

After showering and dressing, I set off for the Cowley Road, hoping to get some after-the-event chaos shots. Once there, however, I'm not too surprised to see the council's been out and cleared up. There isn't that much to capture debris-wise, but the stage is being taken down and there are a few people sleeping where they fell, so I get out the Canon and take one or two shots. Then, at the best café in the street, I eat eggs Benedict, followed by French toast with maple syrup and bacon.

Finishing up my coffee, I go through

yesterday's digi-photos. Some of the first I come across are of Cait in the churchyard. Black and white and, if I say so myself, not bad. Maybe in future I should always have a drink before picking up a camera. Cait might be a bit on the mature side, but she's definitely photogenic. And attractive. Actually, really attractive in these photos. Nice legs, I notice again. I'd given her a kiss, I remember, before she went off with the tosser in feathers. Had that been a reaction to Charlotte? Christ, Charlotte. I click back to the pictures of her and delete them. Suddenly it's easy.

Checking the time, I curse and quickly pay up. There's a big shop to do, the ink cartridge to find, and then I really should show my face at the Italian Job.

On my way home to drop the cameras off and pick up the car, I bump into a rough-looking Zac, who says, 'Hey, what you up to?'

'Food shop.'

His face lights up. 'Out of town?'

'Yep.' For financial reasons, combined with laziness, Zac rarely leaves the city. 'Come with me if you want.'

'Cool.'

In the car he talks about the festival, mostly who'd been playing and where. He says he managed to pick up an American tourist, who kept him in drinks all afternoon, until everyone went back to Barney's for a smoke and some food.

'Daniel, the Yank, came too. He was really cool. And like a visiting professor or something. History, I think. Anyway, you know how clever and like well-informed Faiza is?'

'Uh-huh.'

'Well, multiply it by a gazillion and you've got Daniel. Or maybe by ten, because Faiza did get a first at Cambridge and does teach philosophy at Brookes. Anyway, he crashed at Barney's but this morning he'd disappeared, which was a bit gutting because I thought we might get some breakfast together.'

'Right.' I don't have that much to say about the festival, since I'd slept away the late afternoon in the churchyard, then – being old and boring – gone home and watched TV.

Zac rubs his middle. 'And I could really do with some breakfast, man.'

I look over at my scrawny friend. We'd gone through school together up to sixteen, but then Zac failed all but one GCSE (incredibly, French) and has been hanging out in Oxford ever since, never holding down a job for long and going on incapacity benefit at every opportunity on account of chronic fatigue syndrome. I once asked how he got chronically fatigued doing nothing and Zac said he did a lot of thinking. He's barred from his academic parents' home for stealing and selling their things, so moves from one shared house to another, where he tends to piss people off by helping himself to fridge stuff. Despite this, he's got far more friends than I have. Maybe because he makes everyone feel like a success story.

'You can get breakfast in the supermarket café,' I tell him, 'if you want. My treat.'

'Pain au chocolat,' Zac says, almost to himself and with perfect pronunciation. 'Cheers, Joe. I'll owe you one.'

'Yeah, right.' I ask him how the job-hunting's going.

'Er, well, not much around, that's the trouble. I don't suppose the Italian Job–'

'Nothing at the moment.' The one time Zac worked for us, complaints rose, profits dipped and he put on weight. 'Sorry.'

'Let me know if–'

'Will do.'

Back at home, Zac and I put things away, but our methods are quite different. I take an item and put it on a shelf, whereas Zac takes an item, opens it, helps himself to whatever, then puts the item on a shelf. By the time all the bags are emptied, he's had another meal.

I make up a plate of cold food, which I take into Dad's bombsite of a study. 'Ah,' he says, pencil in mouth, feet on desk. 'Ink.' He takes the cartridge from my hand, ignoring the food in the other. 'Excellent.'

'There's artichoke in the salad,' I say, knowing how much he likes it.

'Splendid, splendid,' he says, lifting his printer lid and fumbling around.

'And boiled skunk in the tortilla wrap.'

'Jolly good.' The printer buzzes and chugs and installs the new cartridge. 'Thank you, Joe.'

'You're welcome.'

Back in the kitchen, Zac's head is in the fridge and he's humming Pink Floyd's 'Money'.

'I've got to get to the café,' I tell him. 'What are your plans?'

Zac's eyes wander from stacked fridge to refilled wine rack. 'OK if I chill here?'

Caitlin We've done Christ Church cathedral (beautifully cool) and Christ Church meadows (baking) and those who don't want to punt – me and the blonde women – have an hour and a half to kill before the literary tour. I debate with myself whether to spend the time looking for Ralph, or to mosey around the shops. Surely a man at least six-two tall can look after himself in a small friendly city? I wonder if he's too embarrassed by his body paint and singed hair to make an appearance, but I'm not sure Ralph does embarrassment.

'Not punting?' someone asks.

I turn and see it's the American, Daniel.

70

'Oh, you're back!' I exclaim, sounding more pleased than I intended. Out in the brightness his hair is darker, his skin more olive. I'm guessing there's some Spanish or Italian in him.

'I spent this morning in my room,' he says, 'sleeping.' His eyes, not quite as dark as his hair, are fixed on mine. 'Got kind of caught up in a carnival yesterday,' he adds.

'Me too!' I say, amazed.

'Yeah, I ran into Ralph.'

'Today?'

'No, yesterday.'

'Oh. He still hasn't come back, you know.'

'Having too good a time, I guess.' Daniel gets out his camera and shows me a funny photo of Ralph dancing with some children.

'Yes,' I say, 'he certainly throws himself into things.'

Daniel switches his camera off and puts it away in a little leather bag. 'Listen, if you're not punting, how about a stroll? We could maybe go see the Botanic Garden, since we both missed it yesterday?'

I spot the blonde women heading our way and quickly say, 'Yes! Great idea!' wishing I could stop being so effusive.

I'm not sure we notice much of the walled garden or the large unbearably hot greenhouses, so busy are we filling each other in on our lives up to now. We have lots to say and I find myself really liking Daniel.

We sit for a while on the river bank, chatting and watching punts and rowing boats go by. But we're without shade and after a while we stand up dizzily and make our way back to the High Street and an air-conditioned restaurant, where we both, perversely, go for hot tea. Sometimes we sit in a not-uncomfortable silence, flicking through the day's papers and occasionally fan ourselves with them.

As he reads, I shoot quick glances at Daniel. He's forty-five too, he told me, and used to live with someone but has no children. He teaches American political history and is currently writing a book on the George W. administration. I asked if that was really history, and he informed me, laughing, that even this morning is history.

By the time we meet the others from their punts, I feel pleased I've befriended the best-looking man in the group. That doesn't, however, stop me scanning the streets throughout our literary tour, hoping to catch sight of Joe, perhaps heading to or from work. We're told about Tolkien, Lewis and Carroll. About Dexter, Pullman and Murdoch. Val throws in historical or architectural detail: 'Cistercian monastery... Bridge of Sighs... Oxford Movement... Divinity School...' She talks enthusiastically on vaulting, parapets and pediments, but not much sinks in. In fact, none of it does. Joe has an Italian café, that much I know, so when Val announces after the tour that she's booked a table at an Italian restaurant, I'm suddenly paying attention. My heart does a skip or two and I run a comb through my hair.

But in the restaurant, Joe's nowhere to be seen. This isn't too surprising, since I counted at least four Italian eateries on our tour. It's also good, because I can relax and concentrate on what Daniel's saying. It's a popular place and he's having to shout above the other people shouting. He's telling me about the parts of the UK he's hoping to visit before his flight home.

'And I'd love to see Wales,' he says.

Without thinking, I invite him to stay. 'I've got converted outhouses for guests,' I add quickly.

He lifts one dark eyebrow. 'I wouldn't want to impose.'

Perhaps he doesn't really want to see Wales, I think. Was just being polite. I nevertheless take a business card from my bag and hand it to him. 'You're welcome to come for a couple of days, or longer, if you want. But I expect you've got things organised.'

'Uh, no, I haven't.'

He's giving me a look that makes me think he's reading more into my invitation than I'm offering – which, if I hadn't been ruined by the attentions of an almost-thirty-year-old, I might be.

'*Fettuccine Alfredo?*' asks the waiter, and I put my hand up.

'Great,' Daniel says to me. He smiles his attractive toothy smile and tucks my card in his wallet. 'Thank you.'

During desserts, when the restaurant has quietened considerably, Ronald stands up and thanks Val, Gemma and Ben for giving us all 'such a wonderful time'.

People say, 'Hear, hear,' and then we drink a toast.

Val also stands. 'And thank *you*,' she says, 'for being such a super party. One of the best I've had!' She then suggests going around the table, each saying what the highlight has been for us so far. 'Feedback is terribly useful.'

Some vote for their Shakespeare-in-the-rain experience, others the literary tour. Pauline enjoyed the punting best, she says, and then all eyes are on me and I'm a bit stumped. I can hardly say sitting in a churchyard with a pheremonal young man, so I rave about the concert, even though I missed the first half-hour.

Next it's Daniel's turn and he says, 'This meal?' causing a few chuckles. Then he adds, 'And meeting Caitlin,' which makes me blush to my roots because people start clapping, although not the two tarty women.

'Sorry,' he whispers afterwards, clearly distressed. 'A bit too much sun, I guess.'

Back at the college, in the moonlight, we all sit on the grass of the Chapel quad – which I suspect is forbidden, but Val is quite tipsy – and play games.

'I went to market and bought a hat,' begins Val, and off we go, around the circle. Ronald has the worst memory, failing at round two. And Daniel is the winner, beating Liz when she forgets what came after 'bananas' and goes out.

'A chip butty,' Daniel tells her. 'Whatever that may be.'

Daniel's not so good at charades, though, having never heard of *The Bill* or *Emmerdale*. When it's his turn he raises the tone somewhat by miming some Hemingway – *The Old Man and the Sea* – which I get fairly quickly.

'Come again?' says Barry.

Shortly before midnight, when I flop naked on my bed with my new unopened paperback, my head – in the quiet and stillness, after all the activity – starts filling itself with Ralph and whether he's OK. So I get up, put my clothes back on and go down to the lodge and ask the night porter for his room number. I then find the room, knock on the door and call out, 'Ralph?' Then a much louder, 'Ralph!' I bang several times but there's no answer. I think perhaps I should let Val know I'm concerned, but not right

75

now. An elderly lady and myself can hardly go hunting for him in the dark.

Back in my room, naked on the bed again, unopened paperback still unopened, I scrub Ralph from my thoughts and go back to the churchyard.

FOUR

Daniel I look at the day's itinerary. 'A.M. Visit University Church and climb tower.' I picture some of our party struggling with the latter, or worse, wedged in a spiral stairwell. Not Caitlin, of course. This afternoon we have a minibus tour of the Cotswolds, to include an early supper in somewhere called 'Lower Slaughter'. And we wonder why English place names don't lend themselves to song.

Heading for the Hall, I step into the quad to discover it's not as cool a day as my dark and thick-walled room had me believe. In fact, it's already a shade too hot, and before breakfast too. Once indoors again, I fill a tray with the least fattening items at the buffet and join Caitlin, who only has tea and looks a little tense.

'Hi, there,' I say. 'You OK?'

'Yes, thanks. Well, no. I just think someone

should be looking for Ralph. I got the porter to open up his room earlier and it's obvious he hasn't been back since we went out Saturday evening. His case isn't unpacked. Where is he? The worst thing is, I feel partly responsible.'

'Well, you mustn't.' I don't want to alarm Caitlin further, but I think it's odd too. It is possible Ralph has met with misfortune. Fallen in with some of the unsavoury types I spotted at the carnival. Fallen in the Thames. 'We should tell Val,' I say, 'and she can inform ... well, whoever.'

'The police? Yeah, like they'll do something. He's a grown man who skived off the moment he arrived.'

'Pardon me?'

'Um ... played hooky?'

'Ah. Aren't you eating?'

Caitlin shakes her head. 'Too much Italian food yesterday. Not that I don't like Italian food. In fact, I was thinking of trying another Italian place this evening.'

'Aren't we supposed to be dining in Lower Slaughter?' I chuckle again at the name, whilst Caitlin just shrugs. 'You're skipping the Cotswold trip?' I ask.

'I think so. Er, bit of a headache. I'll be OK to do the church visit, but I'm not up to a minibus journey. I'll rest, or potter around Oxford.'

Now I don't know what to do. I'd love to

spend the day with her but she hasn't exactly suggested it. I'd also like to see those Cotswold villages, which I've heard from fellow Americans are beyond cute. For fear of appearing overly keen, I say, 'I'm kind of looking forward to getting out of Oxford.'

Caitlin laughs. 'I love the way you say that.'

'What?'

'Hey, here's Val!' Caitlin jumps from her seat and goes and corners our leader. I see Val frown and scratch her chin, then nod and take out her phone. She looks at a piece of paper, tries a number, shakes her head and puts the phone away. I can only guess she was calling Ralph's cellphone, although Caitlin told me he'd lost it.

Caitlin returns and says, 'Val's going to tell the police.' She sits down, picks up her cup, and as her eyes roam around the tall, wood-panelled room she shudders. 'Suddenly, I'm feeling homesick,' she says.

I too take a good look around the hallowed room – all those dead guys on the walls – and know what she means. To dispel the gloom, I get us on to the weather, the costs of things here compared to the States, and guessing Val's age. Caitlin's on her second tea when Val comes over in her long, lilac classy-looking dress and seats herself beside us. Anywhere between sixty-five and eighty, we'd decided.

'I thought I'd try Ralph's home first,' she tells us. 'Just in case he shot back to Lincoln for some reason.'

'Good idea,' says Caitlin.

'Yes. Only I got ... his wife.'

'The cad!' I cry.

'No, no,' says Caitlin, placing a very welcome hand on mine. I believe it's the first time we've touched. 'Don't be too hard on him. He, er ... well, he was only here to do a spot of research. Said he wants to start something similar in Lincoln.'

'So his wife explained,' says Val. 'Rather naughty, but I suppose I should be flattered. Anyway, Hilary seemed terribly concerned about her husband, but told me Ralph *is* rather excitable and impressionable, and forgets to consider the effects of his actions on others. He's probably gone off on one of his little adventures, she said. She couldn't talk for long, what with her terminally ill mother and working full time.'

'So you're not going to the police?' I ask.

'Hilary suggested leaving it one more day. Now we know a little of Ralph's character, that might be wise.' Val stands again and turns to the group. 'So,' she calls out, 'who's for some splendid views of Oxford?'

Almost at the top of the church, after a 124-step climb, is a stone viewing platform that surrounds the tower. Only five of us have managed it – myself, Caitlin, Barry (astonishingly) and the interneters. Barry has binoculars, which Caitlin borrows and then stands in one spot looking through.

Having done a circuit, squeezing past Japanese tourists and others, I come back to where Caitlin is still peering east. 'There are some great views round the other side,' I tell her.

'Uh-huh,' she says, not moving.

'Are you hoping to spot Ralph on a rooftop somewhere, frantically waving for help?'

'Oh, it's not Ralph I'm looking for,' she says, now training the binoculars on the High Street.

I decide not to ask.

It's two thirty, it's hot and the beauty of the Cotswolds is beginning to pall. When you've seen five achingly beautiful, sleepy, warm-stoned villages with not a piece of thatch out of place, you feel you're ready to jump ship at the next tiny railroad station and get a train back to Oxford. Which is what I do.

An hour and a half later, I'm walking toward the city centre, looking up Caitlin in my cellphone. Luckily, we'd exchanged numbers last night. My idea. But when I try her, there's no answer. I wonder if she's still unwell, so head back to Peterchurch to find out.

However, on knocking on Caitlin's door, I'm greeted with disappointment. I try her phone again, but once more it rings and goes to voicemail. I imagine her fully recovered and meandering around a museum. Pretty as a picture, finger on chin, the sound muted on her cellphone.

It's four thirty. I could seek out a delicious tea-and-scone deal somewhere quiet and cool, or I could go see what the Cowley Road looks like when not in carnival mode, and maybe check out any Italian restaurants in advance. Each plan has a certain appeal, and after a shower and a change of clothes, I decide to do both.

Caitlin It's with some trepidation – no, a lot of trepidation – that I press the bell of the tall terraced house in Divinity Road. I've dressed myself up a bit and I'm even wearing earrings. While I wait, I arrange my face into a friendly but slightly worried expression, which I hold until the door opens and there's Joe.

'Hey,' he says, breaking into a smile. 'Forgotten your college again?' This time he's in a white T-shirt, which is snug and contrasts fabulously with his silky brown hair and tanned arms and face. 'You OK?' he adds, when I find I can't speak.

I nod and clear my throat. 'I, er, just wondered if you've come across Ralph at all.

81

He's sort of missing. Basically, since I left the churchyard with him on Sunday. He stopped to have his body painted and didn't come back to the college. Anyway, we're all really quite worried, especially his wife.' Now I've started, I can't stop. 'Yes, he's married, but apparently she knew Ralph was here. He was just carrying out some research into singles' weekends for the over ... more mature people.'

'Come in,' says Joe. 'You'll swelter out there. Can I make you a smoothie?'

'Yes,' I expire. 'That would be nice.'

He makes a great smoothie – kiwi fruit, everything – which we sit on the patio drinking, under the shade of a vine-covered pergola. I ask Joe where his father is.

'In his front-room study, working. I kept that separate when I knocked the walls down, so he can focus on whatever he's doing. Once Dad starts a project, he just goes at it till it's done.'

'And are you like that?' I want to ease the conversation round to the café, so I can find out the name of it. 'I mean, you must have had drive to open ... er, what did you say your restaurant was called?'

He smiles. 'I'm not sure I did. The Italian Job.'

'Really?' I was in there earlier, on the verge of asking if a Joe ran it, but wisely not doing so. It was sweet and informal, unlike some of the other places I'd popped my head in, with their crisp white cloths. 'Good name.'

'You think? I was never sure. Yeah, it took some drive, I suppose. My mum and I inherited a chunk of money from my grandfather a few years ago. I came across Carlo with his idea for a sort of relaxed Italian café in the city centre, then it all happened quite quickly. It was a fifty-fifty investment in the business, but we don't own the premises. Carlo sees to the food side and the accounts. I go in and help out front most days and do the marketing.'

'And do you enjoy it?'

'Yeah. I'd rather be a world-renowned photographer, but hey.'

'And what did you do before that? Sorry, I'm being nosy.'

'No, you're not. I did a fine art and photography degree, then got a job on a local paper as a lowly photographer. Lots of golden anniversary couples. Boring as hell.'

'Well, at least you were out and about. I did admin in a builders' merchants when Frankie was little and we were hard up. There wasn't a day went by I didn't want to torch the place.'

'I can imagine.'

Joe's got a small scar, I notice, on his left cheek, not far from his eye. I want to know how it got there, whether he'd had stitches. He asks me what my husband did.

'Oh, mostly he had affairs,' I say, a bit too flippantly, perhaps.

Joe shakes his head. 'But why?'

I'm not sure how to answer this, so just shrug and get back to Ralph. Joe asks if we've been to the police, and I tell him Val's about to do that. I'm exaggerating everyone's concern, of course, otherwise he'll think I'm here on a pretext. 'It's cast quite a cloud over things,' I say, as solemn as I can manage.

'If you want, we could go out now and have a bit of a hunt for him? Ask around.'

It's a thoughtful offer but I don't want to go anywhere. I think quickly and say, 'Someone in the group has a picture of Ralph in his camera. It might be worth getting a print of that, then asking people if they've seen him.'

Joe looks down and nods. I'm not sure, but he may be eyeing up the legs I fake-tanned this morning. 'About the churchyard the other day,' he says, lifting his gaze. 'Sorry if I was a bit ... you know, out of order.'

I wave a hand at him. 'Oh, don't worry.' I want him to stop before he tells me he must have been out of his mind too.

'My girlfriend and I recently split up.'

'Oh dear.' I'm not sure I want to hear about his girlfriend. 'Gosh, it's warm,' I say, fanning myself with a hand.

'I'd just bumped into her at the carnival, you see ... and well, anyway, I'm sorry.'

'There's nothing to apologise for, Joe. It was very pleasant. Sitting there. In the shade.'

'Yes.' He puts his empty glass down and leans my way. 'Is it too warm out here for you?'

'Um...' I want to put my glass down in case another kiss is coming my way, but find I can't move my arm, or any part of me.

'Shall we go in?'

I hear myself swallow. 'OK.'

Joe scrapes his chair back and stands, just as my mobile starts up, somewhere in the depths of my bag. I let it ring, then let it ring some more.

'Aren't you going to answer it?' Joe asks. He seems bothered that I'm not.

'Yes, of course.' Now I feel silly. I put the glass down, unzip the bag and find the phone. I catch the name 'Daniel' only when I've pressed reply. I've already ignored two calls from him.

'Hi, Daniel.'

'Hey, Caitlin. How's the head?'

'Er, better. Thanks.'

'Good. Where are you? I was wondering if you'd like to hook up. We could maybe go get some Italian food.'

'Aren't you in the Cotswolds?' I ask, confused.

'Got a train back. Listen, I have a bit of a lead on Ralph.'

'Great,' I say, suddenly not caring a jot about Ralph.

'Can we meet in around thirty minutes? Say at Carfax?'

'I, um ... well...'

'It's quite important.'

'It's just that...' It's no good, I can't come up with an excuse. 'Well, OK,' I say, wishing I'd never laid eyes on Ralph. But then I'd never have laid eyes on Joe. 'I'll see you there.'

'Who's Daniel?' asks Joe, when I hang up.

I stand and hook my bag over my shoulder. 'Oh, just a guy in the group.' I would add more but Joe's giving me this look.

'Do you have to go?'

'I think so.'

'Then come back some time? Not this evening – I'm at the café later. But maybe tomorrow? I'd like to take more photos of you, if that's all right? You're a good subject. I'll pay you, of course. Listen, why don't you give me your mobile number, then we can arrange something?'

On Sunday I was very pretty, today I'm a good subject. Ah, well. I read out the number from my phone screen, then tap his in. 'Are you sure you want to take pictures of me? My husband used to say I wasn't photogenic.'

Joe grins. 'If you ask me, your husband was an idiot.' On that fairly high note, I leave.

Daniel and I are seated in a café waiting to order before he explains. 'Earlier, I wandered through town to the Cowley Road, just for something to do, really. When I was there, I met this guy I know, Zac.'

The waiter comes over and we order. 'And?' I say, when we're alone again. I wonder how he knows Zac, but am keener to hear about Ralph.

'Zac hangs out in that neighbourhood, so I showed him the photograph of Ralph on my camera, and he said, yeah, he had seen him. Last night.'

'Oh, good.'

'However, Zac said Ralph was with a bunch of people you'd cross the road to avoid. Lots of muscle, lots of tattoos. He didn't recognise them.'

'And how do you know this Zac?'

'Met him at a workshop. African drum.'

'Ralph wanted to have a go at that,' I say. 'Ralph wanted to have a go at everything.'

'It was great,' Daniel tells me with a big smile. 'You'd have loved it.'

'Really?' Suddenly, I'm regretting sitting in a churchyard with Joe when I could have been drumming with nice Daniel. Why is that? What's the matter with me? 'Listen,' I say, 'I wonder if we should do something about Ralph. After all, his wife said he was impressionable. He could be caught up in something heavy.' It might be fun going on a Ralph hunt with Daniel.

His face lights up. 'Sure. Why don't we take a look round the area, after we've eaten? Maybe we'll come across him.'

'OK.'

I beckon the waitress over and we order from the wine list, then Daniel says, 'Blenheim Palace tomorrow. Churchill's birthplace. Think you'll be going?'

'Oh, yes,' I lie. 'Really looking forward that.'

Later, we amble along the Cowley Road, all the while keeping an eye out for Ralph. We stick our heads in various pubs, check out the takeaways and wander through the little park. Obviously, I've got Joe on my mind too, but he had said he was going into the café later. On our way back, we try the supermarket.

We've walked up and down half the aisles, when a woman all in black comes and gives Daniel a hug. 'Where did *you* run off to yesterday?' she asks in a husky voice. I experience a twinge of jealousy, and wonder where that came from. The woman leans her head back and her eyes bore into Daniel's, while a hand runs up and down his back. She's older than us, big-boned and smells of garlic.

'This is Olive,' says Daniel, once free. 'Olive, Caitlin. Listen, gotta hurry. Great to see you, Olive. I'll be in touch.' He takes my arm and gently yanks me away.

'But you don't know my...' Olive's calling out.

By around half nine we're ready to give up, but before going back to the college we stop for a drink in a dinky, low-ceilinged pub. It's while we're at the bar, ordering two more wines, that a man in the far corner welcomes everyone to open-mike poetry night.

'Great!' says Daniel.

'Hmm,' I say, not so sure. Amateur poets?

We get the last small table as the place fills up. It's by the propped-open door to the garden, so we're in a welcome breeze. We also have a good view of the performers, the first of which is a middle-aged man with waist-length greying hair. He unrolls a wad of A4 paper and perches one buttock on a bar stool.

'Hey, it's Barney,' says Daniel. He puts his glass down and claps along with the others.

'But how do you–' I begin in the general applause and whistles. This Barney's obviously a popular guy, but how does Daniel know him?

Barney's poetry is really comic verse. Topical and very funny, with the odd in-joke that has the regulars roaring. When his turn is over and an intense-looking young woman in earth colours approaches the mike, Daniel and I decide to leave. On our way out, Daniel waves at both Barney and a dark and sultry woman at the bar. As we stroll towards Peterchurch, I'm desperate to ask Daniel about his double life. But, since I'm leading one myself, and since he's not volunteering anything, we talk about American poets. Well, he does.

Our timing is unfortunate and we arrive at the college just as the others are returning from the country. Daniel says a quick good night and darts off to his room, while I stay out in the quad, taking in the honeysuckle and the last of the evening light.

Val approaches and says, 'Headache all gone?'

'Yes, thanks.'

'We couldn't keep Daniel away from you an entire day. I do so adore our little success stories. Perhaps you and he would agree to appear in our literature?'

'No!' I tell her, then see the wounded look. 'I'm sorry, but nothing's, you know, happening. Daniel and I are just friends.'

'But it'll blossom,' she says, rubbing my arm sympathetically. 'Mark my words.'

'Listen, about Ralph,' I say, keen to switch subjects. 'There have been sightings in east Oxford – you know, Cowley Road. Well, one sighting.'

Val's crêpey hand leaves my arm and flies

to her chest. 'Oh, goodness. I do try to tell my groups not to venture further east than Magdalen Bridge. Not if they can help it.'

'No?'

'No, dear. Far too dangerous.'

I'm tempted to agree, thinking of Joe, but thank her for the tip and wish her good night.

On the bed, naked again in the still and stifling night-time heat, I wonder if I've been wrong about Ralph. Maybe he's not a jolly Blyton character, after all. Perhaps he likes hanging out with thugs... My eyes close and I listen to my breathing deepen and lengthen, then the paperback dropping to the floor. The Famous Five swim around in my head... I'd loved those books as a child, and had even forced Frankie to read them, aged eight. He liked Dick best. But now Dick is fat and tattooed and wears a boy-band T-shirt, and George, always my favourite Blyton girl, is in combats and mugging someone. Timmy's a bull mastiff... It's horrible, and I'm still feeling disturbed when the mobile rings and my eyes snap open and I'm suddenly talking to Frankie.

'Where's the Vanish?' he asks.

I sit up and cover myself with the sheet, as though he can see me. 'What have you stained?'

'Nothing.'

'Then why are you phoning me in the

91

middle of the night asking where the Vanish is?'

'I just wanted to know, in case I do stain something. And it's only half ten.'

'Not my fabrics?'

'Look, forget it, yeah? I'll get some tomorrow. Just in case I do happen to have an accident. Say with red wine or something. You all right?'

'Yes, thanks. Hot, tired.'

'I'll let you get to sleep, then.'

'It's on top of the cupboard in my workroom. Occasionally, I drip coffee and things on material.'

'Cheers,' he says. I hear him whisper, 'Top of cupboard in Mum's workroom.' Then to me – 'I'd better go. Bye.'

I settle down again, throw off the sheet and try to decide what would be worse – the carpet or one of the sofas. And who was Frankie talking to? A girl? I wonder if I should have left him in charge of my home and livelihood... I wonder if I should go home and take control... I wonder again, and as others must have done, if George was a lesbian.

Daniel That was quite a day, I decide, lying on my bed and trying to read. An action-packed one, for sure – church climb, Cotswolds, coffee with Zac, dinner with Caitlin, the Ralph hunt, the pub – and all in such intense heat. This is way too hot for the UK, surely?

I close my book and fan myself with it. The very best part was being with Caitlin. We seem to get along well and I'm finding myself more and more drawn. In the pub, my eyes had wandered between the inscrutable, curvaceous and stunning Faiza, leaning coolly on the bar, and pretty, skinny Caitlin, laughing unreservedly at Barney's verses with Guinness froth on her upper lip. No contest, really.

Tomorrow we'll explore Blenheim Palace together. If I'd thought about it, I'd have bought a book, absorbed some facts and been able to impress Caitlin as we wandered round the house and grounds. There may still be time.

FIVE

Joe I'm having a well-deserved lie-in, semi-awake after a knackering night at the café. God, I hate tourists, but obviously I love them too. I can tell without opening my eyes that it's another glorious if unbearably hot day, but guess my father won't see much of it. I'll get up and make us both breakfast soon, even if Dad will forget to eat what I take him on a tray. Later, I'll probably give Cait a call about the photo session. Do I just want photos of her, or do I want more? I'm definitely attracted. An older woman – why not? The younger ones can be so tedious, and what's eight years or so? I see it's eleven thirty, then my eyes close and drift back into sleep until my phone starts up. I reach for it and read 'Cait'.

'Joe?' she says.

'Yeah. Hi.' My voice is croaky and I clear my throat.

'I've woken you up.'

'No, I'm just being lazy.'

'Sorry. It's just that I've got some free time and thought you might want to take those photos.'

'Yeah, OK. I, er, just need to get myself organised. Where are you now?'

'Downstairs.'

'How did you manage that?'

'Your father let me in.'

'What?' Dad never hears the doorbell when he's working.

'Sorry,' she says again. 'I shouldn't have–'

'No, it's fine. Great, in fact.'

'Tell you what, I'll go and get a coffee somewhere, then come back.'

'No, don't do that.' What if she doesn't come back? Too embarrassed.

'No?' she asks softly. There's something in that 'No?'. Something like, 'I'm not really

94

here to have my picture taken, and we know that.' Maybe.

'Listen, why don't you come up?' I reach out to my jeans and feel around for gum, grimacing while I wait for an answer.

After a longish silence, during which I think I might have totally misread things, she says, 'Where are you?'

'First floor, back room.'

When two tense minutes have passed and Cait hasn't shown, I get up and poke my head out the door. There's no sign of her but I do hear voices, and one of them sounds like Cait and the other like my father. After throwing on clothes, I bound down the stairs and find the two of them chatting in the kitchen.

'Dad?' I say. 'How come you're...?'

'Finished the paper. And another truly ground-breaking piece of work it is too. I found your charming but neglected guest here trying to locate the bathroom.'

Cait bobs her eyebrows at me in a hey-ho way. She's looking particularly nice in a strappy flowered dress. I say, 'Cait's come for a photo session.'

'So I gather.' Dad's taking things from the fridge. 'Let me see ... smoked salmon, cream cheese, bagels. Ah, jolly good, water-cress.' With his arms full, he turns to Cait and me. 'Anyone for a spot of brunch?'

My dad's always had this ability to charm attractive women – though not when he's on a maths mission in underpants, obviously – and, once again, I watch him in action and wonder how he does it. Could just be the drawling public-school accent and his wide range of adjectives – sublime, towering, zestful, heady – casually dropped into his stories to make them all the more colourful. It makes me realise how limited my vocabulary is. But on the other hand, how ridiculous we'd sound – me, Ozzie, Tim, Zac and everyone we know – if we started saying, 'Yeah, Dysexlia were really zestful last night.'

Dad's telling Cait about his conference in Kiev at the time of the Orange Revolution. 'I spent an entire exhilarating day in Independence Square, wearing a supportive but unflattering orange cap under my Cossack fur hat. I assumed the Ukrainians chose heart-warming orange to combat their joyless, veritably glacial, weather.'

I look at him and sigh, knowing I'd have said 'freezing cold'. I imagine his school timetable – '9–10.45 Double Adjectives' – and almost feel sorry for him. Actually, I do feel sorry for him because he loathed his boarding school, being what he calls 'a complete duffer at games'.

'Wow,' says Cait, all wide-eyed and impressed. 'Er, what kind of fur was it – the hat?'

'What? Oh, mink, I believe. Terribly effective.'

Cait sort of purses her lips and Dad says, 'I sense you disapprove. But, believe me, when one's ears are about to be lost to frostbite, one opts for expediency over conservation.'

'I'm sure one does,' says Cait, then she laughs in quite a flirty way. I'm not too bothered, though. She wouldn't go for someone with ear hair.

'Coffee?' I ask her. My first contribution to the conversation. 'Or shall we get on with the photo session?' I wink, knowing Dad's still somewhere in Kiev.

'And do you believe Yushchenko was poisoned?' Cait asks, her hands clasped under her chin. 'Just as Litvinenko was?'

'Oh, undoubtedly,' says Dad.

I go and make the coffee, anyway.

Daniel I'm worrying about Caitlin. Yesterday a headache, today she has sunstroke. It could be she doesn't take good care of herself, although you'd think growing organic produce and so on would ensure healthy eating. I decide, when we're on our third state room with tapestry-covered walls, that once back in the city I'll pick her up some vitamins.

'Just think,' says Sheila, when we've

moved on to Churchill's *actual* birthplace. 'In that very bed!'

'Incredible,' whispers Pauline, and Hamid agrees with an awed shake of the head.

The interneters never stray too far from me, and after a while I don't mind, because one of them, Sarah, appears to know more about the original Duke of Marlborough, Queen Anne, Louis Quatorze and the Battle of Blenheim than the guide herself. She whispers additional information to us such as, 'Basically, John Churchill saved Europe from French domination.' Or, 'Anne had seventeen pregnancies but only five live births.'

I discover, when we're having tea on the terrace, that Sarah not only teaches history, but has written books for children, mainly on kings and queens and great battles. I ask the other interneter, Liz – perhaps the prettier of the two – what she does, and it turns out she's a palaeontologist.

I say, 'Wow, I had no idea,' my eyes avoiding the deep cleavages opposite.

'I tend to keep quiet about it,' says Liz, 'particularly since taking early retirement. I think it might have been putting men off.'

I suspect it's inadequate clothing putting them off, but can hardly pass that on. Instead, I say, '*Very* early retirement, surely?' and she laughs. I'm beginning to like the interneters, but like Caitlin more. Sunstroke? It's possible, I guess. Especially if you're used to the rain, which I've heard is prevalent in Wales.

I excuse myself and slip indoors, where I try calling Caitlin to see how she is. She doesn't reply and I picture her resting in her cool dark room. After our exploration of Woodstock, we're due back in Oxford at around four, when there's free time until dinner in a French restaurant. I form a plan to skip the restaurant and spirit Caitlin off to the Cowley Road for a little more Ralph-hunting. We could also dine cosily and exotically together – Indian? Japanese? – maybe revisit the poet pub...

'Really, Daniel,' says Val, sidling up to me. 'I saw you flirting with Liz and Sarah. Don't tell me you're switching affections already?' She giggles and floats off in cream linen. 'Minibus in ten minutes!' I hear her tell the others.

Woodstock is an attractive and bustling little Cotswold-style town. It's nestled right beside Blenheim and I'd have preferred to walk here through the palace park than take the three-minute ride. Being herded around is not something I'd normally go for, but sometimes you just have to shake off your ego and climb into a sweltering minibus with a genial smile.

We're given forty minutes and I wander,

alone at last, around the stores looking for gifts. Some to take home and perhaps one for Caitlin. My sister is easy. A pot of local honey. As is my mother. A scarf. For Caitlin, because I can't decide and am running out of time, I buy a bar of natural sandalwood soap, hoping she doesn't take offence. During my sprint to the bus, I spot a pharmacy, so dash in for multivitamins. But once I've paid, I have second thoughts. I wouldn't want to offend her – 'Here, take better care of yourself.' Or, worse still, come across as too eager to please. Desperate, even.

On the journey back, I fake a doze and think about the summer stretching before me. Connecticut with my mother for two weeks, two weeks in New York visiting friends, then back to London and some serious work on my book before students descend in early fall.

I'm not sure what I'd envisioned when I signed up, post-divorce, for these two years in the UK. A period of healing, certainly, in a place a long, long way from Lauren. Meeting someone new and exciting, I guess. Whisking her back to the States for some late-in-the-day babies... I don't think I imagined sitting in a crowded minibus listening to Pauline talk dental implants. But as my head nods against the window, I see Pauline and the others as part of life's rich tapestry, and then I think of the Blenheim tapestries, and then I do actually doze for a while.

I knock on Caitlin's door and to my joy it opens.

'Hi,' she says. 'How was the trip?'

'Great. Interesting. Hot. Here, I got you a gift. Well, two.' I hand over the soap and the vitamins and can see she's stumped for a response. Now I regret both purchases. Am I telling her she's unclean and unhealthy? 'Sorry,' I add. 'Was sort of in a hurry. And the vitamins are to ... you know.'

'Yes,' she says, smiling at me prettily. 'I expect I could do with supplements.' She sniffs the soap. 'Mmm, thank you. But really, Daniel, you shouldn't have.'

'Well...' Rather than hang around and not be invited in, I tell Caitlin I need to go shower. As I reverse, I say, 'Any sign of Ralph?'

'I checked out his room an hour ago. No change.'

'Oh dear. Kind of worrying.' I frown and squeeze my chin and hope she's convinced by my acting.

'Yes,' she says, also frowning and possibly acting too. Hard to know.

'How about we go looking for him again this evening?' I suggest. 'We'll likely miss some amazing French food, but we could find something on Cowley Road.'

'Yeah, OK. I had a big lunch, anyway.

Meet you at the lodge in an hour?'

'Sure,' I say, surprised at how easy that was. I turn and skip gaily, as I'd guess many an undergraduate has, down the old wooden stairs.

Caitlin We're in the poetry pub again, just for a quickie. We haven't eaten yet and the Guinness is going to my head. Daniel's telling me about the studio flat he's renting in London, and how he can open the fridge, close the window and take clothes from the dresser, all without leaving his futon. 'Lucky I'm not claustrophobic, only with London prices, that's all I can afford.'

'Oh dear,' I say.

'Nah, it's OK really. Kind of cosy. But anyhow, I usually eat out, and often colleagues take pity and have me over for dinner.'

I wonder if he goes on dates too. A mid-forties man with charm, looks, hair and no flab must be in demand in London. Or anywhere. It's a hard subject to bring up, though – 'Have you slept with many women since you arrived?' And, besides, why would I want to know? Has Joe now got me interested in any attractive man?

I'm saved from this line of thought by Daniel asking about my place. I tell him how I'd moved to the cottage from Bangor after the divorce, wanting a fresh start, a different kind of life for myself and Frankie. New work, new friends. How I'd fallen for the cottage and its location on my first viewing.

'It was early summer and everything was warm and colourful. The owners had already established the vegetable patch, and I immediately had the idea of expanding it.'

I can see from the enchanted look in Daniel's eyes that I'm painting too idyllic a picture. 'However, in the winter,' I continue, 'we're in mud to our knees and the draught through the bedroom window makes my neck stiff all day. In fact, that can happen in summer too. When it freezes, I have to wear a coat while I'm sewing and keep the gas cooker alight.'

'But the views,' says Daniel, staring over my shoulder at some imaginary scene, 'must make up for all that.'

'Yes,' I have to admit, 'they do.'

His warm brown eyes are back on mine. 'I was hoping to come visit next week, if that's OK?'

I'm momentarily taken aback, having forgotten, what with all the Joe stuff, about my invitation. 'Yes,' I say, 'next week's fine. But give me a day or two to organise the guest accommodation. Sometimes the hens wander in there.'

'What fun.'

Someone's come up to our table. A skinny

guy with shoulder-length fair hair, pale skin and even paler blue eyes. 'Hey,' he says. 'Daniel.'

'Zac. How you doing? This is Caitlin. Caitlin, Zac.'

'Hi,' we both say.

Zac sits and adds another Guinness to our little table. 'This is so cool, bumping into you all the time. Did you find your friend?'

'Unfortunately not,' says Daniel. 'Have you seen him since?'

''Fraid not. So, what are you guys up to tonight?'

'We're about to go and eat,' I say. I feel Daniel's knee nudge mine under the table. 'Then we'll look for Ralph again.'

'Right, right.' Zac takes a sip and nods for a while. 'You know, there's this Thai place down the road, where the food's out of this world.'

'Oh, yes?' Again I get the nudge from Daniel. I wish he'd stop, because I'm quite liking it. 'Sounds great.'

'Yeah,' says Zac. 'I'll show you where it is.'

Daniel slumps back in his chair and goes quiet, while Zac describes some of the dishes on their menu, and yes, they do sound heavenly. When he's finished his Guinness, he stands and says, 'Coming?'

Daniel and I drain our glasses too – Daniel slowly. On our way out, Zac shouts, 'Cheers for the drink, man,' to a guy at the bar.

At Thai Chi we ask for a table for three and are put in the window and handed extensive menus. We rely on Zac's recommendations and when the waitress returns, let him do the ordering. Daniel looks miserable but resigned, then when the starters arrive seems to perk up.

While Zac tells us about his plans to travel, once he's got the cash, I watch passers-by for signs of Ralph and a gang of no-gooders. That is, after all, what we're here for. It's Wednesday, and his things have been untouched in his room since Saturday. There has been one sighting by – I look over at Zac – a perhaps unreliable witness. And on the basis of just a photograph. It might not have been Ralph at all with that gang. Or Zac could have been spinning a yarn, in the hope of getting a meal or two out of Daniel. I realise now what the knee nudging was about, for Zac has mentioned, more than once, how 'massively broke' he is. He's job-hunting again, he's telling us now, because being a traffic warden involved getting his personal space invaded too often.

'I saw it as a job with green credentials, yeah? You know, get the bastard car drivers. Then one guy – this hard dude with a blow-up hand giving the finger on his dashboard – said he knew where my mother lived. I said, oh yeah, where's that, then? You know, like laughing. And he told me. Turned out I'd been at school with him. I'd issued the ticket and couldn't do anything about it.'

'God,' I say, 'how awful.'

'Made my mum get a chain for her door.' Zac scoops up the last of the starters, then says, 'So what do you do, Caitlin?'

I tell him, and occasionally Daniel jumps in with details. I see the same faraway look form in Zac's eyes that had been in Daniel's earlier.

'Sounds cool. And do you take on wwoofers?'

'Er, no. Not enough work, really. And it's hardly a farm. But maybe when my son leaves home.'

'Wwoofers?' asks Daniel.

'Willing workers on organic farms,' says Zac. 'Because if you did, Cait, I'd be like really interested.'

I laugh, partly because he looks so weedy. 'Well, give me your phone number and I'll let you know.'

'Er, no phone at the moment. Maybe if you give me yours?'

I see Daniel tensing in a don't-do-it way. I wait for another knee nudge. 'OK,' I say, when it doesn't come. 'Later.'

'Cool.'

By the time the array of main dishes arrives I'm full, so I take it slowly, sitting back and watching the men dig in. For someone so thin, Zac tucks away a lot of food. At one point, he calls the waitress over and asks for another bottle of wine. 'Is that OK?' he asks after she's gone, and Daniel simply nods.

When Zac raps loudly on the window and shouts, 'Hey, Joe!' my heart stops and I look back at the beautiful blue eyes staring at me through the glass. In the seconds it takes Joe to come in and reach our table, I've sort of composed myself.

He stands with his hands on his hips, looking slightly windswept, as though he's been hurrying. 'Zac? Cait?'

'Hi, Joe,' I say.

'You two know each other?' asks Zac, and Daniel's looking baffled too.

'Joe put Ralph and myself up last Saturday night, when we were...'

'A bit lost,' says Joe diplomatically. He sits on the fourth chair, directly opposite me.

'Are you on your way to the café?' I ask. 'Oh, this is Daniel, by the way.'

Joe grins. 'So you're Daniel.'

'Ye-es. How do you—'

'Oh, um, Zac told me about his American friend.'

'Ah.'

'This is too weird,' I say, laughing. I then tell Joe we're about to search for Ralph. 'He's been missing since Sunday, you see.'

Joe feigns surprise. 'Really?'

'But then we bumped into Zac,' says

Daniel, 'and got sidelined into all this food.'

Joe nods. 'Yeah, food usually happens when you bump into Zac. No, I'm not going to the café, Cait. I was on my way to the river, to take photos. You know, people falling out of punts.'

'Really?' I give him a wish-I-could-come-with-you smile. 'Sounds fun.'

We'd had a fun, if slightly frustrating, photo session at Joe's house. After the long, filling brunch, Julian had charged around the mostly open-plan ground floor, sorting out things he'd let pile up and singing along to the 'Hallelujah' chorus.

At one point, while Joe repositioned me, he'd stroked my cheek and whispered, 'We could go up to my room.'

'Might be a bit obvious.'

'True.'

'And I'm not sure I could... you know... to the "Hallelujah" chorus.'

'No.' Joe had looked around at the vast space that incorporated hall, stairs, dining room and kitchen. 'Sometimes I wish I hadn't knocked so many walls down.'

'Caitlin?' Daniel's saying.

'Sorry?'

'I said, what do you think?'

'About...?'

'Joe's offering to print out copies of my photo of Ralph at his house, so we can pass them around, post them in shops. Maybe

108

Ralph himself will see one and get in touch.'

It seems a bit over the top, but spending more time with Joe sounds good. 'Great. Shall we get the bill, then?'

'Hey, what's your hurry?' says Zac, beckoning the waitress. 'Man, you *have* to try their coconut pudding.'

'*Zac*,' snaps Joe.

'What?' He puts his hands in the air, all innocence. 'They're getting the bill, OK?'

Joe's father rushes to the hall and says, 'Ah! Company! Come in, come in. How are you, Zac? Long time no see. Or do I mean, long time no cook for you, ha ha?'

Julian's in a short terry robe and has quite good legs for an ageing academic. Something Mahler-ish is belting out of the kitchen. Joe goes and turns it down, while we all hover in the living area, where I introduce Daniel and Julian to each other.

'American?' asks Julian.

'Yep. Ever been?'

'Indeed, yes. I spent two very productive years at Yale.'

Joe returns and says, 'Dad, you're always very productive. Now, where's your camera, Daniel? Let's get this picture printed. How many copies shall I make? Six?'

'Why not?' Daniel hands over the camera, then tells Julian he comes from very near Yale himself. 'Around an hour from New Haven.'

'Ah, how fortunate you are. You have the most resplendent autumns.'

'Yes, we do.'

'Want to come and help?' Joe asks me quietly.

'OK.'

When Zac starts following us up the stairs, Joe stops. 'Hey, Zac, why don't you help yourself to ice cream or sorbet, or anything you want?'

'Cool.'

'And maybe you'd like something, Daniel?'

'Sure.'

'Dad, would you...?'

'Of course.'

Once in his room, Joe locks the door, takes my hand and leads me to his king-size bed with brown leather surround. Habitat? I'm wondering, as I land on Egyptian cotton and watch Joe, above me, take his T-shirt off.

'This is mad,' I tell him.

'I know.'

'We really shouldn't.'

'No,' he says, and we kiss, slowly. Then we kiss again and again.

The others are in the garden now, talking. Mostly Julian. I hear 'coarse', 'lure', 'rod', 'fly' and 'tackle'. He could be talking sex but I think it's fishing.

A hand has worked its way up my top. I help out by undoing the tiny buttons. 'This is so nice,' says Joe.

'Yes.'

'I really want you.'

'Me too.' Our lips meet again, our hands are everywhere. Joe has such beautifully smooth skin. I love it. I love the taste of him, the look of him. We roll over and I'm on top, hoping my chest isn't too small.

'Lovely breasts,' he tells me.

'Thank you.'

'Think I'll go check on my camera!' we hear Daniel say, and Joe and I freeze. 'Wouldn't wanna lose any photographs.'

'First floor, back bedroom!' calls out Julian.

'Got it!'

Joe puts his T-shirt back on, I do my buttons up and we get off the bed. Joe then switches his computer on, while I flatten both the duvet and my hair. We both dash to unlock the door, semi-collide, open it, have a last snog, then part.

'Hi,' says Daniel with a soft tap, tap. 'How's the printing coming along?'

'Yeah,' says the young man behind the counter, 'he was in here earlier today. Only without the hair.'

'Bald?' I ask. It's past nine and we're on our fifth shop, a health food one.

'Yeah, bald,' says the guy. 'But I'm certain it's him.' He's pouring something I don't recognise through a funnel and into a jar. 'Tall, yeah?'

'Yes.'

He puts the sack of whatever down and takes the picture Daniel's holding up. 'It's definitely him.'

Zac, inspecting the freezer, says, 'Was he with some like well-hard tattooed buffoons?'

The young salesman cocks an eyebrow, scans the shop and says, 'Hardly.'

'On his own?' asks Joe.

'No, he was with Luna.'

'The white witch?' asks Zac.

'Yes, that Luna.' The photo gets turned towards us. 'The guy even had those two moles. There. He and Luna were here some time and bought a lot. Pulses, herbs, gram flour.'

We all lean in and examine the two moles.

'So,' says Daniel, 'now we're looking for a bald man eating lentils.'

I ask the shop guy if Ralph seemed OK. 'Not hurt or anything?'

'A couple of nicks on his head. I think he must have used a razor. Luna made him buy calendula cream.'

Daniel turns to me, but his eyes keep darting to Joe. 'Maybe we should give up on this search. Ralph obviously has some kind of agenda – research, whatever. He's doing

OK by the sound of it, and we do have our trip to Stratford tomorrow, Cait.'

And another Shakespeare play. 'Hmm,' I say. If I dropped out of the holiday would Val give me a refund?

Now Daniel's making firm eye contact with Joe. 'You wouldn't believe our schedule,' he says with a shake of the head. 'It may be a week for the over forty-fives, but they sure pack the visits in.'

I feel my face flood. I want to dive behind the organic aloe display, dig a hole, tunnel my way back to Peterchurch. Instead, I turn to the freezer and say, 'Er, how much are your soya choc ices?'

'One twenty. But I'm afraid we're closed. I just had the door open for air.'

'Oh, sorry.' Now I feel even sillier.

At this point, we can do nothing but apologise, thank him for his help and leave. None of us even asks where this Luna hangs out. Ralph, I think we've all decided, can look after himself.

On the pavement, I can't look at Joe's face in case he's horrified. I should have told him my real age because now he's probably wondering if I'm *well* over forty-five. I fix my eyes on a discarded organic cereal-bar wrapper, wondering why the health-conscious person who bought it wasn't litter-conscious too. Meanwhile, Zac's telling Daniel they should really meet up again before he leaves and Daniel gives a tepid, 'Sure.'

Joe's being quiet. I know he's still here, I can see his nice shoes.

'Well,' Daniel says, 'I guess we'd better head back.'

'Hey, Cait, how about your phone number?' asks Zac. 'In case you need a wwoofer.'

'Don't worry,' says Joe. 'I've got it.'

Back at Peterchurch, I lie on my bed and let resignation wash over me. Tomorrow I'll act my age. Minibus, Anne Hathaway's cottage, cream tea, *Troilus and Cressida* and chitchat with the others. Maybe I'll even get to know their names. I'll talk about glucosamine, Des Lynam and how peppers no longer agree with me. (They don't.)

I reach for the mobile and phone Frankie again. 'Hi,' I say. 'How's things?'

'Er, not that different from this morning.'

'Merlin OK?'

'Mum, are you bored or something? I mean, when you're at home you don't always speak to me twice in one day.'

'Bored? No, no, no. I'm having masses of fun.' I hear the catch in my voice and so does he.

'Are you upset?'

'Don't be silly. Oh! Someone at the door, gotta go. Bye. Lots of love. Bye. Bye.'

This is ridiculous, I tell myself. You made a fool of yourself, yes. You made a bit of a fool of Joe too, but not deliberately.

'Just get over it,' I say out loud. 'No one died.'

I should do something, I decide, getting up. Have a shower. Yes, a shower. I gather washbag, shampoo, conditioner, two towels and a razor for my legs. The razor gets put back – no point – then I do, funnily, hear a knock at my door. I open it, expecting Daniel but finding Joe.

'You wouldn't believe,' he says, shoulders hunched, hands tucked in his jeans pockets, 'how hard it was getting your room number.'

SIX

Joe Barney and Faiza called in late afternoon, not for any particular reason, and just sort of hung around. Now, at eight, we're eating one of my father's ratatouilles with potato dauphinoise. Dad's on good form, talking Middle East with Faiza, then talking Bob Dylan, the poet, with Barney, the poet. Over dessert, we move on to yesterday's stabbing on the Cowley Road.

'Right by the cash machines,' says Barney. 'You won't find me using those again.'

'I heard it was personal,' says Faiza. 'Rather than some hapless cash withdrawer almost getting slaughtered for fifty quid. Rumour has it the victim was Asian, which is unfortunate, so soon after our multicultural celebration.'

I sneer. 'Better if he'd been white?'

'Well, that would depend on the ethnicity of the perpetrator. A white guy stabbing a white guy would have been the best scenario. I mean, the least aggravating, inciting... But anyway, whoever did it is still out there, and as an Asian, I won't sleep soundly till he's caught.'

'There must have been witnesses,' says Dad. 'More potato, anyone?'

'Thanks,' says Faiza. Apparently, the police are looking for a man caught on camera, running away from the scene.'

'And his ethnicity?' I ask. Sometimes I love Faiza, other times she really gets on my nerves. Tonight she's annoying me for some reason.

'Caucasian, I think.'

'And if he's a white witness does that make it more, or less inciting?'

'Just shut up, Joe, if that's all you have to say.'

I grin and she smiles back. Maybe I just fancy her.

I'm a bit shocked when the doorbell goes and I find Cait there. 'Didn't you go to Stratford?' I ask, and she shakes her head.

We have a quick cuddle on the doorstep, then I take her through and introduce her to Faiza and Barney.

'Hey, you're the poet,' Cait says. 'We saw you the other evening.'

Barney shrugs. 'Oh, that. I get free beer for bringing more punters in.'

'I thought you were good. Very funny.'

'Cheers.'

Cait joins us for coffee and when the other guests leave and Dad's settled down to *Newsnight*, Cait and I go to my room, and she tells me she's spent the whole day pootering around the colleges and plucking up the courage to call round. I'm not sure I know what pootering is, but I tell her she can come any time. And then we make love. Properly, this time, not like last night's rushed affair on her single bed.

'I'm forty-five,' she'd said then, mid-sex. 'Sorry, Joe.'

I'd told her she didn't look it and that, anyway, I fancied lots of women in their forties.

'Really?'

'Fifties, even. Well, Kim Basinger.'

But tonight, none of that tension's there. Until it's over that is, and Cait says, 'God, I wish your birthday was sooner. Like tomorrow. I wouldn't feel half as bad sleeping with a thirty-year-old.'

'Why would you feel bad,' I ask, 'if I don't?

It's not like you're corrupting me or any-thing.'

'No,' she says, giggling and stroking my hair. 'You definitely didn't need corrupting.'

A taxi comes for Cait just after midnight.

'Will I see you again?' I ask.

'Are you kidding?' she says, pecking my cheek. She stops halfway down the front path, turns her head and gives me a little wave. In the moonlight, she looks about twenty.

Back indoors, I find Dad sitting at the kitchen table, deep in a book and scooping up leftovers with a spoon. 'What are you reading?' I ask, not that it'll be something I've heard of.

'Oh ... nothing of any import.' He snaps the book shut and looks embarrassed. After tucking it under his arm, he fills the dishwasher, switches it on and wipes the table and all the surfaces. I've trained him well since moving back home. 'Good night, Joe,' he finally says.

'Night,' I say back, a bit intrigued by the book still wedged in his armpit.

When I hear him go to the bathroom, I take the stairs two at a time, tiptoe into his room and check out his bedside table. *How to Find a Partner When You're Over Fifty* says the cover in shocking pink lettering. *The Essential Guide to Late Love*. I put it back the way it was and creep out and into my bedroom, where I lay on my bed, a bit stunned, to say the least.

I suppose I've always thought Dad was married to his work, liked his space. Maybe wasn't even aware that life could be different. Not only does he want things to change but he's been into town and bought a book with a bright pink title. I try, for a while, to think of someone I could match him with. A clever and cultured woman who wouldn't mind talking to herself for weeks at a time. There's Ozzie's mum. Come to think of it, half the people I know have single, divorced mothers. And surely some of them would jump at the opportunity of getting together with Julian Sollars, academic extraordinaire? I'll work on it, I decide.

I go downstairs and switch things off and lock doors. Then back in my room, trying to sleep, I have an image of someone like Cait getting together with my dad. Only not Cait, of course.

Daniel Having decided I couldn't compete with handsome young Joe, I'd thrown myself into the Stratford trip – flirting with the interneters on the bus, holding forth on *Troilus and Cressida* (the Trojan War, Ajax, Achilles and Ulysses) over our cream teas, and generally being far more gregarious than comes naturally. In the evening, when we were finally seated and the actors charged around the stage shouting their lines, my mind slipped back to the Caitlin issue. She hadn't joined us again today (another headache) but I could, roughly, guess what she'd been doing.

If I hadn't seen them kissing through the gap in Joe's bedroom door, I'd never have known why I wasn't getting anywhere with Caitlin. I'd have sworn she was interested in me, but apparently not. Women, it seems, are becoming as base as men. Chasing after youngsters they can't possibly have anything in common with. I must say I'm hugely disappointed in her. OK, I'm jealous as hell. And, yeah, I do understand. If I were attracted to men and wanted a light-hearted holiday fling, I'd choose Joe over me any day.

Having tortured myself enough, I turned my attention to Ajax beating his servant Thersites in a pretty convincing way. But then you'd expect no less from the RSC.

Having established myself as an expert on the play, questions about the plot, characters and background mythology are fired my way in the minibus, making the journey home far speedier than the long haul there.

Before I know it, we're disembarking by the lodge, some being helped from the bus by the driver. Others, such as Barry, shunning the proffered hand. We're a sorry-looking bunch, ready for a nightcap we won't get, since it's almost 1 a.m. The blondes hobble off to the bathroom, something they'd been yearning for, out loud, since Long Compton, while Ronald takes Sheila's arm and offers to walk her to her room.

'Just one moment,' comes an unfamiliar voice. Ronald and Sheila stop in their tracks and we all turn toward the street. Two men in suits are approaching. They take badges from pockets and flash them at us. 'Police,' they say, then each gives his rank and name. 'We'd just like a word before you disperse. Could someone retrieve the two fair-haired ladies?'

'I'll try,' says Val, still looking chic despite the long day. 'Call of nature,' she adds with a wink at the better-looking policeman. 'May I ask what this is about?'

'You may,' he says, in that nasally British-cop way. 'We're here with regards to this man.' He holds up a photograph, then moves it in a slow semi-circle, so we can all get a glimpse. It's of Ralph, minus hair, and almost certainly came from a CCTV camera. 'We believe Mr Higson is one of your party?'

'Was, more like,' says Barry. 'Ent bin sight nor sound of him since Satdee.'

'May I ask why...' begins Val, but the policeman is staring at her in such a grave way that her voice trails off, as though she's waiting for the very worst of terrible news.

121

Which I think we all are.

'We'd like to talk to him,' he says, tucking the photo away, 'in connection with a stabbing.'

During a good deal of gasping, I catch sight of Caitlin getting out of a taxi, then walking toward us. She's staggering a little – the cobbles? drunk? – and is swinging her purse, as a happy carefree young girl would. Or maybe like someone who's had lots of sex would. She reaches us and finally looks up.

'Hi,' I say with a curt smile. 'Headache better?'

Ralph Gosh, what a week it's been so far. The fantastic carnival, then getting in with Lenny and his mates simply by wandering into that pub. That all started with a bit of a misunderstanding. They thought I'd been sent by someone called A.J. – or Ajay. I never was sure, but wrote A.J. in my notebook. 'Yeah, old A.J.,' I said and went along with it for a laugh.

After the night in the van, Lenny and his 'missus', who looked worn out and smoked non-stop, kindly put me up in their cramped council house. Cramped because of the four children, four cats, and two large hounds who barked if you so much as sniffed. In the evening, Lenny's wife made a pig's of cutting my singed hair, and Lenny ended up shaving me with his razor, on the setting he uses. This has left me bald and a little bit sore, but strangely liberated. Like I'm really hardcore, or something.

I slept on a small mattress on the floor in the twins' room, which although they're only ten, had topless women on the walls and an ashtray of cigarette butts under the bottom bunk. Still, I kept thinking, all good material for an author, and only for one night.

My notebook was filling up nicely, but then the next day, while Lenny, myself and the others were hanging out on the Cowley Road, came the unfortunate fracas over ... well, I'm not sure what it was over. There was a bit of a crowd of us, on the street corner. Some young blokes I hadn't seen before too. When I caught a glimpse – just a quick flash – of a knife, I was out of there, sharpish. There's such a thing as carrying your gritty-urban-novel research too far.

The last thing I heard, as I fled down the road, was a gut-wrenching howl that may well have come from an actual gut-wrenching. I come over funny just thinking about it. Now, I'm sort of in hiding from Lenny and the others, because I was, after all, a witness. Sort of. They'll think I was, anyway. I've heard from Luna that someone's in hospital 'fighting for life'.

What a stroke of luck it was coming across her in the first shop I dived into. And another stroke of luck that she's a white witch, because otherwise she wouldn't have taken any notice of me, standing there shaking and pretending to be interested in crystals.

She could see I was in a state, so came over, her hands full of joss sticks, and said, 'You look troubled. Would you like a spell?' I thought she said 'smell' and looked at her incense and said, 'OK.'

Next thing I knew I was being led to her canal boat, where she lit loads of candles, which I personally wouldn't do in a wooden vessel with only one tiny door to escape through. She asked if I wanted a love spell, a money spell or a banishment spell. I said, since I was married, I'd like the last two, please. But mostly the last. I described the people I wanted banished – Lenny, Dog and the others – and asked if she could banish the memory of a nasty incident too. She said she'd have a go, but obviously failed because the sound of that howl is still with me, especially in the night, when I can't sleep on Luna's skinny sofa because I think big fat long-tailed water voles might gnaw their way into the boat and run all over me.

The worse thing I did was to tell Lenny about my singles' week and, worst of all, where I was staying. No, worse than that even, was telling them where I'm studying. They're not supposed to give out home addresses at the university, but with a knife at your throat you might cave in. It was when I first came across Lenny and co. that I blabbed too much, not having guessed they were hardened criminals. After all, not everyone who looks like a psychopath is one these days.

Anyway, I can't go back to Peterchurch College. Lenny or Trev, or worse, Dog, will be waiting behind my door, I know it. I can't go home either, not till Dog, or Trev or whoever had the knife and did the stabbing, is caught and banged up. I can't even phone home in case Hilary's been contacted about me going missing. She'd give me such an ear-bashing, I know it. Threaten to kick me out, I'm sure, and keep the entire house, even though I put 40K capital in – the profit I made on my starter home before I met her. She's got friends who are lawyers, so I know she'd find a way. I'd ask Luna to banish Hilary, only my money might get banished with her.

SEVEN

Caitlin Unbelievably, it's our last full day. Where did the week go? We're supposed to be doing the Oxford Story and a boat trip to Abingdon, but Daniel and I are back in the health-food shop asking the same assistant where we might find Luna. Down on the canal, we're told. He gives us directions and the name of her houseboat.

After hopping on a bus back into town, we take the towpath, then find ourselves passing dozens of floating homes. Some are beautifully painted with well-kept tiny gardens in front and potted plants and wind generators on top, while others are quite plain, even scruffy. It takes a good twenty minutes of walking before we find *Angel Dust*, which is maroon and covered in little pink stars. I can't believe we'll find Ralph inside this little Barbie boat, and we don't.

'He left this morning,' says Luna, a big woman of around fifty, whose wild ginger hair clashes with her paintwork. 'After he saw his photo in a shop window.'

'Oh dear,' I say. 'That was our doing. Any idea where he went?' I'm feeling frustrated and cross. Ralph is becoming hard work, and there are more pleasant things we could be doing with our last hours in Oxford.

'Ralph had a bit of a plan,' Luna says, 'but refused to tell me. "If you don't know, you can't snitch," he said.' She laughs, then turns serious. 'You haven't mentioned me to the police, have you?'

'No,' says Daniel. 'We haven't told them anything. We're guessing Ralph's in hiding from whoever did the stabbing.'

'Yes, poor love. He didn't exactly witness

126

it but they don't know that. I'm confident he's safe, though, since my spell to banish the gang from his life. Would you like to come in for nettle tea?'

'No!' cries Daniel. 'Uh, thank you.'

I ask Luna if she thinks Ralph might be heading home to Lincoln, and she says definitely not. 'He's more terrified of his wife than he is of Lenny and Dog ... I mean...'

'So,' says Daniel, lifting an eyebrow. 'Lenny and a dog?'

'It's a person, not a dog. But I haven't told you that, and if you have any sense you'll erase the names from your minds. In fact, if you'd like to come in, I could conjure up a little spell to–'

'We have to go,' I tell her. 'On a boat. To Abingdon.'

'But thanks,' says Daniel.

We return to the college to check Ralph's room. It's another equator-hot day, and although it's not yet noon, I'm shattered. A late night followed by all the walking is taking its toll, and when we have Ralph's door unlocked for us, my initial urge is to go and collapse on the unused bed. But then I see how empty the room is and the shock wakes me up. I ask the porter if the police have taken Ralph's things this morning, since they left empty-handed last night.

'So far as I know,' the porter says, 'both

spare keys have been in the lodge all morning.'

'Hmm,' I say. 'That means Ralph himself must have been back and collected his stuff.'

The porter nods and rubs at his chin, like Watson to my Holmes. 'There's been two of us on, so I haven't seen everyone that's come and gone. But I reckon you're right. He must have nipped in and out. Wanted by the police, I hear. If he's buggered off with the keys, there'll be a charge.'

'When we find him,' says Daniel, 'we'll be sure to pass that on.'

We step into the quad to see Ben and Gemma counting heads.

'Ah,' says Gemma, spotting us. 'Here's the missing two. Now, does anyone think they might get queasy?'

I put my hand up and am told to see Ben, who's got the Sea-Legs. 'We may as well go on this trip,' I whisper to Daniel. Joe's at the café all day, plus the river sounds cool and calming. 'It's not as though we know where to start looking for Ralph.'

Daniel agrees. 'And who knows, Abingdon might be a jewel of a place.'

After tagging on, as the party strolls down St Aldates towards the river, I ask Gemma where Val is.

'Oh, she'll be with one of her other groups.

She's just started some more, you see.'

'Oh?'

'One for under forty-fives and one for over sixty-fives.'

I say, 'This under forty-fives group...'

'Yes?'

'Can you join it if you're actually forty-five?'

'Er, yeah. I think so.'

'Oh. I wish I'd known.'

'But surely,' says Daniel, beside me and listening in, 'it's better to be the spring chicken of the party than the mother hen. And, besides, what the heck would you have in common with thirty-year-olds?'

At least he didn't say 'old broiler', but I still feel insulted. There's a hint of venom in Daniel's voice, and I wonder if he once suffered at the hands of a younger woman. 'I'm sure I'd find something,' I tell him, thinking of Joe.

'No doubt,' says Daniel, while Gemma points out a museum to our left.

'It's the Bate Collection of musical instruments,' she says, pronouncing them 'musicawinstruments'. 'Val always says there's a gem every ten yards in Oxford, so be sure to point them out. And down here's the police station that got featured in *Morse*.'

'Oh, yes!'

'But I don't think in *Lewis*, only I'd have to check.'

Daniel takes his camera out and snaps the building. 'For my mother,' he explains, when I laugh. 'Big fan.'

It's lovely gliding along on the boat, passing cows, stopping occasionally for a lock, picking at the buffet provided. I discover the names of the two women who obviously fancy Daniel (Liz and Sarah) and what's more, I really like them. Liz is a keen hill walker and knows a lot about Wales, the north in particular. Sarah tells me all about the Welsh revolt against the Normans under William II, and about the end of Welsh independence. She doesn't leave me embarrassed that I don't know, or at least have forgotten, all this stuff. For a while, I talk to Pauline about dogs, then with Barry about boats. Well, he does the talking, me knowing nothing and him being a boat builder. And, as we enter Abingdon, Daniel and I are chatting to the round blonde women, who want to know what I've been up to all week.

'Oh,' I say, 'what with the headaches and things, I've just been mooching around.'

Daniel says, 'So that's what you Brits call it,' and wanders off. I think something's troubling him, and it's not Ralph.

St Helen's, built circa 1100, is the second-widest church in the country, we learn from the vicar, being three metres wider than it is long. We wander round looking at churchy things, then afterwards walk up the ancient and lovely East St Helen's Street to visit the museum in the Old County Hall, which stands all alone beside the market place.

'Sometimes,' Ben tells us before we enter, 'someone throws buns to the crowd from the top of this building.' He points up, in case we don't know where the top is.

'When do they do that?' asks Sarah.

'Oh, um... special occasions, I think. Gemma?'

'Yeah, I expect so.'

'Who throws them?'

Ben pulls a face. 'I'm not sure.'

'And why?' persists Sarah.

'Er, tradition,' chips in Gemma. She shrugs. 'It's called bun throwing.'

Sarah tuts and the others snigger. I think they're all missing Val. We take a quick tour of the old abbey buildings. After ice-cream cornets, we return to our cruise boat, most of us commenting on the attractiveness of the town, the loveliness of the weather and, amongst ourselves, the uselessness of our guides.

It's while we're negotiating Sandford lock that my phone rings and I see it's Joe.

'Hi,' I say, turning away from the others, then making my way to the far end of the boat. 'Where are you, at work?'

'Yeah, unfortunately. But I popped out

earlier and thought I saw Ralph.'

'Oh?'

'Getting into a taxi. I was very close, and I'm sure it was him. Same voice.'

'Right.' I see Daniel glowering my way. What on earth's the matter with him? 'So what did you hear?'

'He said, "The railway station, please. And don't spare the horses." Only the driver was Asian and I'm not sure he understood.'

'What time was this?'

'About eleven.'

'Why didn't you call me before?'

'Jesus, Cait. It's not like I haven't tried.'

'Oh. Sorry. We all put our bags in a pile on the boat on the way here. Saved having to carry them round.'

'See what I mean about...'

'Old people?' I laugh and change the subject. 'Have you seen the local paper?'

'No, thanks.'

'Well, take a look. The police want to talk to a witness in connection with that stabbing. It's Ralph. There's no picture, luckily. But they were here last night, showed him caught on camera.'

'Jesus, no wonder he was in a hurry to leave town. Listen, I'd better go. We're really busy. See you later?'

'I hope so.'

When we hang up, I see I've missed four calls, all from Joe. From now on, I decide, my mobile will always be on my person and I will always answer it.

It's truly terrible of me to skip the 'last supper', as Val's calling it, and I can see Daniel's gutted when I say I have a blinding headache that's making me too nauseous to eat. I feel bad and would actually like to go. But of course I can't.

Once the others set off, I call Joe and arrange to be at his house at eight. Having missed the group outing to the launderette, I'm down to two clean outfits. I opt for the red dress because, since my late afternoon nap, I'm in a red dress sort of mood. By half seven, I'm on my way, determined to make the most of the evening. After the past three relationship-free years in Wales, I know this might be my last ever physical encounter with a man. Boy. Whatever.

Julian's out, which is unusual. 'My uncle's here for the weekend,' says Joe. 'They've gone to a concert at the Sheldonian. Have you been there?'

'No,' I say, while Joe pours us a glass of wine each and hands me mine. 'But I expect the others have.'

Joe shakes his head. 'This trip's been a bit of a waste of money, hasn't it?'

I put my glass down and pull him towards me. My face is level with his shoulder, which I kiss through his shirt. 'Worth every penny,' I say, wondering where this new bold me has come from.

But Joe then takes the lead and, before I know it, I'm back in the locked bedroom for the last time, wishing I never had to leave.

Daniel We eat Slovak, around a big table. The food is sensational and the immediate company – Sarah to one side, Liz the other – is most pleasant. If a waiter had only taken away Caitlin's place setting and empty chair, I might have made it through the evening without thinking of her. But there, directly opposite me, and for the full two hours, sits the cutlery, wine glass and napkin she'd have used, if she hadn't had been busy screwing Joe. I have to keep swallowing my bitterness, as well as the *bryndzove halusky* – a dumpling surely made in heaven.

Toward the end of the evening, it's clear Val has drunk a little too much, for she begins flirting outrageously with Ronald – one arm around his very straight back, the other spooning Slovak fruit dumpling into his moustached mouth. Sheila takes umbrage and I fear the night will turn nasty if somebody doesn't intervene. That person is Sarah, who hoists our leader very carefully from her chair and guides her to the ladies' restroom. Hopefully, she'll encourage Val to put one or two fingers down her throat, although that would be a shocking waste of some fine food.

They're gone a while and I talk to Liz about the week, and those who've paired up – Ronald and Sheila, Pauline and Hamid. 'Not a bad success rate,' I say.

'No,' sighs Liz, stirring her coffee a little too frantically. 'A little disappointing for myself and Sarah, though.'

'And me,' I add.

'But you've had Cait.'

'Well, not really.' Should I tell her about Caitlin's toyboy? It's tempting, but it wouldn't make me look all that good. 'She's had all those headaches ... you know.'

'Mm. Anyway, I'll certainly be coming on another of these weeks.'

'You will?'

Liz nods. 'Oh, yes. Both Sarah and I have decided that if it attracts men like you, it's worth having another stab.'

I laugh and thank her. If only Caitlin were sitting opposite to hear.

Caitlin Around ten, I'm woken by my mobile. I'm wrapped in Joe's arms and feel that's a good enough excuse not to leap from the bed and rummage in my bag. We must have been asleep an hour.

'Aren't you going to get it?' murmurs Joe, arms loosening up.

'Mmm,' I say groggily. 'I just need to find ...

135

oh, it's stopped.' I expect it was Daniel, worried that he can't get a response from my room. When it rings again, I quietly curse, then go and answer it in the semi-dark. 'Hi.'

'Hi, Mum.'

'Hi, Frankie. Why are you calling? Spilled wine again? Snowdon erupted?'

'Er, not a volcano, Mum. Are you drunk, or something? You sound weird.'

'You woke me up, that's all.'

'Right. I just thought I'd call because there's this guy here, wanting to stay. Says he met you in Oxford. Only he seems a bit wound up. He keeps looking over his shoulder and jumping when I slam the kitchen cupboards. Anyway, I'm not sure about him, that's all.'

'Don't slam the cupboards, Frankie. You'll break the hinges again.' I suddenly feel self-conscious, all naked in the middle of the floor, and look around for something to wear. 'Hang on,' I say. I put Joe's shirt on, mobile still in hand. 'My son,' I whisper. 'I think he's got Ralph.'

'In Wales?'

'Hi,' I say into the phone.

'Are you with a man?'

'Try not to sound so surprised. Anyway, this guy. Is he bald and called Ralph?'

'Bald, yeah. But he says his name's Derek. Only when I said, "Do you want a drink, Derek?" he didn't answer. He must have thought I was talking to another Derek. Not that there's one here. Or maybe there is.'

Suddenly, I hear the background hubbub. 'How many people have you got there?'

'I dunno. Forty?'

'I don't want them there when I get back.'

'Not even Derek?'

'Especially not Derek, but I think I'm lumbered. Listen, Frankie. Put him in the guest accommodation and tell him I'll see him tomorrow. OK?'

'You don't want to talk to him? Oh. Actually, I can see he's dancing with Megan. Ha! Fucking hilarious.'

'Don't swear. And no one's to dance on the vegetables.'

'Mum, have you ever tried dancing on vegetables?'

'Well, no. Listen, I'll get back as soon as I can. See you then.' It's only when I hang up that reality hits me. A man on the run from a potentially murderous gang, not to mention the police, is hiding in my isolated home with my much-loved only child. I'm not sure how Ralph found it, but I did see a computer screen through one of Luna's porthole windows. My website announces the address to the whole world, potentially murderous gangs included.

Joe gets out of bed and comes over. Are you all right?'

He sits beside me and I lay my head on his

shoulder and sigh. 'I wish we'd gone to Worcester.'

Ralph Great party! And what a fab spot Cait lives in. As remote as I'd imagined and the perfect hideaway. I know Frankie's her son, but have no idea who the others are. Mostly his school pals, I think. All young, but I think I fit in well. Being a bit of a dancer helps.

The music suddenly gets louder, which shouldn't be a problem. I didn't see a single house anywhere near here on the taxi ride. It's good just blending in with this crowd because it makes me feel safe at last. Since spotting that 'Have you seen this man?' poster of me in the newsagents, boy, have I been on edge. Just a mobile number to call at the bottom. Lenny's after me. Possibly with a knife. If he found me here he couldn't do much, not with dozens of partygoers surrounding me. I don't recognise any of the music playing. It's all a bit technical and eerie with no lyrics. I'm about to see if they've got 'Wake Me Up Before You Go Go' when this young guy asks me if I want a tab.

I say, 'What do you mean?' and he shows me some little squares of blotting paper with drawings of strawberries on them. Suddenly, I'm back in Oxford being offered something similar, only I can't remember what the drawings were of that time – a bird or a squirrel, maybe. I'd got myself fairly drunk by then, trying to keep up with the others. I ask this boy what it is and he asks me if I'm saying is it the real thing, and I say, 'No, I just meant, you know, what is it?' Then he laughs and says, 'Acid, Granddad,' and I say, 'You mean LSD?' and go a bit funny, because when I was offered the bird or squirrel or whatever it was in Oxford, I'd said, 'Cheers,' and swallowed it with some water, carefully copying Trev. I'd just thought it was rice paper or something. Some game or silly ritual. But no, it was an extremely illegal drug, and explains why the next twelve hours had been mind-blowing. Literally.

'No, thanks,' I say to the boy. 'I had one the other day.' I can tell I sound pleased with myself, which in a way I am. 'I once tried LSD,' I'll be able to say in future to people I want to impress. Well, if Lenny lets me have a future.

EIGHT

Daniel I find a note from Caitlin slipped under my door.

Daniel,
   Had to leave early. Crisis at home! Really

lovely to have met you, and so sorry not to have said goodbye. Do come and stay anytime!

Love, Caitlin

Her note is both disappointing and encouraging. It also worries me, and continues to worry me over breakfast, where the party has that sad-but-pleased-to-be-going-home look. Although some just look sad. 'What sort of crisis? The chickens eaten by foxes – worse, maybe. I think of Caitlin and her teenage son dealing with whatever it is. Just the two of them. It doesn't seem right. Although not the most practical of guys, I'm sure I could be of help.

I consider calling her, but Caitlin, being a plucky Brit with an independent streak, will no doubt refuse my offer. Has her son done something stupid? Something alcohol- or drug-related ... trashed a car... If so, Caitlin would be alone with her crisis.

As I wade through bacon, eggs, etc., I know my thoughts are leading me toward taking a train to Wales to see Caitlin's OK. Hiring a car even. *Do come and stay anytime!* I pull her business card from my wallet and read 'Cait's Kiddie Clobber'. Once more, I wonder what hitting children has to do with dressmaking. Well, maybe I'll find out.

I say my farewells, which involves much hugging, particularly on the interneters' part. I then go and thank Val, who I'm sensing has come to make a farewell speech I don't intend to hang around for.

'Such a pity about the Ralph business,' she says. 'One hopes details of our singles' weeks won't be bandied about in the local press once he's found.'

'They say there's no such thing as bad publicity.'

'I'm not sure Oscar Wilde would agree.' Val chuckles, then goes on to say how pleased she is to have facilitated 'a little bit of a match, perhaps?' between Caitlin and myself.

'Oh, we'll definitely be keeping in touch.'

'And where *is* Caitlin?' she asks.

'She had to leave early.'

'Oh. I rather hoped she'd make a participant's entry.' Val points toward a large open book containing a pen on string. 'Would you mind...?'

'No, of course not.'

I tend to avoid visitors' books because I can never think of a thing to say. 'A great week!' I write pathetically. 'Daniel Sanchez, London.'

I'm wheeling my suitcase through town, when I see Zac coming my way, head bowed. I try hiding behind a chunky lamp post, but it's not chunky enough and when he looks up he spots me.

'Hey, Daniel. You leaving?'

141

'Hi, Zac,' I say, stepping to the side of the post and yanking on my baggage. I won't tell him where I'm headed (the information centre) or why (to discover where to rent a car) because I have a horrible feeling he'll end up coming to Wales. 'The week's over. Guess I should get back to – 'I don't even want to say 'London' in case he'd like to go there – 'business.'

'Ah, gutting. Barney's having a birthday party tonight. He wanted to know if you could come, but mostly it was Faiza wanted to know. She's hot for you, man, I tell you.'

I let out a shocked sound, not quite a laugh. 'What makes you think that?'

'Mentions you like a *lot*. Says, "I wonder what Daniel would say" about loads of things.'

That doesn't sound as though she craves my body, but maybe Faiza's passions take a cerebral form. 'Yeah?'

'Says you look just like the first lecturer she ever slept with. Gordon.'

I do the not-quite-a-laugh thing again. 'Gordon?' I ask because I can't think what else to say.

'When she was eighteen.'

I nod and gather my wits. 'And how old is she now?'

'I dunno. Thirty-seven. Thirty-eight.'

'And she's not attached?'

'Nah. Guys are mostly petrified of her. So,

142

where you off to, then? The States? I'm planning on going to New York, soon as I've got the cash together. Got to see the Grand Canyon too. San Francisco ... downtown Hollywood...'

While Zac lists places he'll never get to, I mull over my options. Uninvited and perhaps unwanted guest in Wales. Invited and perhaps lusted-after guest in Oxford.

'No, not the States,' I tell him, after a couple seconds' thought. 'Not yet. Matter of fact, I'm hoping to stay on in Oxford a little longer. Beautiful place. Just heading for the information centre to find accommodation.'

'Oh, man, you'll get ripped off. Come with me. I'll find you somewhere to stay.'

'But I like ... comfort.'

'No prob. You've seen Joe's place, yeah?'

'Yes, but I can't–'

'Don't worry, there's loads of room. Joe took off first thing this morning and didn't tell anyone till he was on the road. I got a visit from Carlo, asking me come help in the café later. He's well pissed off.'

'Do you know where Joe went?'

'Er, no.'

Of course Caitlin would get Joe to help with her crisis. Obviously, I'm disappointed. But with all compulsion to rush to Wales gone, I suddenly feel like partying. 'Well,' I say, 'if Julian doesn't mind.'

'He won't.'

Joe One of the neat things about going to Wales is you tune the car radio into a Welsh-speaking station and you suddenly feel you're abroad. I tell Cait this and she says, 'Uh-huh. Any chance of going faster?'

'Not really.' I was a boy racer once, just after passing my test. Then one day a tree came up and hit me. I got off lightly with a broken arm and gashed face, but it pretty much slowed me down to granny speed for the rest of my life. I tell Cait this and add that we're now on narrow roads in unfamiliar territory and any more than fifty would be pushing my luck. 'Do you want to drive?' I ask, not for the first time.

'Too tired,' she says again. 'And besides, it's not much further.'

With Bethesda behind us, Cait grows more concerned about her son and what scenes of mayhem we're about to come across. And not just because of the party. She thinks 'the gangsters', as she keeps calling them, will have followed Ralph to her home and committed unspeakable acts with a knife. This worry, shared slightly by me, isn't helped by the fact that Frankie isn't answering either of his phones. Cait tries once more.

'It's still only ten,' I say, looking at the clock and yawning. 'If he's had a party, he's bound to be asleep still. Lucky bastard.'

Cait puts a hand on my knee. 'Sorry about the early start. And thanks for coming with me. Driving me.'

'That's OK. Are we nearly there?'

'Half a mile.'

I see the scenery's great but am too tired to get excited. What does excite me is the thought of parking the car and switching the engine off. We'd stopped only the once, for the toilets and a rip-off breakfast.

'Next left,' I'm told. Cait points through her window. 'You can see the house. Up there.'

I turn and duck my head for a view. 'God, that's amazing. It's so ... um...' As I look at the distant stone cottage and outbuildings, I try to come up with a word that isn't 'isolated'.

'So *not* Oxford?' asks Cait.

'Yeah.'

A strange mongrel of a dog does backflips at the sight of Cait, then a tall and skinny guy we've obviously woken up meets us in the kitchen. Frankie, I assume, when Cait rushes over, hugs his tummy and says, 'Thank God you're OK!'

'Christ, Mum,' he says, peeling her off. 'I'm almost eighteen and it's only been a week. What you on about?'

'Is Ralph still here?'

'You mean Derek?'

'Yes.'

'I think so. But check the guest rooms.'

'This is Joe, by the way. Who kindly drove me home.'

'Oh, yeah?' Frankie looks me up and down suspiciously.

'Hi, Frankie,' I say, ultrafriendly.

While he makes us tea and the dog calms down, Cait and I poke our noses into one of the outhouse conversions. A nicely done conversion, actually. Characterful but modern. And minimalistic – unlike Cait's cluttered kitchen. One door leads to another door, which opens on to Ralph, looking exactly as I'd seen him a week ago, asleep on a sofa. But this time without hair. Various others are asleep too, all on the floor. I count seven bodies, then am pleased to be outside again, away from the fugged-up room.

'They're really not supposed to smoke in there,' says Cait, following me out and fanning her face. 'Shall we wake Ralph up or wait till we've had a sleep?'

I'm all for waiting, and all for having a kip. 'We could leave him a note to say we're here?'

This we do, pinning it to the inside of his door. And while Frankie cooks some food we don't want any of, we trudge upstairs to Cait's pretty, but again jam-packed room. There's a huge pinkish-red stain on her patchwork quilt and she swears and says,

'*Frankie,*' and insists we change the sheets. When we finally get into bed, I start drifting immediately.

'I should really tell Daniel,' she says quietly on the next lacy-edged pillow.

I come round and find Cait still beside me and also awake.

'What's that noise?' I ask.

'Rain.'

'Ah. And what's the time?'

'Half eleven.'

'Oh, good, we can carry on sleeping.' I throw an arm around her and we have a lazy cuddle.

'I suppose we should go and see Ralph,' she says.

'Mm.'

'Hear his side of things.'

'Mm.'

When I wake again, Cait's gone. I get up, dress, use a bathroom with a spectacular view, then find her downstairs with lanky Frankie. She's got her head wrapped in a towel and is putting cream on her unmade-up face.

She smiles and says, 'Feeling better?'

'Yes, thanks.'

'Coffee? Bacon sandwich?'

'Please.' I take a seat at the solid old table and have a look around the room, which someone has tidied since we arrived. I like it, I decide. I personally couldn't live with the girlie this and rustic that, but it's sort of welcoming. 'So where's Ralph now?' I ask.

'He went off to climb Snowdon with a couple of my friends,' says Frankie. 'Climb some of it, anyway.'

'In the rain?'

They both laugh at me for some reason. 'Yeah, in the rain,' says Frankie, laughing longer than his mother. I don't think he's taken to me.

'So did you get to talk to him?' I ask Cait.

'Uh-uh.' She's peeling bacon slices from a packet and laying them in a pan. It's odd watching Cait in her own home, in her dressing gown, doing domestic stuff, being a mother. 'They left over an hour ago.'

After breakfast, and after Cait's got dressed, she takes me on a tour – the chickens, the goats, the rows of vegetables, beans on canes, fruit bushes. It looks like hard work, but then so is running a café. We collect some eggs, then I give her a kiss behind a redcurrant bush – in the rain, which is warm and refreshing and even a bit erotic.

'Well, well,' says Cait, pushing me away. Still no make-up, I notice. I think she'd worn quite a lot in Oxford.

'What?' I ask.

'I thought you'd go off me when you met my son, saw my chaotic house, realised what a whole different world I live in and how much older than you I am.' She bends and picks up the basket of eggs. 'Looks like omelette for dinner,' she says, smiling and walking off.

'Sounds good,' I say, and catch up with her.

'Listen, I've got masses to do this afternoon, Joe. Think you'll be able to amuse yourself?'

'Er, yeah. But I could help you, if you want?'

'No, no. Thanks, anyway.'

Something's changed, I'm beginning to realise. I'm just not sure what, or how much.

Caitlin Late afternoon, I get to work. Frankie's good at watering things, feeding things and milking things, but he has a blind spot when it comes to weeds. I should really dock the hefty allowance I pay him, but that might be petty. In the house, he and Joe are watching some awful DVD – Frankie because he loves it, and Joe... I don't know, maybe because he's still knackered, maybe because he loves it too. I'd gathered, on the way here, that Joe's movies of choice are definitely not mine. 'You mean you've never seen *The Matrix?*' he'd asked. 'How about *Blade Runner?*' This macho film choice didn't quite go with the 40 m.p.h. he was driving us at.

I pull up a few carrots as I go along, realising how pleased I am to be home again. It doesn't feel exactly like home, though, what with having a handsome young lover and a fugitive staying. But just being back in my patch, tugging at weeds and carrots, is comforting somehow, after the excitement of the past week. Hopefully, things will calm down now. Ralph will see sense and go home to Lincoln, maybe give the Oxford police the information they want.

And Joe will also leave my life. It's been an ego boost and hugely enjoyable, but it can't go on. What seemed risqué and fun in Oxford feels inappropriate in the cold light of Wales. Plus, you get to know a person quite well on a long car journey. Too well. And I can tell Frankie disapproves. Not that I'd take notice of what Frankie thinks. Actually, I would. The weird and annoying thing is, I keep thinking of Daniel. Wondering if I made the wrong choice. He's attractive, we could talk about all sorts of things...

'Oh, for goodness' sake,' I say, then manage to push both men out of my thoughts and get on with the job in hand.

By five o'clock, the wheelbarrow's full of weeds and the ground isn't. I rub at my aching back, like the old lady I am, then push the barrow round behind the big shed to where I hide the ugly stuff, such as compost bins, leaf mould, Frankie's broken bikes. It's when I emerge again, having leaned the barrow upright against the fence, that I hear car doors slam and see Frankie's friend Ioan approach, wet and exhausted-looking. His older sister, Beth, overtakes him, looking a lot less exhausted.

'You should *never* try climbing Snowdon with a hangover,' says Ioan.

Beth tuts. 'Serves you right.'

'How far did you get?' I ask, looking over their shoulders for signs of Ralph.

'Quite high. Derek was behind, but then suddenly he wasn't. So we went back to look for him.'

'And did you find him?'

'You mean he's not here?' ask Beth. 'We thought he must have given up and come back somehow. Only it was a bit odd, we decided, because he kept going on about what a brilliant time he was having.'

'No, he's not here. Unless he slipped past while I was weeding.'

We go and check out his room. It's empty. Then the house.

'Shit,' says Ioan, when we're back outside and he's looking at the dark mountainous view, hoping to catch sight of Derek. 'There's quite a mist coming down too.'

'What's up?' says Joe, joining us and rubbing sleep from his eyes.

'Derek's missing,' I tell him.

'You mean Ralph?'

'What? Yeah, yeah. Ralph.' I introduce Joe to Beth and Ioan, then explain what happened.

'It's looking very cloudy,' says Joe, a hand shielding his face from the non-existent sun.

'Yes,' says Beth, smiling Joe's way.

'Maybe I'll go back and look for him,' says Ioan.

'I'll come with you,' says Joe.

Beth grabs his arm. 'God, no. We don't want two lost newcomers.'

Joe looks relieved rather than insulted, and we all go inside to get a hot drink inside the climbers.

'No way am I going up there,' I hear Frankie say. 'We'll never find him in that fog and then it'll get dark. And for all we know he'll turn up here while we're risking our lives. We should leave it to the mountain rescue team, only they won't take it seriously yet.'

'When will they?' asks Joe.

Beth shrugs and gives him a flirty twinkly-eyed look. 'Tomorrow?'

'Hands off!' I want to tell her, but then I remember *The Matrix* and the fact that I've been missing Daniel.

'Oh,' Joe says. He sits down and Beth joins him at the table.

'At least the gangsters won't find him out there,' I say, attempting a laugh but secretly furious with the hapless Derek. Ralph.

'Gangsters?' Beth asks, and between us, Joe and I tell the entire Oxford story.

When we've finished, Frankie snorts in the stunned silence. 'What a dickhead. And he actually *likes* the Space Hoppers?'

'He seems to like everything,' I say.

'Yeah,' says Beth. 'He was well into mountain walking, until he, you know ... fell, or whatever.'

Frankie shakes his head. 'Fucking ironic, yeah? You're running away from people who probably aren't murderers, and might not be after you anyway, then you fall off a fucking mountain and die.'

'Frankie,' I say, 'stop it.' But I can't keep a straight face, and neither can the others.

'I think I'll phone mountain rescue,' I say when everyone's calmed down and Ioan's filling the kettle at last.

Daniel It's not often you find yourself being taught nine-wicket croquet in an urban backyard by a math professor and his equally brilliant brother. I'm quite hopeless, but they want me to become good. They insist on game after game, in that obsessive/compulsive way of geniuses, and before I know it, Zac has arrived to take me to Barney's party. Surely it's not that late? I think, and it isn't.

'Thought we could have dinner first,' he says.

I'm tempted to thwart Zac's plan to get

153

another meal out of me by simply refusing. However, I'm quite hungry, and since Julian and Francis show no signs of putting their sticks down, I say, 'Why not?' The prospect of an evening, and who knows what else, with lovely Faiza is making me expansive, I guess.

'Where shall we go?'

'Greek?'

'Sure.'

We eat – a lot – only to arrive at the party and find piles of food. Zac carries on dining, while I talk to a Buddhist called Doug about competitiveness. A bad thing. He goes on to talk about the extinguishment of all craving and desire. A good thing. He almost has me convinced, but then Faiza walks in the room in a flimsy white dress that shows off her beautiful brown shoulders and thick black hair so nicely. I tell Doug I'll definitely try the extinguishment thing, but maybe not till tomorrow. Then I excuse myself and go to where Faiza is being handed a drink.

'Daniel!' she cries loudly and unexpectedly. 'How fantastic that you're still in Oxford! I thought I'd have to hunt you down on the internet. God, this wine's foul. Where's the bottle I brought?'

She goes to look for it, leaving me fairly giddy at her greeting but worried that I might somehow fail. Fail to enthrall her with my conversation. Fail in the sack. 'Guys are mostly petrified of her,' Zac had said, and that may explain my sweaty brow, dry mouth and knotted stomach.

While I wait for Faiza to return – if, indeed, she intends to – I feel a hand, which I'd guess to be on the large side and maybe even male, fondle my left buttock.

'Hi,' says Olive's throaty voice. 'Still around, then?'

I turn and she plants the kisses I didn't get from Faiza on both my cheeks.

'Hi, Olive,' I sigh. 'Listen, could you remind me where the bathroom is?'

I'm stoned, I'm a little bit drunk and I've run out of things to say about Third World debt. The party's down to the usual suspects, who I guess will sleep on Barney's floor. I, myself, don't want to sleep on Barney's floor, but Faiza hasn't given any indication that I might be doing otherwise, and I'm so lacking the energy to get home that I suspect I will end up on the floor. Then, in my foggy mind, I remember I'm staying just one block away.

I stand, wobble and announce that I should be heading off now. If I'd known that was all it would take to get Faiza up and in the street with an arm around my waist, I'd have done it much earlier.

'Joe's house is nearer than mine,' she says,

almost sweeping me along. This feels some-thing like an order but I don't care.

There's an attempt at lovemaking in Joe's guest room, but Faiza is very vocal – loudly so – and I'm conscious of Julian in his attic bedroom, maybe going over Fermat's last theorem as a little light reading. He'd let us in, as I forgot the key he gave me, and I can hear he's still awake.

Faiza moves my hand around and issues instructions – 'There...! No, there...! Oh, yes...! That's it, that's it... More pressure...! Less pressure! Mmm, that's good.' And so on.

I'm beginning to feel like her personal masseur/chiropractor, and a very tired one at that. When my vital equipment fails to work, owing I hope to drink and dope, Faiza doesn't take it personally. Which is some-thing. There's no sobbing, 'Don't you find me attractive?' Instead, she finishes herself off beside me, and is soon quietly snoring.

I get up and go to the kitchen for much-needed water, then back in the bedroom I pick up and fold our clothes, making his and hers piles on the dresser. When my cell-phone falls from a pocket, I'm surprised to see there's a text message for me. I'm not a texting kind of guy, so never receive them.

It's from Caitlin. 'Ralph now in Wales but had mountain fall. In hospital unconscious

156

after helicopter rescue! Thought you'd like to know. Caitlin x.'

I rather like that x. I see also that she'd tried calling when I was mid-party. It occurs to me, as I slip back under the sheet, that Caitlin might have been calling for help, support. Perhaps Joe had to leave Wales under pressure from his business partner. Who knows, maybe he's been in the next room all along, fingers in his ears to block out Faiza sounds. My eyes grow heavy and I ponder on what an eventful day it's been. Caitlin's goodbye note, croquet, almost getting laid... Though not as eventful as Ralph's, I'd imagine. I'll text Caitlin in the morning, I decide. No, better still, call.

Ralph I hear voices, see images, but mostly I sleep. Or am I hearing and seeing these things in my sleep? 'Tall people aren't always that sure-footed,' says Cait. I'm sure it's Cait. 'I expect he tripped or something. We've seen him do it before, remember? Over the gravestone.'

They laugh. Who's she talking to? If I could only open my eyes. There's something in my mouth and, I think, up my nose. *I didn't trip!* I want to tell them. 'Has his wife been contacted?' It's a voice I don't recognise. A bloke. *Please God, not Hilary.* She'll kill me to get the house, if they don't get to me first. Lenny and Dog. I see it all again. They're big

157

blokes and they're panting like mad, but that doesn't stop them running at me when I turn to the sound of my name. 'C'mere, Ralph!' Then a bloody great hand that doesn't smell too good covers my mouth and nose to stop me calling the others, further up the track. Beth and Ioan disappear round a bend and I know I'm done for. 'Just checking you didn't see nothing,' says Lenny. 'Like you didn't see no one get stabbed, yeah?' Dog grunts a couple of times. I'm not sure I've ever heard him speak. Maybe he can only grunt. Hence the name. 'Even if you did, you wasn't gonna tell anyone, was you, Ralphy? You won't say nothing, will you?' I shake my head beneath the hand. 'I won't say nothing,' I mumble. 'I mean, anything.' Lenny says, 'And where's your poncy little notebook? Eh? Eh?' He's going through my pockets. How do I tell him I lost it, with the hand clamped on my face?

'They can stay like this for months,' I hear Cait say, 'before they regain consciousness.' The notebook's on Luna's boat. I left in a hurry and forgot it. First my photo in a shop window, now this. Lenny and co. were going to great lengths to find me, obviously. Find me and kill me because I witnessed the stabbing, or so they think. But first, it seems, they wanted all the incriminating stuff I wrote down – names, places, amounts, prices – when they trusted me, thought I was one of them. Why did I do that? I don't know why I ... oh yeah, authenticity, that was it. Vital when you're writing an urban thriller. 'Nah! Not on him. Take your hand off, Dog. Only no shouting to your little mates, Ralphy boy. Or you'll be down there before you know it.' He points to the sheer drop beside us. Dog obeys, and so do I.

'There's not much we can do,' I hear the unknown man near my bed say. 'And you need to get back to Oxford, Joe.' That's Cait. 'Don't you?' 'I suppose I should,' the man says. 'But I'll talk to Carlo. Did you say Daniel's coming?' All these names. Who are they? Joe sounds familiar. We're in a dark churchyard. 'Ralph, this is Joe. Joe who put us up last night.'

Lenny does an armlock on me. 'Where the fuck is it, then?' I'm being pushed further towards the precipitous edge. Off the track now. Lots of rock underfoot, some of it loose. 'I lost it,' I tell them. I can hear my voice is all shaky. I might be crying. I won't tell them it's on the boat. They'll ransack it and maybe harm Luna. I try to tell Cait. *Houseboat!* Angel Dust! *Get the notebook!*

'Nine thirty,' says someone in a singsong voice. A woman. 'Visiting time's over, I'm afraid.' *Oh Christ, don't leave me on my own. They'll only find me. Do me in with a syringe and make it look like a hospital error. Nurse! I need a cop guarding the door – a big one.* 'Shall

159

we take the grapes with us? He'll hardly be eating anything, and Frankie loves them.' I hear the door shut. 'You fucking expect me to believe that?' Lenny says, on the slippery rain-covered rocks.

NINE

Joe When I tell Cait that I've called Carlo and he's cool about me taking time off, she says, 'But doesn't he need you? Peak season and all that?'

I'm definitely picking up some vibes here that don't feel good. Daniel's on his way, apparently. He phoned this morning, she tells me. She's going to meet him in Bangor later. Thinks they'll go for a coffee and catch up. I say, 'But you only saw him Friday.'

'Well, a lot's happened.'

There's a bit of a silence, then I say, 'I think Carlo's got Zac in to help.'

'Well then,' she says laughing, 'he'll definitely need you!' She comes over and hugs me. 'If I'm going to Bangor station anyway, I could give you a lift.'

'But I've got my car.'

'Ah! Silly me.'

I push her away and hold her at arm's length. 'What is it?'

160

Cait sort of slumps. 'I'm sorry. I'm being horrible, aren't I?'

'Totally. Why? Were you and Daniel ... you know?'

'No, absolutely not. Look, Joe...'

Oh, right, here goes. How many times have I heard 'Look, Joe...'?

'It's just that–' she says, only Frankie comes in from walking the dog and tells her Merlin's been chasing sheep again, and she turns and flies out the door shouting, 'Someone will shoot you, you stupid boy!'

I decide not to hang around for the end of the 'Look, Joe...'. I go and pack my bag, a bit puzzled, but not all that surprised. Last night, when we'd got back from the hospital and opened a bottle of wine, she did bring up our ages, and the fact that I'm going to want a family soon, and how she's way too old and busy to contemplate that. It all felt a bit heavy, not to say unexpected. I wasn't giving a thought to the long term, but ... well, could be she's got a point. It's just nice having nice sex with a nice woman for a change. Not that there's been any since we got here. I thought that was because of Frankie's presence, only now I see it's more than that.

What is it about me and women? I come across mirrors, I know I'm good-looking. I'm a decent enough bloke, and do things like drive a person in need all the way to Wales. That could be it, I suppose. Too nice. Maybe I should work on finding my inner bastard. Start treating them rough. 'Ah well,' I say, checking I've packed everything.

I'll go back to running the café, seeing my friends occasionally and looking for yet another girlfriend. It might not be that hard, since I can't stand Frankie. It would have been good to explore the area, though. Have a go at Snowdon. I look at it through the bedroom window. Or maybe not.

I'm just zipping up my bag when I hear a car pull up. Cait back again? I leave the bag and go down to find Beth knocking on the open door and saying, 'Anyone home?'

I tell her Frankie's in his room, but she says she hasn't come to see Frankie, she's come to see me, and did I fancy going for a walk. It would have been rude to say, 'Not really,' since she'd driven here especially to ask me out – as it were. Instead, I say, 'OK,' and go and change my shoes.

When I return, I find her doing press-ups in the living room. I watch for a while, then clear my throat.

'Ready?' she says, suddenly on her feet and all flushed. But not out of breath, I notice.

Caitlin I am so, so looking forward to seeing Daniel. As I zip along in my lovely old car, on the roads I know so well I could drive blindfolded, I have this unexpectedly warm feeling and try to work out why. It's the one you get when you're about to see an old friend you've got masses to say to. One who's also interesting and probably knows things like where exactly Oman is, and who's the president of Uruguay.

I'd had two stabs at world events with Joe on our long drive. I don't know, maybe he was just tired, but there seemed to be little interest and even less knowledge. 'Yeah, it's a fucked-up world,' he said a couple of times, without going into specifics. A generation thing, I decided, and blamed Thatcher. We went back to Joe's comfort zone, namely Oxford, his childhood, his friends, pubs, cafés, Italian food, photography, movies and evil Charlotte. Who doesn't sound that bad to me. Quite good fun, in fact. 'She was always nagging me to go travelling with her,' Joe said. 'India mainly. But India sounds such a nightmare. All those women begging with one-armed children.'

'They say it changes you,' I told him.

'Exactly.'

My plan is to pick Daniel up from the railway station, go and have a coffee or a drink, then pop into the hospital to check on Ralph. Hopefully, wife Hilary will come at some point, although when I spoke to her yesterday she'd said how difficult it would be for her to get away, what with her job and her terminally ill mother having just moved in.

'She won't be with me much longer,' Hilary had said, 'whereas I'm sure Ralph will.' She'd chuckled, a bit half-heartedly, and added, 'He always bounces back from these things, bless him.' I'd wanted to ask exactly how many times Ralph had been comatose in hospital, but Hilary hurriedly wound down the conversation, saying she had to walk the dogs now or she'd be late for her shift at the children's home. 'I'll keep calling the hospital,' she'd said. 'Check he's OK.'

It's weird, but I even have a few butterflies when I walk into the station and wait for the fourteen fifty-four to arrive. I take some deep breaths and think back over the week in Oxford. Daniel and I did get on well, didn't we? There were a few moments towards the end when I wondered... He'd been a bit moody. But by then the heat was making everyone snappy.

The train's late and I pace up and down a while, until the announcement is made that it's arrived. At the very last minute, I dash into the ladies and check myself in the mirror, run a comb through my hair, wash my hands, dry them, decide I need the loo, go, then wash my hands again and comb my hair again. Out in the hall, where a small crowd passes through the station, I spot Daniel and make my way over.

'Hey,' he says. 'How you doing, Cait? My God, it's beautiful up here. The scenery from the train was so dramatic, I can't believe I'm in Britain.'

'Oh, Daniel,' I say, and I give him a long hug. 'How lovely that you've come.'

'Well,' he says, stepping back. 'Quite a greeting.'

It's then that I spot the familiar woman hovering not far from him. She'd been in the poet pub, and then at Joe's house.

'I think you know Faiza?' Daniel asks. 'She insist– uh, said she'd like to come with me. I guessed you wouldn't mind.'

'Yes, we've met,' says Faiza. 'You're Joe's girlfriend, aren't you?'

'No!'

'No? Oh, I thought...'

'Friend. Just friend.' As from about an hour ago.

'Is he still here?' she asks.

'Yes,' I say, looking at Daniel. His demeanour's changed, just slightly. 'In the guest accommodation.' I'll see to that when I get back. 'You two can have the one Ralph was in, until his tumble.'

'Oh, I don't think–' says Daniel.

'It's got twin beds,' I add, seeing the look on his face.

'How quaint,' says Faiza. 'I can't remember the last time I slept in a single bed.'

We make our way outside, in silence,

where I lead them to my car. 'Did you want to go and see Ralph?' I ask.

'Of course,' says Daniel.

'Do we have to?' asks Faiza. 'I can't bear hospitals.'

'You can stay in the car,' says Daniel, opening the back door for Faiza, but joining me in the front.

It's all a bit confusing emotionally – have they become an item? – and I still feel truly terrible about Joe. And also worried about myself. How could I be so fickle? Did I just use Joe? Surely he's not got serious about me? He seemed a bit shocked earlier, rather than heartbroken. And now Daniel's here and I do so like him. I'm even feeling physically drawn, but is that because he's got himself an exotic girlfriend? I look over at him and smile. I don't know why, I just feel better having him around.

Joe Beth is just about superglued to me. She's actually quite attractive, I notice after a while, with long, really fine blond hair and pale blue eyes – neither of which quite goes with her strong body. Maybe athletic's the word. But she's shapely with it, not straight up and down like Charlotte.

We're all waiting for a dinner that Cait's cooking with a lot of interference from Faiza. Cait should never have gone for a Middle Eastern tagine of chicken and artichoke.

166

'You need saffron threads,' says Faiza.

'I don't have any.'

'Then we must get some.'

'Yeah, right,' snorts Frankie. 'I'll just pop out to our Lebanese deli.'

They compromise and use saffron powder, which Cait says is a bit old, but everyone agrees that they don't mind. When ginger becomes an issue – 'Ground, not stem,' Faiza insists, even though Cait has neither – I leave the room, then the house, closely followed by Beth.

'This way,' she says in the garden, and we end up on what turns out to be a really pretty walk. Another one. She talks about her family. Parents, one brother and two sisters. Beth's the oldest, then the sisters, then Ioan. She teaches games in a secondary school and still lives at home. She knows she'll have to leave one day, but can't bear the thought of it.

'But what do you do round here?' I ask. 'You know, for fun.'

'We've got hills, mountains, rivers, the sea,' says Beth, waving an arm at the scenery. She's frowning at me, like she doesn't quite get my question.

'Yeah, but what do you do for *fun?*'

She laughs and says, 'I read a lot.'

'Right.'

'And we often play cards and board games.'

'We?'

'The family.'

'Ah.' Dad and I sometimes play croquet, but I don't think we've done snakes and ladders for a while.

'I'm the Scrabble champ,' says Beth. 'And Ioan's a whiz at gin rummy.'

'Uh-huh.'

'But what do you do with your friends? When you're not in the mountains and so on.'

'Go to the pub, of course.'

'Thank God for that. It was all sounding a bit wholesome.'

She rolls her eyes. 'So what do you do for kicks, city boy?'

'Go to the pub, watch TV and DVDs.'

'Huh. I'm amazed you've got such a good body.'

'Have I?' I ask, although I know I have.

I tell her about the café and all the rushing around and sweating. Then out of the blue she says, 'In that case, race you to that big rock?' We're on a bit of a hill and my legs tell me we have been for some time.

'Er, OK.' I don't really see the point, but want to prove an urban life doesn't necessarily mean an unhealthy one.

'Ready...' she says. *'Go!'*

Obviously, as she's a girl, I let her beat me.

There's definitely tension at the dinner

table, and a lot of the conversation takes place between Frankie and Faiza, who can't agree on anything. Immigrants, private schooling, farming methods. Frankie's about as right wing as they make them at seventeen. Every now and then he says something in Welsh to Ioan and Beth, then laughs. Cait says, 'English, Frankie,' each time, but it doesn't stop him. Meanwhile, she and Daniel are barely saying anything, Ioan is eating and eating, and Beth keeps accidentally touching my arm with hers.

Once or twice, Cait gives me these looks, like she's saying sorry or something. So when she goes to the living room to answer the phone, I decide to take a bathroom break. The call is to do with her work, and I hang around till she's finished.

'Are you all right, Joe?' she asks. 'You know, about...'

'I'm absolutely cool with it.'

'Sure?'

'Sure.' I realise, as I speak, that I am.

'Friends?'

'Yep.'

'Joe, you're food's getting cold,' says Beth, suddenly in the room.

'Coming,' I tell her, and Cait gives us both this funny look. Jealousy? Regret? Somehow, I doubt it.

At the table, things gradually get more strained between Daniel and Faiza. After dessert, while Faiza is telling us, in great and quite boring detail, how a real tagine of chicken is made, Daniel says, 'Why don't you show me your workroom, Cait? I'd love to see it.'

They're gone a while, and Faiza keeps glancing at the door they left through. Finally she jumps up, claiming she too would like to see Cait's room. After she practically runs out, long hair flying behind her, Frankie says, 'Fuckinell, she's scary.'

'Oh, not really,' I say, mainly because I like disagreeing with him.

'Do you know Faiza well?' asks Beth. Something in her tone is asking if I've shagged her.

I shrug. 'Fairly. She's more a friend of a friend, really.'

'Ah,' says Beth and our bare arms touch again. She smiles at me. 'Fancy another walk before it gets dark?'

Three walks in one day? Jeez. After such a big meal, all I want is to flop somewhere, preferably in front of a screen. But Beth's got a sort of glow to her, and somehow gives the impression that one last hike would be a blast.

'Well...' I say, 'OK. Only I'm not racing you again.'

'But it's fun having races.'

'For you maybe, but not for me.'

Ioan sniggers and says, 'That's right, you

tell her. Imagine being her little brother for seventeen years?'

I want to say I've known far bossier women, but Beth's suddenly helping me from my chair and brushing crumbs from my T-shirt. 'Let's go!' she says, and we do.

TEN

Ralph 'I'm surprised there hasn't been any media coverage,' I hear the American say. 'Even local.' Then Cait – 'Oh, people get rescued from Snowdon all the time. It only makes the news if they die. Want another sandwich?' 'Thanks,' says the bloke. Daniel? I've heard him a bit over the past week. And the other one, Joe.

Every time I come to and find I'm still alive – alive and unable to move for some reason (trauma? exhaustion?) – I feel just that little bit more safe. Gradually, I'm thinking that Lenny and Dog just assumed they'd bumped me off. That no one could survive such a dramatic fall. Another option is that they don't care if I'm alive because they know (quite rightly) that they've scared me off forever. It's only thoughts of Luna spoiling this ever-increasing peace of mind. Whether they got to her. Set *Angel Dust* on fire to destroy incriminating evidence. Evidence of what? Not the stabbing...What did I write in the book? Something. Listened in, wrote things down. It didn't bother them at the time.

'All your own produce?' I hear. 'Yep,' says Cait, 'apart from the bread and butter.' They laugh, even though it's not funny, then stop talking while they eat. Things are much quieter when she comes with Joe.

One time I heard another voice – a kid. He said, quite close, like he was centimetres from my face, 'Jesus. If I'm ever in this state, unplug the fucking machine, won't you?' Cait said, 'Don't swear in a hospital, Frankie,' and then I remembered the son. As tall as me only a lot thinner.

Anyway, I'm getting to like it here. Haven't let them know I can open my eyes every now and then. They might start thinking I'm rapidly recovering and shift me to some less safe place. Like home. Boy, am I going to be in for it.

'Heard from Faiza?' Cait's saying. It's tempting to open my eyes just a titchy bit. See what the yank looks like. He says, 'No, and I guess I won't now.' I can smell the sandwiches, strangely. Strangely, because my nose is under the mask still. Cucumber, definitely cucumber. Might be imagining it.

'I know about...' says Daniel. 'What?' asks Cait. 'Well, for start, I saw you kissing in Joe's room.' It goes quiet again and I see *Angel Dust* all ablaze. Neighbouring boat people trying to get to Luna.

'Oh,' says Cait. 'That. Yeah, OK, we did have what you might call a holiday flingette. Then he drove me up here, which was lovely of him, and I realised it was all wrong. Not just our ages, other stuff too.' Actually, I wish they'd take the mask off because it reminds me of Dog's hand over my face. Maybe it does come off sometimes. Does it? I try to remember, while the yank's saying, 'No, not really. Just a few kisses and cuddles. Faiza's ... well, full on. Too much for me.'

They laugh again, and I risk opening my eyes a smidgeon. They're looking at each other, in that way. Will anyone ever look at me in that way again? I let my eyes close and hear wrappers and things being put away. 'I'll give his wife a call, tell her there's been no change since she was here. She seemed like a nice woman, didn't she? Such a lot on her plate, though.'

Hilary was here? When? Chairs get scraped suddenly and noisily, and my mind jumps, even if my body can't. They're running at me again, up the track. 'C'mere, Ralph!' Scaring me rigid. Just the sight of them. What's Hilary up to? Being 'nice' when all she probably wants is power of attorney and the whole house in her name. She'll see to it she gets everything, I know she will.

173

'Oh, Daniel,' comes Cait's soft, slightly Welsh voice. She's at close quarters now. 'There are tears. Look. Oh God, how awful. Do you think he's crying in his sleep, or coma, or whatever it is?' I hear soft footsteps and Daniel says, 'I dunno. I guess that can happen.' It's then that I open my eyes and make Cait practically scream the hospital down.

ELEVEN

Joe It's good to be back, I'm thinking, slowly waking up to the sound of Dad lah lah-ing Tchaikovsky in the garden. And I know Carlo was relieved to see me yesterday.

After closing the café at midnight, following a ludicrously busy day, I'd got a taxi home to find another email from Beth. When was I coming back to Wales, when would be a good time to visit Oxford? She's keen, that's for sure, but then they all are at first. Trouble is, Beth's idea of a good time is canoeing in rapids after a long mountain hike with a two-ton backpack. I kept finding excuses not to fish, camp, canoe, horse ride and so on, until she finally gave up and watched Frankie's DVDs with me, all snuggled up.

I'm not sure why I stayed after Cait dumped me, but maybe it was good just being somewhere completely different for a while. And maybe, after all, I quite liked all the attention from Beth. We'd ended up spending a lot of time on our own in the guest room I moved into when Daniel and Faiza arrived. They'd taken over Ralph's room, but then Faiza stormed off back to Oxford the next day. Insisted on getting a taxi, which must have cost her some. I'd have given her a lift but she didn't ask.

Daniel was still in the guest accommodation when I left, but I'll bet he isn't now. There was definitely something happening between Cait and him, even if it wasn't all-out sex. Not that I cared too much in the end. She's lovely, but I hadn't exactly fallen for her. And when you've seen a woman milking a goat in wellies, dressing gown and reading glasses, you sort of go off the idea. It was the first time she'd actually looked her age. I couldn't make out what the glasses were for until I got closer and saw the book on her lap. 'Oh!' she'd said, jumping and covering her white knees, then laughing. 'Some days, this is the only time I get to read.'

So, last night, although it was late, I clicked on reply and typed 'Hi Beth'. I told her all about the busy day, but didn't mention her coming to stay, or me going back to Wales. I'm not sure why I didn't. I signed off with 'Love Joe' but didn't return the four kisses she'd put on hers. I mean, it's not as if we'd been intimate. We'd been on the verge, on Thursday, the night before I left. I'd stopped things, though, after a sudden loss of confidence. That's never happened before, and I could only put it down to too much healthy air. 'I just think I function better in a city,' I told her, and she said she'd be coming to find out if it was true. It's hard to imagine her in Oxford. Even though I like her a lot, I find the whole idea of Beth quite alien, especially now I'm home.

I finally get up, have coffee with Dad, then set off to find Luna and her boat. Something I promised Cait I'd do. I never have quite got these little floating homes, like sheds on water. Mostly, I'd worry about getting attacked on my way home at night.

I've been walking quite a while and I'm thinking how much I like life's little luxuries – a proper toilet, being one – when I read *Angel Dust* and see a large ginger-haired woman sitting on a chair beside the path, drinking from a mug with 'Luna' conveniently written on it. I introduce myself and – feeling like someone in a Shakespeare play, before phones and things – tell her I've come with news of Ralph.

176

'He's in hospital in Wales,' I say. 'Unconscious, after a mountain fall.'

'Do come in,' says Luna, standing and almost reaching my height. 'I expect you'd like a refreshing drink on such a hot day.'

'Uh, yeah, OK.'

We step into the boat and go through a door, then without asking what I'd like, Luna puts the kettle on. She doesn't enquire after Ralph, but just looks me up and down a lot in a vaguely spooky way. I'm beginning to wish I hadn't come.

'Let me think,' I say, five minutes later. I'm perched on a slim sofa with a mug of something horrible-looking. 'Just the love spell, if that's all right?' This is a bit of an unexpected bonus for my trouble – a free spell.

She's already done something for Ralph, which involved incense, candles, a notebook of his and some chanting. 'There,' she'd said, finally opening her eyes, 'that should get him on his feet."

'Good,' I said, like I believed her, then went back to my slimy dead-grass tea, which wasn't that bad.

'Do you have a love interest in mind?' she's asking me now.

I tell her no, and explain how I don't have a problem attracting women but can't hang on to them.

'Are you faithful?' she asks.

'Absolutely.'

'Attentive?'

'Very.'

'No unpalatable habits?'

Luna's beginning to annoy me. 'Not that I know of.'

'Hm,' she says, stroking her chins. 'Then it must be boredom driving them away.'

Now she's really annoying me, although I think she's right. 'I don't know. Maybe.'

'You might not need a love spell, John.'

'Joe.'

'It may be best to go for charisma instead.'

I'm insulted but strangely glued to the slim sofa. 'Well, OK,' I say. 'But this won't get out, will it?'

'Don't worry.' She places a pale veiny hand on my knee. 'I have a strict witch/customer confidentiality code.'

Customer? 'Er, I'm sorry, but do I have to pay for this?'

'Well,' she says, the hand moving upwards. 'Maybe in one form or another, if you get my meaning?'

So she does have a sense of humour. I laugh and stand up. Even though we're not moving, I feel sea sick. 'If it's all the same, Luna, I'll work on the charisma thing on my own. But cheers for the offer.'

Once outside, on nice firm land, I hear her call out, 'Silly boy! Of course I'll cast you a spell for free.' But I don't go back. Instead, I peep through one of the little windows. Luna has picked up the phone I've stupidly left behind. She lights two large red candles, then sits on her stool again and taps away at my keys. I want to go back in and snatch the phone, but again I'm glued to the spot. Luna stops the tapping, nods, holds my mobile aloft and starts chanting again. Every now and then she spins the phone around her head – once, twice, three times. I wait till she's finished and refilling her whistling kettle before I knock and push at her door.

'Sorry,' I say. 'Did I leave my mobile?'

'The one with Beth in?'

'Er, yeah. That one.'

'Here,' she says, handing it over with a wink. 'Let's see how you get on now.'

Part of me wants to ask what she's done. Did she read Beth's texts? What does she think will happen? But the rest wants to get out, go home and wipe the smell of incense off my phone.

'Oh,' she says, when I turn to leave, 'you may as well take this.' She reaches for the notebook she'd held earlier. 'Ralph might want it when he comes round.'

I have a quick look through, and see pages and pages of notes in tiny writing. At the front it says 'This notebook belongs to Ralph Higson. If lost please return for a small reward.' Underneath is his address and mobile number. Cait had told me he was writing some novel, so this could be connected. 'Maybe I'll send it to his wife,' I say.

'No, no. Hilary won't take care of it. You should take it to him.'

'In hospital?'

'Yes.'

'In Wales?'

'Yes.'

'It's quite a way.'

'True,' Luna says. 'But I sense some urgency, John.'

Back in the land of normal people, I have a quick energising espresso before changing and going out front to welcome and seat lunchtime customers. And, if Zac doesn't show again, serve non-stop until we close and count up the takings.

Zac doesn't show, and it's knackering. When I finally reach my bed, I think about going back to Wales. But I don't think about it for long. Apart from Carlo killing me, Beth would only try to get me in a canoe again. Hyperactive Beth. Strange that she hasn't emailed this evening ... or sent any texts since ... since Luna cast her spell?

Daniel We're all supposed to have a spiritual home, somewhere. And I can see why many would feel that North Wales, with its dramatic slatey scenery, might be theirs. It has a vaguely hippy community of both

Welsh and English people, some of whom have dropped in on Cait since my arrival, often when she's working, and often with children called Shiva or Ned, and jars of sugarless homemade jam we're told to eat quickly. There's a broad spectrum of occupations, from single mom on benefits to biomedical scientist at Bangor University. Many have little businesses of a crafty nature, similar to Cait's. All of them are nice. I wouldn't say this place is my spiritual home, but it's feeling good for now.

Of course, that might have something to do with Cait and my growing affection for her. I can't yet tell if my feelings are unrequited, but Cait sure is playing it cool. I suspect, and hope, this is because she so recently hurled herself into an unsuitable liaison and is being excessively cautious with me.

Anyhow, I shall continue to help around the place, visit Ralph, shop – as I'm doing now – and hope that one day I'll get enough alcohol into Cait for there to be no going back for us.

In Bangor I have a good haircut. That surprises me, but I don't know why it should.

Next, I buy a dark grey shirt, mushroom-coloured chinos and a pair of strong leather shoes that could double as hiking boots should the occasion arise. Cait keeps mentioning a mountain walk, but so far the sewing has taken up her days, as well as most evenings.

'I should never have taken a week off,' she said last night. 'So many orders to catch up on.'

'But I'm glad you took that week off,' I told her, and she'd looked up and smiled at me ... in that lovely way she does. But this time in a very tired way too. I wanted to carry her upstairs, slip her shoes off, put her in bed and tuck her up. But to have suggested such a thing would have been fatal, so I offered, instead, to give her a neck and shoulder massage, then held my breath waiting for an answer.

'OK,' she said, putting her glass down and sitting up. 'I didn't know you could do that.'

It was news to me too, but I made a good show of knowing what I was doing, until Frankie walked in and snorted and walked out again. I think the kid has a problem with me. Having lost confidence, I stopped my gentle, probably useless kneading and Cait thanked me and yawned and lied about how relaxed it had made her, then went to bed unaided.

I buy socks and boxers too, although I don't know why. I have plenty. Maybe I'm thinking new clothes, new beginning? Maybe I'm just nervously shopping because I don't know what else to do whilst Cait chugs away on her sewing machine. (Alas, not the old treadle that stands decoratively in the living room.) She may not have much time for me but I don't want to leave. And I get the impression, through all her busyness and guardedness, that she doesn't want me to, either.

I go to the parking lot, throw my purchases in Cait's old car and head for the hospital. This is my third visit without the overworked Cait. Sitting alone with a guy who can only wiggle his digits and blink 'yes' and 'no' isn't a heck of a lot of fun. But, since his wife hasn't returned and no other friends or family members have materialised, we're stuck with being the only ones concerned for the poor guy. Once, a middle-aged man had been coming out of Ralph's door, just as Caitlin and I arrived. I went to speak, but the guy said, 'Wrong room,' and hurried off. For a moment, we'd thought Ralph might have a pal.

What I do is take a newspaper with me and read out the least depressing stories. The last time I was here, three days ago, I asked Ralph if he liked me doing this and got one blink for 'yes'. So today, I stop at the hospital shop for a broad-sheet, and as I walk the passages and take the elevator, I pick out one or two interesting articles that don't involve death, serious injury or long-term hospitalisation. However, when I reach his small ward, Ralph's bed is empty and his few personal things are gone from the cabinet. I check the other three beds for Ralph, then go to the nurses' station and ask where Mr Higson has been moved to.

'Discharged himself yesterday,' I'm told.

'Pardon me?'

'Since he was up and about and only had the one broken arm, there wasn't much we could do. Once we got him on his pins, the recovery was rapid. The doctors think it was a temporary paralysis, brought on by trauma.'

'Ah.' I take a seat, which I think might be for nurses only, and digest the news. 'Did he say where he was going?'

'Many times,' says the nurse, 'while he was pleading with us to let him go. Something urgent he had to do in Oxford, apparently.'

'Did he say what?'

'No.' She gives me a look that might be asking for her chair back. 'Oh, he could have mentioned a boat, but that was all.'

I stand and thank her, then go to the hospital restaurant. There I have a curry and rice, which isn't at all bad, and mull over this new information. I call Cait.

'Hello,' she says, and I hear the machine going in the background. I picture the phone tucked between shoulder and chin while I tell her what's happened.

The noise stops and Cait says, 'Talk about a quick recovery.'

'Miraculous.'

'Sounds like he's going back to see Luna.' Cait giggles endearingly. 'Maybe they had a thing going.'

'I guess she could have cast a spell over him. Thinking about it, she'd have to.'

'Now, now,' says Cait. 'Tell you what, I'll give Joe a ring. See if he'll go and check on things.'

'Are you sure?' I'm not keen on the idea of Cait calling Joe. 'Ralph's hardly our responsibility any more.' And never was, I want to add.

'Yeah, I know. But I do have his luggage, remember. Well ... I think I do.'

'You'd better go check,' I say. 'See you later.'

Back on the road and heading home – home? – I ponder at length on whether Ralph's going will leave me no good reason to stay.

Caitlin Ralph's case is still in his room.

'Bugger,' I say, wishing he'd crept up in a quiet taxi and taken it while I was working. How blissful it would be to no longer have a link with this person. This person I barely know, and who hasn't spoken to me since, over two weeks ago, he'd said, 'Hey, body painting! See you back at college, Cait.' I've recently spoken to *him*, of course, but had no reply. Just the blinks. It's bizarre that he's

185

suddenly upped and gone, and without a cheerio or a thank you. Above all, I feel sorry for Hilary. Life with Ralph must be quite a roller coaster.

Pulling the extendible handle, I wheel the case over to the house and down the cellar steps. 'There,' I say, climbing back up and switching off the light. 'Out of sight, out of mind and out of my life.'

I get back to work, but then start wondering if I should phone his poor wife and let her know he's OK. Surely he's done that? Although knowing Ralph ... not that I do know him. I go wrong, swear and have to unpick a row of stitching. What would I tell her, anyway? That he's taken up with a white witch on a canal boat? No, his marriage is none of my business. When Hilary phones the hospital, as she'd told me she does most days, they'll let her know what's happened. I block out thoughts of Ralph again and get on with some work.

Orders have flooded in recently. Although I've got two outworkers running up things, they have five young children between them and can't do more than part time. Normally, I wouldn't mind. I love designing and creating these little items of clothing. Things we could never have afforded to put Frankie in. What worries me now is Daniel, and how I might be neglecting him, and how he might just leave. It bothers me that I like having him around so much. He's easy-going and helpful, even cooking dinner sometimes. He's funny and he's growing more and more attractive. I know he likes me, and I'm sure he knows I like him. What he doesn't know is that, as much as I want things to move on, there's the whole Joe thing, lurking and spoiling everything. I'd feel cheap, that's the problem. Jumping into bed with Joe, then doing the same with Daniel. If I were twenty-five, not forty-five, I'm sure I'd think nothing of it. And if I wasn't the mother of a judgemental seventeen-year-old, I might think nothing of it.

I blame Ralph. If he hadn't led me astray, I'd never have become besotted by Joe. Then Daniel and I may well have got together, if only for the week. Daniel told me he'd wanted to come and sit with me after the introductions. That he'd 'gotten waylaid'. I make another wrong turn on the machine and decide to give up and have a cup of tea.

In the kitchen, mug in front of me on the table, I think about Daniel and do a lot of sighing. I know he has a flight to the States booked for next week. He hasn't mentioned visiting other places in Britain, and keeps asking if his hanging out here is OK. 'Oh God, yes,' I'd said last time he asked. He'd broken into his lovely toothy smile that makes him look so American. He's Hispanic on his father's side, he tells me, with a WASP mother, whose parents disapproved of her marriage. 'I sometimes think our class system is worse than yours,' Daniel had said. I'd expected him to laugh but he didn't.

I finish the tea and give in to Merlin's pleas for a walk. Although he can roam around our small patch of land, we have to keep him fenced in for his own sake. Nearby, there are precious Suffolk sheep, which take precedence over a dog any day. 'Fetch your lead, then,' I say, and he does.

Today is the best, weatherwise, for a week, and the intense afternoon heat takes me back to Oxford. Again, I mentally kick myself for the Joe thing – but then remember the ego boost. And who knows, maybe it intensified Daniel's interest in me.

Daniel ... oh God. Now Ralph's better Daniel's bound to leave. My insides churn slightly at the thought of that, then they churn even more at the thought of making love with him. It's all so unsettling, and also ridiculous for a woman of my age and independence. I think back three weeks, to a time when men, romance and things carnal didn't feature at all. Life was so easy, if a little dull. Shall I just drag Daniel to bed the moment he returns from Bangor, and to hell with my self-esteem and reputation, and what Frankie thinks? But what if I really fall for him and then he disappears back to

London and it's never a proper relationship?

'Merlin!' I snap, when he spots sheep and starts pulling at the lead. 'Grow up, will you?'

Of course, if Merlin could speak, he might well tell me to do the same.

Daniel's back by the time I get home. He's picked up the one or two things I'd asked for and I get going on dinner, while he sits at the table watching and telling me again about the hospital business. At half seven, he pours us both a glass of white wine, and by eight we're out on the patio, enjoying the sultry warmth, my vegetable lasagne, and the fact that Frankie's out for the evening.

'I feel very comfortable here,' Daniel says after a while.

I freeze, not knowing how to respond. He could be saying he feels comfortable with *me*. That he'd like to stay for ever. But then he could be talking about the area. I fork food into my mouth and nod, giving myself time to think.

'With you,' he adds.

I swallow and take a gulp of reinforcing wine. 'Well, I do like to make my guests comfortable,' I say, then laugh.

'You know what I mean, Caitlin.'

I nod again and eat again. Why can't I react appropriately? Thank him flirtatiously, and say I feel the same. Or, better still, tell him exactly what's been going on in my head. Perhaps I'm scared of giving in, going to bed with Daniel, and then have him go off me. He seems very interested all the time I'm unavailable. Fun of the chase ... who knows?

'What happened with you and Lauren?' I ask.

Daniel puts his fork down and leans back in his canvas chair. 'Aahh, now there's a long story.'

I look at my big man's watch. 'I've got time.'

'Well, let me sum up. Boy meets girl. They fall for each other, decide to shack up together. Girl has fling with boss, boy graciously forgives on girl's declaration that it's now over. When girl, still with same boss, receives two promotions in six months, boy gets suspicious and starts following girl.'

'No!'

'Desperate measures, but boy has to know for sure. Anyhow, boy's suspicions confirmed on one so-called weekend business trip.'

'Oh, poor boy.'

'Yes.' Daniel shakes his head. 'And poor boss's wife and kids. Last thing I heard, he'd moved out and was living with Lauren. It's so classic, it's corny.'

'Yes,' I say with a sigh. I'd glossed over my own marital trials with Daniel, but now I tell all. For a while afterwards, we just look at each other, like two people who've been through a similar hell. I want to touch him, hug him, make love. But then Joe pops into my head and I feel tacky again. I straighten my back, stack the plates, smile at Daniel and ask if he'd like some sorbet. The moment's gone, just like that.

TWELVE

Ralph What bad luck. All that effort to get myself discharged. Bombing down to Oxford on the train, even though I felt like poo. Then finding Luna's only gone and given my notebook away to someone called John. She wasn't even under any pressure, she told me. Just offered it to the guy. A complete stranger. 'He said he'd take it to you in hospital,' she told me, a bit apologetically because she could see I was cross.

I also came over funny. I couldn't remember a John in Lenny's crowd, so asked her to describe him. Luna put a hand on her chest and did this weird thing with her eyes and said, 'Divine.' Which didn't help a bit. I asked if she knew anything about him, anything at all, and she said 'Yes, he's got a girlfriend called Beth. Well, he will have by now, if my little spell worked.' Beth? The one

I went up the mountain with, or another one? I asked Luna if Beth was Welsh and she said she didn't know because text messages don't have an accent. Sometimes, I think she should be called Loony, not Luna.

I asked if this John was Welsh and she said he didn't sound it, but he knew I was in hospital in Wales. Had Lenny and the gang been watching the hospital? Seen me leave, even? I told Luna I might need to crash on the boat for the night and have a bit of a think. Now, four days later, I'm still here and still thinking. My original plan had been to just get the notebook away from Luna, then go and find Lenny and give it to him, in the hope that he'd realise I'm not going to cause trouble, and maybe let me live the rest of my life in peace. Or just let me live.

Obviously, that's no longer a plan. But still, I'm getting used to being here again. Luna cooks lots of witchy stews, which are good, considering the minute stove. She pampers me, and that's just what you want when you've only got one useable arm. Left, unfortunately. Mostly, I just slob out all day watching her spotty portable TV screen.

There are things I should be doing, I know. One, taking the letter the hospital gave me to my GP. Only my GP's in Lincoln, so that will have to wait. Two, going home and talking to Hilary about our marriage. But I'd need to get legal advice first and not be so emotionally fragile. Three, ask Cait to check with the hospital to see if a notebook's been handed in, or if a guy called John has shown up anywhere.

Trouble is, Luna dropped her phone in the river and can't afford another, and her laptop's being fixed (which is why she can't afford a phone) and although I keep thinking I should go and find an internet café or library and email Cait via her website, or just get her number and call her, I'm too scared to leave the boat now I'm here. It could be this John guy's got a contract to carry out on me. Maybe they think I've photocopied my notes.

Luna's done a few spells – one to get the arm better, one to banish John from my life, and one she wouldn't tell me about, but just said, 'Let's wait and see.' I think Luna might be after my body, but can't let that thought hamper my recovery, or get in the way of my what-to-do-next plan, when I come up with it. Every night she says I'd be more comfortable sharing her bed, and I say the sofa's fine, thanks, even though it's like sleeping on a tightrope and the world's thinnest mattress. Still, shouldn't be for much longer.

All I need is for my head to clear a bit and a plan to pop into it. Nice to have a place to crash in the meantime, even if it is short on facilities. One thing I don't understand about Luna is why she couldn't do a spell to mend her laptop, or bring another mobile into her life.

Joe Faiza comes to the café and starts slagging off Daniel. She asks me if I'm pissed off with Cait, and I tell her no. I take a break and we sit chatting over a coffee, then Zac rolls up and the conversation moves on to other things, thank God. Considering Faiza says she can't think of a single thing she needs a man for, she seems a bit cut up about Daniel. My guess is she's used to doing the rejecting.

'So what's this farm like?' asks Zac.

'It's not a farm,' I say. 'Cait grows fruit and vegetables. Keeps a few chickens and two goats. But mostly she makes kids' clothes.'

Faiza says, 'It's horribly rustic.'

'Only I was thinking of going and helping,' says Zac. 'Leaving the urban jungle for a bit.'

'I'd hardly call Oxford an urban jungle,' says Faiza.

'Not even when people get stabbed, in like broad daylight?'

'Oh, that was just kids, it seems. Messing about with knives they shouldn't have had.'

'Really?' I say. I think about Ralph fleeing the crime scene, then running to Wales and changing his name. About the thugs Zac had seen him hanging out with. 'Are you sure?'

Faiza sips at her coffee and nods. 'Brothers,

apparently. Couldn't be named, it said in the *Oxford Times*, because they're too young. Anyway, one's recovering and the other's devastated. He claims it was an accident, so the police aren't going to press charges. I'd imagine this friend of yours, Ralph, was in the vicinity when the stabbing happened. Running away because he doesn't like the sight of blood, or because he thought he was next.'

'Hmm,' I say. She could be right. 'Also, some kids are huge these days, so he might have thought they were older. That they'd come after him because he saw what happened.'

'Man, someone should tell him,' says Zac, finishing off the last bread stick. 'Go to the hospital and do like sign language or something.'

'He can hear perfectly well,' I say. 'And, anyway, he's not there, he's in Oxford.'

Cait had called and asked if I'd go to Luna's boat to check he's on it and if he's OK. I told her I would, even though I'm not keen to see the white witch again. For one thing, I haven't heard from Beth since Luna manhandled my phone, and she's not answering my calls to her mobile. I'm thinking maybe Luna sent a rude text or something. I could go and see Beth, I suppose. Just tell Carlo I'm taking time off again. We've got two new members of staff starting, so maybe

I can. Beth and I might be chalk and cheese, but, weirdly, I keep thinking about her.

'We're guessing he's with Luna again,' I tell Zac and Faiza. 'Probably still in hiding.' It occurs to me that these young brothers with the knife were called Lenny and Dog – the names Luna had given Cait.

'I could like milk the goats,' says Zac. 'Make cheese.'

Faiza goes, 'Ugh.'

'You'd only eat it all,' I say.

'But I gotta get out of here. Oxford's doing my head in.'

'I can recommend a billion nicer places to go,' says Faiza.

'But the mountain air. All that exercise. Just what I need, man.'

I say, 'You know it rains all the time?'

'It does?'

'Yep,' says Faiza.

'All the time?'

'A lot.'

'Oh.' Zac gets up, goes and grabs another pack of breadsticks and comes back. 'So, what are you guys up to later? Dysexlia's playing at The Oak, only Sam wouldn't put me on the guest list. Tight bastard.'

As usual, it's late when I get home, and again there's no email from Beth. She was so keen, now she's gone off me. Same old story. I write her one more email, promising myself it will be the last. Just a chatty, hey-are-you-all-right? message. If she doesn't reply to that, I'll give up. Or go and see her. I don't know ... maybe she's ill.

The hardest thing to get my head round, as I toss and turn in bed, is why this is bothering me so much. Eventually, I give up and switch the light on and send her an email saying I'm missing her. After all, she's said that enough times to me in her messages. It could be I've just been playing it too cool. I hesitate for a while, then put four kisses at the bottom.

THIRTEEN

Daniel While the three of us watch TV, I wonder why the kid isn't in India or Thailand or Machu Picchu, or wherever they go these days. Short on dough, perhaps, despite his father's allowance and the money his mom pays for helping her. Caitlin, I know, just makes enough to pay the bills. I'd offer to fund a trip for Frankie, if it wouldn't look obvious. And surely he has a TV in his room? In fact, I know he does, because I hear it in the night, even from my outhouse.

It's a repeat of something called *A Touch of Frost* and Frankie had told us, three minutes in, who the killer is. I'm tempted to suggest going to a pub, but don't want the kid tagging along. And besides, Caitlin is hand-stitching something she claims is urgent. Caitlin still has a stack of urgent orders, but since I haven't sewn since Cub Scouts, I can't offer to help.

I tick off the days until my flight to the States, getting along with Caitlin, if not getting anywhere with her. It's a pleasant kind of existence. I go on short, and sometimes longer, hikes along the beautiful valley we're in, with the Glyderau mountain range on one side and Carneddau on the other. One day I cheated and took the steam train up Snowdon. That was fun, and not everyone was under five or a pensioner, as I'd expected.

I regularly go to Bethesda and the smaller villages of Tregarth and Mynydd, where the locals are forced to speak my language, in order to sell me the groceries Caitlin has listed. Often, I return with the goods and cook for either the two or the three of us, depending on whether Frankie's home or in the pub. I walk the dog, I collect eggs. I've even, once, milked the odorous goats. 'Just don't ask me to drink the stuff,' I told Caitlin, giving my hands a thorough wash.

'She's the next victim,' says Frankie, briefly looking up. He's either texting or playing a game on the cellphone in his lap. 'He strangles her in the multistorey.'

'Thanks, Frank,' I say, then get out of the comfortable old chair with its worn and faded patches, and announce that I'm going to read. Caitlin frowns at me, then goes back to her sewing.

Lying on my bed, staring at the uneven ceiling, I go over my options. I have four days until my flight. I could return to my apartment for two or three nights, but what would be the point? It's much nicer here, and all my friends in London are on vacation.

I wonder when Caitlin last had a vacation, not counting her week in Oxford. She's talked about trips she'd taken to France, Portugal, Italy, but I seem to remember the husband being mentioned. Poor Caitlin. I'd be thinking 'poor Frankie' if I liked him better. What is it about the kid? He's not what you'd call rude. OK, a little. It's more a surliness, I guess. A kind of dark presence. Perhaps Caitlin hasn't taken a vacation of late because how much fun could you have with a morose teen? Although at seventeen, he should be coming out of that. The hormones and neurotransmitters must have straightened themselves out by now. I try to recall myself at seventeen, but remember only intense study and crippling shyness with girls.

How I'd love to take Caitlin with me. Show her New England, New York. I'd happily pay for everything too. But such a grand gesture would be inappropriate, given our relationship status. What if I just mention it, in a casual and jocular manner? Make out she'd be doing me a favour. 'Hey, wanna coupla weeks in the States? All expenses paid? I'd kinda appreciate the company?'

A touch needy, perhaps.

A tap on the door makes me jump. 'Come in!' I call out, and Caitlin appears, sewing in hand.

'Not reading then?' she asks, while I leap from the bed and remove a pile of clothes from one of two wooden chairs.

'Here, have a seat.' I clear the other of books and place it near hers. 'I was just thinking about my trip home,' I say, sitting down. 'Had this idea that you could come with me, ha ha.'

Caitlin's threading a needle, small wire spectacles on the end of her nose. 'I'm sorry?' she says, glasses coming off, needle being lowered, face suddenly flooding with colour.

'Uh...' Oh dear. Now I've begun, however accidentally, I'll have to continue. 'It was just an idea.'

'But I couldn't possibly afford–'

'I'd buy you a flight.'

'Don't be silly.'

This isn't going well but I persevere. 'And once we're there, you wouldn't have to spend a lot. We'd stay with my mom, and I've already paid for the apartment in New York.'

'Daniel...' says Caitlin. Her colour's calmed down and she's looking at me warmly. 'Oh, Daniel.'

'What?'

'It sounds wonderful, but I can't up sticks again so soon. And I can't let you pay for me, either. Goodness!' She leans across and puts a hand on my knee, just lightly. 'But thank you. It's a really lovely offer.'

I'm thinking of putting my hand on hers, when she moves it and goes back to threading the needle. 'You can take Frankie, though,' she says.

'Thanks, but I'm sure you need him here.'

She laughs and shakes her head. 'I had a call from Zac, offering to come and work for only his board.'

'You mustn't do it,' I tell her.

'I know. Anyway, I told him there isn't enough work, but that he's welcome to come as a paying guest.'

'Good for you. Remember what Joe said about Zac in the restaurant. Not always turning up for shifts, then eating and drinking the profits when he did.'

Caitlin colours up again, and I think it's the mention of Joe. She nods and concentrates on her sewing, but continues to blush.

'Caitlin,' I say.

'Yes?'

I inch my chair nearer to her and place a hand on her arm. The needle stays half in

201

what looks like the fancy cuff of a jacket, and Caitlin looks up at me.

'I really, really don't care,' I tell her quietly, 'about the Joe thing.'

She puts her free hand on mine again, and again quickly lets go. 'No,' she says, 'but I do. And then there's Frankie. I mean, what kind of an example would I be... Oh, Daniel. I'm sorry.'

Her eyes are watery, so I smile, stand up and say, 'Why don't we go for a drink? A kind of farewell one. Probably, I'll head off tomorrow.'

I watch her go from red to almost white, and suddenly wish I hadn't been so rash, or so blunt. 'Things to do in London.'

'Oh, of course.' She too stands, then quite unexpectedly falls against my chest. I wrap my arms around her and rub my chin against her soft shiny hair. 'Oh, Daniel,' she says again.

On squeezing her tightly, I feel a sharp and not pain-free sensation in my chest, which can only be the needle piercing me through my T-shirt. 'I'll miss this place,' I say, deciding not to mention the agony she's causing me. 'And you.'

'But not Frankie, eh?'

'Er, well...'

'Hey,' she says, pulling back. 'Instead of going to the pub, why don't we go for that walk we've never got round to? It'll be light a while long– Arggh, Daniel, you're bleeding!'

I look down and see a spot of blood on my white T-shirt. It's in the vicinity of my heart, which is nicely appropriate, considering how broken it feels. 'You know,' I tell her, 'I've often been called a bleeding-heart liberal.'

Caitlin laughs and the eyes well up again, and I tell her I think I'll live.

Joe I didn't have to work this evening because the new waiters are turning out to be really good. I eat at home for a change. Dad's done us roast lamb, steamed veg and sautéed potatoes, and to get us on the subject of relationships I tell him he'd make someone a wonderful husband.

'Ah, but who'd have a curmudgeonly old fart like me?'

'Dad,' I say, 'you've no idea how many lonely women there are out there.'

'Desperate enough to take me on, eh?' He does one of his belly laughs and passes me the gravy boat. We eat in silence for a while, then he says, 'Were you thinking of anyone in particular?'

'No. Only, if you were to ... well, advertise or something, I'm sure you'd get masses of replies.'

'Yes, no doubt that route suits some. Personally, I'd end up feeling like an unwanted fridge. In good working order but missing one shelf.'

'Buyer to collect?'

'Ha, ha. Quite.'

'This lamb's really good.'

'Isn't it?'

'So what happened with you and Mum?' I ask, quite bravely really. Dad and I don't talk about such things. 'No one's exactly ever told me.'

'Ah. Your mother. It all seems terribly distant now. However, I'm still hugely burdened with guilt.'

Christ, I think, now he's going to own up to some affair and I'll wish I hadn't asked.

'It was the long spells of neglect,' he goes on, staring at our American-style stainless-steel fridge with ice dispenser and no missing shelves. 'She claimed that when I was working hard on something, shut away, unaware of her needs, it felt more lonely than had she been on her own. Of course, I didn't understand loneliness then. When one emerged from beavering away on a book or paper, there was the family – you and your mother – for companionship. These days I ... well, I'm able to empathise with how she felt then. An ability she often said I was lacking.'

I suddenly wonder what Dad does in the evenings, when I'm out working, or just out. As far as I can tell, he watches TV, listens to Radio 4 and reads a lot. Among other things, books on how to find love. Now *I'm* feeling guilty. Should I take him out with me? Get him pissed and dancing to stuff like the Space Hoppers? On the rare occasions he has an evening in town, it's to go to a concert. Quite often alone but sometimes with Olive, who's into similar stuff, but a bit more out there. Indonesian gamelan, that kind of thing. Dad and Olive? Maybe not.

'You shouldn't feel guilty,' I say. 'You had your research to do. And like you've said loads of times, you can't do it any other way.'

'Blinkers on, yes. But to the detriment of what could have been a happy and rewarding lifelong partnership? One can't help but wonder if it's been worth it. How are the potatoes?'

'Good. Nice and sweet with the olive oil.' I eat a cube of potato and make the right noises. Dad likes to be praised for his cooking. 'It could be,' I say, 'that as women get older, they become more, I dunno, flexible? So, if you got together now with someone who's been on her own for a while, then she might not mind you being in the zone for a few weeks.'

'Because she's so thankful to have a man?'

'No, because she's used to spending time on her own.'

'Ah. Hmm.' Dad puts his fork down and clasps his hands under his chin. 'So, how do I go about finding this accommodating soul?'

'I'm not sure. I mean, if advertising makes you feel like an old fridge, then you'll just have to get out more.'

'As they say.' He laughs and picks up his fork again. 'Carrots sufficiently al dente?'

'Yep. Perfect.'

After dinner I make coffee and we sit outside under the pergola. I tell him about Wales, and Cait's place, then suddenly I'm also telling him about Beth, which is a bit of a surprise because I've more or less given up on her, and because I stay off girlfriends with Dad, since he told me Elsa had 'the gait of a Canadian goose' and I couldn't stop noticing her waddle after that.

'Your Beth conjures up a picture of a Betjeman heroine,' says Dad. 'Miss J. Hunter Dunn, Miss J. Hunter Dunn.'

'Yeah?' I have no idea what he's talking about. That's probably good because, just in case Beth makes a reappearance, I don't want to be put off her. 'Anyway,' I say, 'not *my* Beth. She's stopped talking to me now, even though she seemed dead keen. I don't know what's happened, only that I might have seemed a bit, you know, not keen.'

'Ah.' Dad's eyes are smiling at me, with all the creases sort of fanning out around them. Charlotte once said she liked the way my father smiles with his eyes. That it was friendly. Other women must like it too. 'Do I detect,' he says, 'that Beth's silence is fanning the flames somewhat?'

'Not at all.' I know I'm sounding defensive and that he's got it exactly. 'I'm just puzzled, that's all.'

'If you'd like my advice... Ha! Listen to me. *My* advice on a relationship issue. That would be like Einstein advising on hair-dressing. Not that I'd have the temerity to compare myself–'

'Go on.'

Dad leans back in his chair and focuses on the impressive sunset. 'I was going to say *audentis Fortuna iuvat.*'

God, I hate it when he does this.

'Fortune favours the brave,' he says, before I have to ask.

'I need to take a few days off again,' I tell Carlo. 'Really sorry.' I've arrived in time to help clear up, and I throw myself into it.

'Thassa good,' he says. 'I go two weeks in Milano in September.'

'You do? I mean, you are?'

'So, you take few days off now. New boy and girl they are shit hot. And they help you good when I go.'

'Great.' This has been easier than I'd imagined. We might have a fifty-fifty partnership, but because he puts in the hours, the passion and the creativity, Carlo's always been top dog. 'I should be back by the weekend. Well, Monday.'

207

'No prob,' Carlo tells me. 'Two chefs and me, we rotate. And now seex waiting boys and girls. Is enough.'

I'm beginning to feel surplus to requirements, which I actually don't mind. Being a sleeping partner's a bit of a dream. 'Cool,' I say, although I'm a bit worried that two chefs and me won't be enough when Carlo's away. People get ill, can't do their shifts.

I do the till, put the takings in the safe, say goodbye and head home. When I let myself in the house, I hear Dad talking to someone in the kitchen. This is a bit unusual at one o'clock on a Tuesday morning. Has he found his accommodating soul already? But there in the distance, through the opening to the kitchen, I see Beth's blonde hair. At the bottom of the stairs is a huge rucksack. Either she's on her way to Everest, or she's come to stay for a while.

'Beth?' I say, walking calmly into the kitchen, even though my heart's pounding. I bend and kiss her cheek. Beth never smells of perfume, I've noticed, but smells good all the same. 'What a nice surprise.'

Dad's pulling a face at me. I think it's saying, 'Fortune favours the brave, remember?' and I realise 'nice' was the wrong word.

'Fantastic,' I add, hoping that's enough.

'Well, I must retire,' says Dad, standing with his mug. 'I fear I've bored your friend enough with my anecdotes, Joe.'

'Oh God, no,' says Beth. She's got that look they all have when he's been talking to them. 'It's been *really* interesting.'

I want to tell Dad to get his own girlfriend, but I know he would if he could.

'So,' I say to Beth when he's gone, 'why haven't you been replying to my messages, returning my calls?' I'm sounding more upset than I actually feel, but I could just be tired.

'Well,' she says, making circles on the table with a finger and not looking at me, 'I got this text, yeah? It came from your phone but was signed by someone called Luna. First, I thought you were, you know, mucking around.'

'Luna? Jesus.' I put my head in my hands. 'Go on.'

'Is it a woman?'

'Yeah.'

'She said ... here, I'll show you.' Beth pulls her phone from a pocket and scrolls through till she finds it.

I take it from her and read, 'Beth, you are bombarding this handsome young man with messages. Take my advice and cease all communication on your part. Then he will be yours. May the angels be with you. Luna, the Miracle Worker.'

Beth laughs nervously. 'I thought *no way* am I going to do as this nutter says. That was after I stopped thinking it was you. But then, I don't know... I just couldn't *not* do what she said.'

'Like you were under a spell?'

'I suppose.'

I'm beginning to wish I'd taken advantage of Luna's skills now. 'You could have kept quiet about this,' I say. 'Let me think you were genuinely pissed off with me all that time.'

'Yeah,' says Beth, crossing her legs in the jeans she fills out nicely. 'But that's not my way. Too open for my own good sometimes!'

'But I like that,' I say. I stretch out and squeeze her shoulder. 'Sleepy?'

'No, not really.'

'I meant, do you want to go to bed?'

'Oh. Sorry. How dense of me. You must think I'm so uncool.'

'Yes,' I say. 'But I like that too.'

FOURTEEN

Ralph First I think it's in my dream, then I realise someone is, in fact, knocking on the window. Tap, tap, tap. Tap, tap, tap. Kids, drunken revellers – they often prat about like this, intimidating the vulnerable canal folk at night. I will them to move on to the next victim, then say, 'Piss off,' under the thin duvet I've usually kicked off by now,

210

due to the heat in this locked-up little home.

Obviously, I don't say it loud enough for them to hear. I turn on my side – which isn't easy in a plaster cast – so my back's to the towpath, and feel sleep creeping up on me. But then I hear the tap, tap, tap again, then again, and I wonder, in my drowsiness, if Luna's managed to lock herself out.

I get up and go and find the torch. I unlock the door, poke my head out and see no one, then climb out of the boat and on to the towpath. The torch lights up patches of the path, but I don't see Luna, or anyone at all. Not until a big sort of shadow comes at me from the trees, then another.

'So,' whispers the first shadow, 'survived your little fall, did you Ralphy?' The second shadow snatches my torch and I'm about to shout for help, when the familiar hand clamps itself over my face, quite hurting my nose, and the torch is shone right into my eyes. At the same time, an arm goes round my waist. I try saying, 'Watch the plaster cast!' but the hand over my mouth tightens its grip, so I give up.

'Who'd have thought it'd be so hard getting rid of one accident-prone witness?' says Lenny, still really quietly. He doesn't want to wake Luna, and I don't want him to either. There's a possibility she might save me, but I don't want her dying in the process. 'Mind you, there's still the little matter of the notebook, isn't there? Eh? Got it on the boat, have you?'

His voice chills me like nothing else in the world and makes my knees disappear with fright. I try shaking my head and it hurts my nose even more. 'Let him speak, Dog. But no shouting, you hear? Not unless you want your girlfriend getting the same treatment, and a bit more, hee, hee, since she's a woman. Know what I mean?' When I got to speak, nothing comes out at first, just a sort of rasping noise. 'Someone called John's got it,' I'm trying to tell him. Lenny leans his head, his ear, right up against my face. 'Say what?' I have another go, forcing the sounds through my throat and out my mouth. If Lenny would switch the torch off it might help. 'Someone called John's got it,' I say, this time a bit louder.

The hand covers my mouth again. 'I thought I told you not to shout? Now, who the fuck's John? Not making this up, are you? 'Cos me and Dog don't take kindly to being told porkies.' I shake my head, then Lenny nods at Dog, who loosens his grip a bit.

'I don't know,' I say as quietly and as clearly as I can. 'He came to the boat and Luna gave him the notebook, and he said he'd take it to me in hospital, but I don't know who John is and neither does Luna, so no point in grilling her, OK?'

When Lenny asks me if I know what this

John looks like and I say, 'Divine,' he doesn't take too kindly to my answer, and before I know it, I'm being bundled to the water's edge and told how effing useless I am.

Caitlin I wipe away another tear and tell myself this is stupid, that I never cry. Only over deaths and divorces and things, and Daniel's leaving is hardly that traumatic. I move my face away from the tiny cotton trousers I'm working on, so they don't get messed up with salt water. Then I rub at my cheeks with my cotton shirtsleeve, sniff, and get on with the seam.

After taking Daniel to the station, two days ago now, I'd come back to a house with a big hole in it. That's how it felt. Still feels. I've always loved my home but now I'm thinking: Daniel sat there and ate his breakfast every morning, he cleaned his teeth there, answered lots of *University Challenge* questions there. Like a lovesick teenager, I still haven't washed up his last coffee mug. Perhaps it would help if I did.

At the station, we'd had a long cuddle before he went through to the platform. A few kisses on cheeks and one quick one on lips.

'Keep in touch?' was the last thing I said, but he'd gone and I don't think he heard.

It's no good, I can't see what I'm doing through the tears. I give up and make yet another cup of strong comforting tea, only it doesn't really comfort. Instead, the caffeine makes me anxious.

'Walk?' I ask Merlin, who's never been known to say no, and we set off in appropriately drizzly weather.

My head often clears and comes up with new designs on walks, but today it's full of doubt, guilt and regrets, with a smattering of anger. I'm not sure who I'm angry with – it could be me, or it could be God. Why did he send me off in totally the wrong direction in Oxford? What was the point of that?

'If you exist,' I say looking up, 'I want you to know I'm really quite pissed off.'

'Sorry!' comes the reply, but it's just the elderly walkers I've let the gate slam into. That's something Daniel said he loved about the British: 'The way you apologise when someone steps on your foot.'

'Sorry,' I say back, and soon the couple are overtaking me, which isn't difficult, since I'm so sluggish today.

It occurs to me, as I'm pulled along by Merlin, that I may have been a bit too moral about the whole Joe and Daniel thing. That I should have said to hell with principles. Put my future happiness before my son's (and my own) opinion of me. Frankie had wanted to know why Joe moved out of my room and into the outhouse, and I was honest with him. We'd had a silly fling, now it was over and we were friends. I'd felt like an old slapper telling him this, but he didn't comment. Just nodded and asked to borrow a tenner to go to the pub. I handed it over, even though the landlord shouldn't be serving seventeen-year-olds. The trouble is, if Frankie didn't visit the Lion, he'd never go anywhere.

Joe had gone with him a few times, attracted by the completely slate pool table, and the fact that he could thrash Frankie at the game, and no doubt impress Beth. Joe's certainly had no trouble jumping from one relationship to another. Now Beth's down in Oxford with him and I'm alone and miserable, and Daniel will come back from America and get into his life in London again, and because of the distance and the time lapse, the friendship will peter out. It's not like me to be so negative, but now I'm in that frame of mind, I can't shift it.

'It's so easy for you,' I tell the neutered Merlin. 'Food and walks and the odd thrown stick, that's all you need.' He reacts to the word 'stick', looking up and cocking an eyebrow at me. But we're near sheep and he's on his lead, and I realise life isn't that much fun for him, either.

When I walk in the house, my first thought is that Frankie's got a new friend round. A guy with long fair hair is sitting alone at the kitchen table with a big pile of toast in front of him. As I get closer I see who it is and stop in my tracks.

'Zac?' I ask, not because I'm doubting it's him, just wondering how he got all the way here.

'Hey, Cait. Cool house, you've got. Wicked views. Is there any Marmite? I couldn't find any.'

I take it from a bag I haven't got round to unpacking, and while I'm at it, put the other stuff away. From the very top of one food cupboard, I lift Daniel's last mug down. I hand Zac the Marmite, then go to the sink, empty the mug, fill it with water twice and scrub at its insides with a brush. When I've finished, I sigh, prop it on the rack and turn to my guest.

'Look, Zac,' I say, deciding to be firm from the start. 'I'm afraid I don't have any work for you, and I can't afford to house you as a non-paying guest, on account of your colossal appetite. Sorry. Only I thought we should sort that out straight away.'

'That's cool,' he says. 'Got a bit of cash, so I'll buy my own food.'

'Really?'

'Well, not that much cash.'

'How did you get here?'

'Hitched.'

All the way?'

'Pretty much. Jumped a train to Birming-ham first.'

'So how long did it take you altogether?'

'Er...' Zac looks at the wall clock, 'two days.'

'No!'

'I kipped overnight in a cab with a lorry driver. Man, he had the worst feet, but he was a decent bloke and put his shoes back on when I like begged him to.'

I laugh and remember how much I liked Zac in Oxford. 'Listen, I'll make you a proper meal because you're probably in need of one, but–'

'Jesus, Mum,' comes Frankie's voice. He's standing in the doorway with his arms folded. 'First Joe, then Daniel. What's this one called?'

They get on quite well, despite the age gap, especially once Frankie realises Zac's not a love interest. The three of us have an early dinner of shepherd's pie, during which he and Frankie talk non-stop, mainly about music. My mind drifts back to Daniel, and how he made us that really good pizza with olives and anchovies and what he called his sexy secret sauce, then suddenly I hear Zac mention his name.

'Fuck, I wouldn't have put him down as a dope smoker,' says Frankie.

'Language,' I tell him. 'Who?'

'Your Daniel. You know, the one who went round waving his hands and opening every window when I lit a roll-up.'

'Daniel's a top bloke,' says Zac, while I pile the last of the pie on his plate.

'Yeah,' says Frankie, 'I really liked him too.'

I stop chewing and stare at him.

Frankie shovels food in his mouth. 'It's a shame,' he says, talking through it, 'that you and him didn't get together, Mum. He seemed perfect, if you ask me, even if he is cleverer than you. But still, better that way round.'

'What?'

'The husband being cleverer than the wife.'

Now he's talking marriage? 'Because men have such fragile egos?' I manage to say.

'No, I mean it's more natural.'

'Man,' says Zac, 'you'd never be able to say that in Oxford.'

Frankie shrugs. 'And it was so obvious he was after you, Mum. Even though you were dead unfriendly to him.'

'I was?'

'Every time the poor bloke suggested you two doing something, you said you had work to do. He was gutted, you could tell. Well, maybe you couldn't. But I could, being the sensitive, caring type.'

'Since when?' I ask. Oh God, had I really been that foul? Suddenly, I feel wretched. And to have produced a child with such appalling views...

'Just think,' says Frankie, 'how cool it would be to have a stepfather with a stash.' He puts his fork down and pretends to draw noisily on a joint, eyes narrowed.

'Daniel's not into it in a big way,' says Zac, laughing at my hilarious son. 'He told me he'd like have the odd toke if there was some going, that's all.'

'Anyway, he's fucking brilliant,' says Frankie. 'Which is just what you want in a stepfather. Not some moronic brutal bastard with only half his teeth, like Matt's stepdad. Daniel got, what, eighty per cent of the answers in *University Challenge*. Didn't he, Mum? Mum, you've gone really white.'

'Frankie,' I say, but I can't express my rage, disappointment, frustration – whatever it is. All I can do is leave the table and then the room.

'What'd I do?' I hear Frankie whisper.

'Search me. Is she coming back, do you reckon, or shall I finish hers?'

Ralph When I wake up in hospital, the first thing Luna says is, 'Honestly, Ralph, why go outside for a pee, when there's a perfectly good toilet on the boat?' While my brain tries to clear, Luna goes on, 'We think you must have walked into a tree, broken your nose, sort of reeled back, maybe a bit stunned, and then fallen in the canal. They did a stomach pump, because you really don't want to be

219

swallowing that water. You're on the strongest antibiotics. But don't worry, I've done a spell and you'll be right as rain in no time.'

I suddenly feel quite sick but that might be psychosomatic, now I know I've drunk canal water. 'Thanks,' I say. I'll tell her the rest later, or perhaps I won't because she'll never sleep soundly again, snoring noisily and relentlessly, the way she does. 'Want a grape?' she asks.

I have to say I'm getting a bit fed up with hospitals. This time my nose is throbbing painfully under a bandage or plaster of some description, and I reach, up and touch it with my one free hand. Still, no masks and tubes this time. 'I'd like to go home to Lincoln,' I tell Luna.

'Are you sure?' she asks and I nod.

If they came after me there, Hilary would either scare them off for good, or side with them and do me in – and I'm beginning to want the business settled, one way or the other. 'Maybe one grape,' I say, lowering my arm. Luna comes and pops one in my mouth and the sour taste of the canal goes at last.

'I'll miss you,' she says.

'What, a clumsy oaf like me?' I ask, and she smiles and feeds me another grape, and then some more, like she's a slave and I'm a Roman emperor or something. Anyway, it's quite nice.

Daniel I go pick up mail and messages from my pigeonhole and ask Fiona if she'd kindly check emails whilst I'm in New England, since I'll be somewhat cut off for a few weeks.

'If anything particularly urgent crops up,' I say, 'here's a contact number for me for the next two, maybe three weeks. But strictly for your eyes only.'

There's something of a glint in Fiona's eyes as she inspects the piece of paper I've handed her. This may confirm something I've suspected for a while, that the homely, thirty-something Fiona is a little sweet on me.

'It'll be a pleasure,' she says. 'And, of course, I'll only call if it's really necessary.'

'Thanks. I'll be picking up messages again in New York. I'll let you know when I arrive.'

'New York. How exciting.'

'Yes,' I say laughing. 'I guess.'

'Are you holidaying alone?' she asks.

I'm taken aback by Fiona's intrusive question, but can see she's just fishing. 'Be meeting up with family, friends,' I say, then wish her a good rest of the summer, although I know she won't be going any-where. 'Don't work too hard.'

She giggles and puts her little secret – my number – in a drawer. 'No chance!' she says, pushing her glasses up her sweaty nose. It's unbearably hot again today and I'm praying New England will be cooler, rather as Wales was.

Wales. Caitlin. Subjects I no longer want to dwell on, I decide, having spent days trying to make sense of it all. She likes me, but she doesn't want me in the way I want her. But then sometimes she'd given the impression she did want me in that way. Women are tricky to read – Lauren had been the trickiest of all – and it probably isn't worth expending a lot of energy dissecting, interpreting and speculating. Especially not with an ocean to cross and some good and dear people to visit. With one day to go, I find myself keen to take to the skies and leave the past few perplexing weeks behind.

Joe Of course, Beth thinks this must be the best place to live in Oxford. On a boat on the canal. 'No cars,' she explains. 'Doesn't the traffic noise do your head in?'

'Er, no. I think I stopped hearing it years ago.'

'It's so quiet here,' she says, striding along the towpath in her snug jeans. Every now and then I lag behind, just for the nice view of her. 'And pretty,' she goes on. 'Almost like the country.'

'Yeah,' I say, 'it is.' Beth's making me see Oxford in a different light. She loves the colleges and quads and all that, and she loves the liveliness of the Cowley Road and its assorted restaurants, but she thinks some of the residential side streets are squalid and littered, which is something else I've stopped noticing. And she's not too keen on bits of the city centre.

'We could be in any boring town in Britain,' she said in Cornmarket Street. 'How could they do this?'

'What?' I said, and she'd made me count the chain stores. She can be quite domineering, Beth.

'We're nearly there,' I tell her now, taking my eyes off her bum and walking beside her again. 'It's the pink and purple one, three boats up. Now, remember what I said about not going in. Luna might have got us together but we don't want to take any risks.'

'OK, bossy boots.'

'Huh!' I say, taking Ralph's notebook from my bag and having one last flick through. Nothing of interest has appeared since I last did that.

Luna's sitting on the tiny deck reading, and says, 'John, hi,' when we stop beside her.

'Joe.'

'And don't tell me,' she says, snapping her book shut. 'This is Beth?' I can't help noticing the book's title – *How to be a White Witch*. I had no idea Luna was still a trainee.

Beth laughs a bit nervously. 'Yes, I'm Beth. And thank you so much, Luna.'

'All in a day's work. Now, why don't you both come in and I'll–'

'Actually we're in a hurry,' I tell her. 'I just

wanted to bring this back because I heard Ralph was here.'

'*Was* here, yes.' Luna takes the notebook from me and I feel instant relief at offloading it.

'Was?' I stick both hands in my jeans pockets, so she can't give it back.

'Had a bit of an accident, poor love.'

'Another one?'

Luna points at the canal. 'Went head over arse into the water at two in the morning. Lucky I heard. And lucky I'm a strong swimmer because Ralph certainly isn't.' She flings her head back and practises her witch's cackle. 'He was flailing around quite helplessly, what with having his arm in plaster. Kept going under.'

'How awful,' says Beth.

Luna does an impression of Ralph and almost topples in herself. 'Oops, steady on, girl,' she says, clutching at a rail. 'Anyway, we think he must have been sleepwalking.'

'And where is he now?' asks Beth.

'In hospital. The John Radcliffe. Just a broken nose this time, thank goodness. Bit of concussion, bit of an infection. They're keeping an eye on him. He keeps saying he must get back to Lincoln, but then changes his mind. I don't think his is a happy marriage. And ... well, I do believe he's growing more and more attached to me.' Luna grins proudly. 'He may be the most accident-prone person I've met but he's such a fun-loving soul.'

It just about matches Cait's description of him, only I think she said childlike. 'Look, give him my best when you see him,' I tell Luna. 'Only it's Joe, not John.'

'Will do,' says Luna. She settles down with her book again and Beth and I head back towards town.

'Do you think she's cast a spell on him?' whispers Beth, even though we're well out of earshot now and on our way to Port Meadow, a place I think she'll like, what with the horses and cows and the river running through it. 'If my parents weren't Methodists, and if I didn't think I'd end up living on a boat, I might try being a white witch.'

'I thought you liked the canal boats?'

'Yeah, they're great. But, you know, you couldn't fit a big family on one, could you?'

'How big?' I ask. I always think just one might be manageable, being an only child.

'Oh, I don't know ... three children? Four?'

It seems to be a question, and I'm not sure what the answer is, so I say, 'Shall we walk all the way round the meadow? It's about six or seven miles, probably.' I'm guessing. I did it a few years back and it was knackering.

'What, just the once?' she says.

Back at home, shattered, I phone Cait to tell

her about Ralph's latest accident. I expect her to find it funny, or shocking or something, but she sounds very flat and just says, 'Thanks for letting me know, Joe. Bye.'

I go back to the living room, where Dad's talking to Beth about the different types of owls there are, where they live and what they eat. 'I read that conservationists are trying to increase the population of barn owls in your part of the world, Beth.'

'With the extra nest boxes?'

'Mm, and not before time. Whilst I was growing up in deepest Herefordshire, aeons ago, it was impossible to venture anywhere at night without bumping into an owl.'

'Not literally?' I ask and Beth rolls her eyes. Sometimes I think it's best not to say anything when Dad's talking to my women.

After dinner, I take Beth to see a reggae band at the Drome, even though I'd rather watch TV because my legs ache. Dad turned down her invitation to join us, saying he had a few calculations to do on something that had occurred to him.

I'm a bit on edge when we arrive, not knowing what Beth will think. But before long she's well into the music and, what's more, dances really well. I don't know why she wouldn't, being the athletic type, but it's still a nice surprise.

'Who is she?' Oz shouts, when Beth's gone to the loo.

'Someone I met in Wales!' I yell back, and we leave it at that, as it's impossible to talk. He just gives me the thumbs-up. I've seen some of Ozzie's women, though, so I'm not sure I want his verdict.

The only light on when we get back is in the study. The door's closed, so I knock on it and call out, 'Hi, Dad!' No answer.

'Maybe he's not in there,' says Beth. 'Gone to bed.'

'No, he's there. He's just not *here.*' I laugh and explain, then lead her over to the sofa, and in the dark start kissing her and undoing her top.

'Joe!' she says, pulling my hands away. 'What if he–'

'He won't. And even if he does, he won't notice us.'

'But–'

'I promise.'

FIFTEEN

Caitlin 'Thanks, sweetie,' I say in the pathetic voice that's become a permanent fixture, but which I can't shake off. Frankie's brought me tea in bed.

'Actually, Zac made it but didn't want to

come to your bedroom. He's been taking calls for you too.'

'Really?' I must have been deeply asleep, not to hear the phone across the landing.

'Some woman wants her bridesmaid dresses, like yesterday.'

'Oh, her. Well, I can't tackle them till I'm better.'

'You look really rough.'

'Thanks,' I say. 'Listen, could you ask Zac to come and see me? I don't mind him in my room.'

Frankie leaves just as Merlin runs in and jumps on the bed. He's expecting a walk but he won't get one from me. I drink my horribly weak tea and wonder when I'm going to get better. Tomorrow? That would be good. One more day in bed feeling hot, shivery and not in the least hungry. Yesterday, I tried and failed to read the novels that have piled up and thought, on and off, about writing a letter to Daniel. A letter I'll never send because I don't have a home address for him.

The past few days have been spent trying to work out how to get in touch with him. I've tried his mobile several times, but it's switched off. Perhaps he's left it in London. How furious I am with myself for not calling before he caught his plane. I'd had time, I just hadn't worked out what to say. 'Daniel, I've been such a fool. And guess what, my son would like you to be his stepfather!' I'd also tried his department to see if they have an number in the States for him, but some snotty woman said they couldn't give out personal details. I hung up on her.

There's an email link for him on the university website, but would he be picking up work messages while staying with a mother who doesn't have a computer? He'd told me he likes to just 'kick back' when he's in New England. I could ask the secretary, but don't feel I can call her again. How wonderful it would be if Daniel phoned me from home, but I can see he'd have no real reason to. I'd made it clear, it seems, that nothing can happen between us. Even Frankie picked up on it.

I might just have to wait till Daniel's back in the UK. Hope he still feels friendly towards me. Hope he hasn't met anyone in the meantime. Or perhaps I could email him a nicely neutral 'Call me?' message, in the hope he'll get it at some point, and phone me before he does meet someone. But that would take effort, and all I want to do is go back to sleep. I put the weak tea down and settle back into the pillow, wondering again if I've got a virus, or if I've just worn myself out, both physically (Joe, Ralph, catching up on orders) and emotionally (Daniel).

There's a knock at the door and Zac sticks his head round. 'You OK?'

'Fine. A bit tired, still. I just wondered

who's been phoning.'

'Hang on.' He goes to my workroom and comes back with a piece of paper, from which he reels off four very clear messages. 'Oh, and Sarah rang to say she's got this summer bug that's going round and won't be able to do the tops you sent over. Her husband's just brought them back.'

'Bugger.'

'Bad news?'

'Mm. It's yet another job to do, and such a boring one. Stitching twenty identical T-shirts I've had orders for. It's so easy, I'm sure I could train Merlin to do it.' I attempt a laugh. The dog's ears prick up at the mention of his name and I give him a limp stroke. 'They're already cut out, but it's time consuming.'

'Maybe I could do them?' says Zac.

'Er, no. I don't think you'd...' I stop, realising I'm about to insult him. '...enjoy it.'

'Yeah, I would. Man, you should have seen my embroidered placemats. Miss Dawson said she'd never have believed it of me.'

'Yes, but–'

'Also, I used to do my girlfriend's hems. Ex, that is. She was like quite short and everything had to be taken up. Honestly, you couldn't tell. She said I could be a professional.'

'Really?' I sit myself up, suddenly feeling cheerier. 'Can you use a machine?'

'No problem. Well, I'd learn quick.'

'Hmm,' I say. 'Perhaps Frankie might show you.' He used to enjoy 'helping' me when he was young and hadn't discovered pubs. I pick up the mug, look at the pale, pale liquid and put it down again. 'I suppose I could let you have a go at one top. They're so tiny, it wouldn't be a waste of too much material.'

'Wicked.'

'Then we'll take it from there.'

'Cool.'

'And Zac.'

'What?'

'Get Frankie to show you where the tea-bags are? I think you might have forgotten to...'

He comes over and peers in my mug. 'Oh, yeah.'

Soon, over a cup of tea with tea in it, I hear the bass of two voices through the wall, then the stop-start whiz of the Singer. I've got three machines, so should Zac cause a huge tangle and kill the motor, the business will still function. So long as I'm functioning, that is.

Properly awake at last, I reach over to the chair for the laptop, put it on the duvet and fire it up. I click on the university website, which is now in my favourites list, then on Daniel Sanchez, then on his email link. I decide to keep it short, especially as someone else might be picking up. 'Hi, Daniel. Hope you're having a great trip. Do give me a call, if you have time. Best wishes, Caitlin.' I like the way he calls me Caitlin.

The cursor hovers over 'Send' while I reread. All my Kiddie Clobber contact details are at the bottom, which gives the email a rather businesslike air, but I want to make sure Daniel has all that. I read the message a third time and suddenly find the tone all wrong. So lacklustre, so reserved. In fact, just the way I'd been during his stay here.

I've deleted back to the *'Hi, Daniel'* when Zac knocks again, then appears with a little stripy T-shirt.

'Crikey,' I say, 'that was quick. Let's have a look, then.'

He brings it over and I'm stunned. I know, for sure, that this isn't Frankie's handiwork. He could never have put the little garment together so well. Even the stitching around the neckline is perfect, and that's often the hardest bit to do, steadily and neatly.

'I'm impressed,' I tell Zac. 'Want to try one more, just to prove it wasn't a fluke?'

'Sure.'

'Only wait for me,' I say. 'I want to come and watch.'

'OK.' Zac stands beside my bed, arms folded and smiling to himself, obviously proud of his achievement.

'I meant wait for me in the workroom. I need to, you know...'

'Oh, right.'

By lunchtime he's done all twenty tops, and the standard hasn't dropped. I ask Frankie to make Zac something to eat because he's earned it.

'Whatever he wants,' I add, then totter on weak legs to my workroom and fish out the patterns for the three bridesmaid dresses of assorted sizes. Having slept all morning, I feel ready to tackle a bit of work, and this is the job I'd most like to get out the way, now I know Mrs Rhys is putting the pressure on. The roll of pink polycotton (the client's tragic choice) is heavy, but I yank it on to the table, unroll a length and start pinning the smallest of the paper patterns to it. It's not often I take on jobs like these, preferring to create my own designs from my choice of fabrics, but Mrs Rhys had known exactly what she wanted – thrusting a photo from a magazine at me – and is paying well.

It's an easy job – sleeveless, collarless, A-line – but it's not long before I come over dizzy, prick myself and need a little sit down. While I watch the spot of blood ooze from a finger, I remember stabbing Daniel the night before he left. I chuckle to myself, but it hurts, so I stop and close my eyes. Time for bed again.

I drift in and out of sleep, half-hearing things – the phone, the sewing machine, distant sheep, male voices, a car pulling up, Merlin barking. Eventually, I become aware of the light fading, and also of a terrible thirst. I heave myself from bed, find flip-flops and dressing gown, go to the loo and then head downstairs for water.

But I stop on the second step because I hear the purr of the sewing machine behind a closed door. Is Zac still doing the tops, or is he making himself clothes with my fabrics? I should check this out, but badly need a drink. Downstairs there's no sign of Frankie and all the lights are off. Perhaps they're both at the Lion and I'd imagined the sound. I knock back a large glass of water, then fill it again and take it upstairs.

There Zac is, I discover, when I open the workroom door. Zooming away on something that looks horribly like a pink bridesmaid dress, his long hair dangling precariously close to the needle.

'Zac?' I say, making him jump.

The machine stops and he turns around. 'Feeling better?'

'Er, I'm not sure.' My heart's thumping, as I pray he hasn't ruined an entire roll of material. Maybe had lots of attempts at getting things right. But I don't see huge discarded remnants all over the floor, just

234

the odd little one. I raise my eyes and let out a shriek at what's before me, hanging on the end of my clothes rail. It's a fully formed bridesmaid dress – the smallest of the three, I'd guess – minus the ghastly bows Mrs Rhys had insisted on, as in the photo. I wonder, for a moment, if I'm still in a feverish sleep and dreaming. If I am, it's a very nice dream, and actually quite funny.

'I'm leaving the hems,' says Zac, 'because I thought you might want to do a fitting first. And I wasn't sure how to do the bows.'

I can't speak, but take the little dress out on to the landing, where the light's much better. I personally wouldn't sew in my room with only the Anglepoise, but it doesn't seem to affect Zac. Everything is beautifully done, even the zip. All these years I've thought I had some special talent, then along comes this whippersnapper to prove anyone can sew. I feel a bit devalued and tearful, but that could be the virus at work, for the next minute I'm wondering what I've done to deserve this godsend.

'You're amazing,' I call out.

'Cheers!'

Back in the room, I ask how the second one's coming along. 'Third,' he says, pointing to the other end of the clothes rail. 'It was dead easy, once I found the first pattern and the photo you'd pinned to it. Took me a while to like match the zip, though. My mum always said I was colour blind.'

'No, it's fine. Exactly right.' I wheel the rail towards me and take a slightly larger dress down and out on to the landing. It's the same story. I want to go and give Zac a kiss, but the last thing I need is for him to get my bug.

'You know,' he says, when I return both dresses to the rail, 'I've always felt sorry for people who become like compulsive about something. Only now I get it, because I can't stop till I've got these all done. I've never had an obsession before, and it's brilliant. Like having a *raison d'être*.'

'Yes,' I say, reversing and thinking about a nice bath. 'Good.' I'm sure Zac's *raison d'être* will be gone by tomorrow, so I may as well let him finish the last gaudy dress.

Back in the netherworld of my sick bed, with body clean and hair damp, I start up the laptop, find Daniel's email link and begin again. I'm a bit woozy as I type and wonder if I should really wait till I'm better, because I'm using words like 'missing' and 'you', right next to each other. I should stop, I think, but before I know it, I've written 'Lots of love, Caitlin xx' and clicked on 'Send'.

SIXTEEN

Ralph Hurrah! Got the notebook back. My plan is to go and find Lenny. With the rusty tyreless car in the front garden, the England flag, the cardboard bedroom window and the noisy dogs, his house shouldn't be too hard to spot, once I'm in the right area. Will just have to trawl around the housing estates on foot, since I can't drive with one arm. Or can I? No, they'd never let me hire a car.

So, I'll give him the notebook, or perhaps set fire to it in front of him. Then promise, maybe on my mother's life, that I haven't made copies, and hope that in the end Lenny's a trusting and reasonable sort of man. I'll also reassure him that I did not see the stabbing take place, and that I shall go to the police and tell them too. Luna said it was just a couple of kids involved, that it was in the paper, only I think the police must have got it wrong, or else Luna's got the wrong incident. Luna's a good soul but she is a bit of a space cadet.

Caitlin I'm teaching Zac a few embroidery stitches, so that he can add finishing touches to the six quilted gilets that parents with planner personalities are ordering for the winter.

'So, do you want me to do these before the eight pairs of girls' shorts, or after?' he asks. 'Or, shall I finish off those boys' tops?'

'Oh, you decide, Zac.' I realise I might be overworking him, but he seems happy enough. I'd do some of the sewing, if I could only apply myself. 'I know you eat a lot,' I tell him, 'but I think we should come up with an hourly rate. Or a piece rate might be fairer. That's how I pay my outworkers. You know, so much per article.' I'm not sure I can afford it, but I guess it won't be for long. Just until I'm functioning again.

'Sounds cool.'

'Are you OK for time, though, Zac? Nothing to get back to Oxford for this week?'

'This week?' he asks. 'More like this decade. This *life*. No, I haven't. It was really hard to leave, even though I was desperate to, if you know what I mean.'

'Sort of.'

'But now I like *never* want to go back.'

'Oh, you will,' I reassure him. Or perhaps I'm reassuring myself. Where exactly was he thinking of settling?

I leave Zac to his embroidery and wander around the cottage garden for a while. Picking at this and that ... sighing ... looking westwards, towards America. 'Pick up your emails!' I will Daniel. But then my insides sort of crumble because I think, oh, what if he has picked them up and decided not to respond? Is he wondering if he could have a relationship with someone who manages three typos in a four-sentence message? Should I email again and explain I had flu? That might come across as neurotic – that I'd gone back and checked a sent email. All the while, though, while I'm wondering if I'd be coming on too strong, too bothered, I remember that this man offered me an all-expenses-paid holiday.

'Walk?' I ask Merlin, and he gives me this 'What, in this heat?' look. He goes and plonks his rear down on a shaded patch of grass, then lowers his front-quarters and rests his chin on a leg.

'Suit yourself,' I say, heading to the kitchen for water. I fill a bottle, grab a hat and bag of peanuts for energy, and let myself out through the gate. With no dog in pursuit it feels odd. A little bit lonely, even. I could be vulnerable too. In theory, I'm no safer with my ageing soft-hearted dog, but weirdos don't need to know that.

How lucky I am to have the Ogwen Valley as my back garden, but how annoying and sad that I didn't find time to share it with Daniel. I know he walked here alone several times, even venturing up the steep sides sometimes in the shoes he'd bought especially. What lovely days out we could have had.

I take a left fork and start climbing up-wards, my legs aching a little from previous punishing walks, and maybe the remnants of flu. After a while, I stop, sit on a rock and eat peanuts. It's hot, despite the odd passing cloud, so I drink plenty of water, then screw the top back on the bottle and hoick myself up again. With the little rucksack on my back, I trudge upwards and northwards, sometimes passing other walkers, who greet me in either Welsh or English.

Daniel had been fascinated by the lan-guage, with all its consonants and its alien, throaty sounds. He'd ask how things were pronounced and smile his toothy smile when I told him. 'I love hearing you speak Welsh,' he finally admitted. I think I blushed and said, 'Well, I don't much like speaking it,' or something equally ungracious. I want so desperately to turn the clock back. Meet Daniel at Bangor station and have a whole different experience of his stay here. I swear out loud and continue with my climb, lots of 'if only's' going through my head, then every now and then, a 'what if?'. What if he's called while I'm out? Zac might be curt with him because he's absorbed in the sewing. What if he comes back to the UK deter-mined to find a partner in the capital, rather than in some far-flung mountainous region? If only I could speak to him, I think, as I approach a particularly gruelling stretch.

'C'mere, Ralph!' someone shouts behind me.

I turn, just as an enormous white beast jumps up at me, places its paws on my shoulders and licks my face. I scream and stumble backwards, then land on my bottom on solid rock. 'Ouch!' I cry, while the dog does as it's told and returns to its owner – a man in a baseball hat who looks vaguely familiar. I'm suddenly tearful, although the pain's now subsiding. The dog is a Samoyed, by the looks of it. They have a friendly and exuberant nature, in my limited experience – not something you want to encounter on a precipitous mountain path.

'Jesus, you all right?' asks the man in an English accent. 'Sit, Ralph. Sit!'

'Yes,' I say. 'I'm OK. Just a bit shaken.'

The man perches himself on a ledge opposite me and puts a hand over his eyes and rubs at his temples. Christ,' he says, 'I knew I shouldn't bring him here again.'

When he lowers his hand, I realise where I've seen him before. 'You were at the hospital,' I say.

'Sorry?'

'We were visiting our friend, Ralph...' I stop and look at Ralph the dog. '...and just as we arrived, you were coming out of his room.'

'Ah.'

'I'm Caitlin, by the way.'

241

'Stuart,' he tells me. 'Yes, I remember you.'

'Did you find the person you wanted?'

The hand goes up to the temples again, and Stuart exhales noisily. 'The guilt's been driving me nuts, so I may as well tell you.'

'Tell me what?'

'The chap. Your friend, Ralph.'

'Yes?'

'Well, it was my fault he fell.' Stuart nods towards the other, much hairier Ralph. 'Big bloody softie, he is. Loves people. The wife's always said he'll kill someone with his affection one day, and he damn near did.'

'Oh?' I'm beginning to get the picture.

'But we love him to death. Sorry, unfortunate phrase. After phoning for help from a call box, I went home and told the wife what had happened. That Ralph had run at this stranger and done his usual over-the-top greeting. Knocked the poor sod over the edge. We decided to keep quiet about it, for obvious reasons. You know, that we might be forced to have him put down.'

Stuart's voice begins to crack at this point, and looking at the huge fluffball of a beast beside him, I can understand why. Maybe it takes one dog owner to empathise with another. 'I'd do the same,' I say. 'You've probably been living in fear, thinking that Ralph, human Ralph, would give a description of your Ralph, and then... There can't be that many Samoyeds round here.'

'No.'

'Only Ralph, my Ralph, has kept quiet about the incident, as far as I know.' Why is that, I wonder. Perhaps he's a dog lover too.

'He has?' says Stuart. 'Thank God for that. Listen, are you sure you're all right? I've got a flask of coffee, if you'd–'

'No, no. I'm OK.' I stand up and brush myself down, keeping a close eye on the dog for signs of excitement. 'But, like you said, probably best not to bring him here again.'

'Yes. Last time I checked at the hospital, they said your friend had left. How is he, do you know?'

'Fine, I think. Actually, he fell in a canal and nearly drowned last week. But apart from that...'

We both start laughing, and Stuart says, 'Well, that makes me feel better, knowing he's accident prone. Thank you. Are you, er, going up? We could walk together.'

Stuart points at the steep path and I shake my head. 'Think I'll head home. I'm expecting a phone call. But thanks.'

'Did anyone ring?' I ask Zac, while I check out the gilets. He has a way with a needle, that's for sure.

'Yeah, here,' he says, sliding a piece of paper over the cutting-out table. He's written down four messages, all business related.

'No personal calls, then?'

243

'No. Oh, yeah, there was one.'

'Yes?'

'Er ... whatshisname phoned.'

'Daniel?'

'No, Ralph.'

'Ralph?'

'Something about his luggage. Said he'll try again later.'

'Right.'

'You OK?' asks Zac, a needle and purple thread in his hand.

'Yes, no. I don't know.'

'Do you want to like talk about it?'

I do, but not with Zac. 'Not right now,' I tell him, then go off to check my emails on the laptop. But there's nothing from Daniel, so I phone Jude in Bethesda and ask if I can come round. Jude is a good listener, has met Daniel and, luckily for me, is between jobs and therefore home.

'I'm amazed you can find the time,' she says, laughing.

I think I was rude when she called in two weeks ago, disappearing upstairs to work and leaving her in Daniel's capable hands. Oh well. I'll pick up some chocolates on the way.

Joe I take Beth to the Italian Job for the first time. I'd avoided going there in case Carlo roped me into doing something, when all I wanted to do was show Beth Oxford. But she's been here long enough for me to take the risk. She'd find things to do, being resourceful.

We're getting on really well, and she's definitely growing on me. I keep waiting for the, 'Look, Joe...' but no signs yet. A good thing is that Dad's working on something, so not only can he not impress Beth with his charm and his stories, but we've also got the house to ourselves.

Beth's plusses are that she's up for most things, easy to talk to and nice to be in bed with, despite getting fits of the giggles. She says she finds it hard to take sex seriously, even though she loves it. I think I know what she means. The minuses are that she's bossy and way too energetic. 'Come on lazybones, up you get!' The other morning, I'd got her to lie in till ten to nine and she said it was a record. Most days she's awake and fidgeting around seven. Just a small thing, I suppose, and maybe she'll adjust, or I will. If she doesn't dump me first.

We stop on the way and go round the Botanic Garden, which I find a bit boring but Beth doesn't. She keeps pointing at stuff and saying, 'I'll definitely have that in my garden.' It's the garden that goes with her fantasy house and family. Somewhere rural – Wales, I'd guess – surrounded by hills and with a stream close by for the children to paddle in. It must be nice to know what you want. 'And a pond just like this,' she says. 'Hey, look, Joe. Newts!'

'Oh, yeah.' Actually, they're quite cute, floating around with their arms and legs spread out. Do newts have arms? Of course not, I decide, pleased I didn't come out with that.

Beth insists on paying the full amount for our meal, which pleases Carlo no end. She tells him in her Welsh accent that she absolutely loves his café. His? And that it was one of the best pizzas she's ever eaten, as good as those she'd had in Venice. He tells her she's obviously a woman with good taste. I didn't know she'd been to Venice. I didn't know girls ate whole pizzas, either. Charlotte used to manage about a third of one, picking bits off she didn't like, while Carlo scowled from the counter. He's not scowling at Beth, though, which makes me stupidly proud of her. Though why I'd want Carlo's approval, I don't know.

I tell him I'll be back in action next week. When he says good because one of the new waiters has left, Beth says, 'I'll come and help too, if you like?' That means she's planning on sticking with me a bit longer, which is nice to hear. That, 'Look, Joe...' is coming, though. I just know it.

We stroll back along Queen's Lane and the

High Street, arms round each other's waists, taking up too much pavement but not caring. I've stopped keeping an eye open for Charlotte as we roam around town. I suppose I thought that if she saw me with Beth she might come up and say something cutting. A put-down, or whatever. But now, I wouldn't care if she did, because it could be a bit of a test. See how Beth reacts. 'You know, you're right, Charlotte. He is boring!'

At the little park beside the medical centre and in front of the mosque, we sit on a bench and watch toddlers on the play things. Beth has this permanent smile that some women get in the presence of small children. She points and say, 'Aah, watch that little one. *Sweet*, yeah?'

'Mm.'

Beth squeezes my arm, kisses my cheek, turns back and says, 'Oh my God! Look!'

'What?' I ask, stifling a yawn. A two-year-old laughing on the roundabout? A baby laughing in a baby swing?

'That man. Isn't it...?' She points to a guy approaching the other bench. 'You know ... Derek.'

'Ralph?' I squint into the sunlight, then put a hand over my eyes and see him. He's got hair now, and his nose is very red, but what with the arm in a sling... The bench is close to ours and when he gets there, I call out, 'Ralph?'

'Hello?' he says, his eyes darting between Beth and me. 'Do I know you?'

I get up and go over to him and Beth follows. 'Joe,' I tell him. 'You stayed at my house one night? You and Cait.'

'Ah, Joe. Yes. And Beth, isn't it? Hi.'

'Listen, are you all right? You look a bit...'

'As though I've been through the wars?'

'Well, yeah. We heard about you falling in the canal.'

Ralph looks over his shoulder. 'Pushed, more like. Long, long story, Joe. Haven't told anyone. Well, Luna, a bit. But not every-thing.'

'Really?'

Beth goes over and slips an arm through his good one. 'Well, you must tell *us*,' she says. 'Come back to Joe's and he'll make you a nice drink and something to eat, and you can share whatever you want with us. Can't he, Joe?'

'Er, yeah.'

'So,' I say, once we're settled at the kitchen table, 'let me get this straight. Lenny and Dog pushed you off a mountain and into the canal because they thought you might grass them to the police over the stabbing, and also because of what you wrote in your note-book about their drug deals. Like names, phone numbers, types of drugs, amounts.'

'In a nutshell.' Ralph shrugs and helps himself to another sandwich. Beth and I aren't eating, what with the pizza. 'I just think if I find him, hand the notebook over, promise not to go to the police, or to go to the police and say I didn't witness anything...'

'But you know it was just a couple of kids involved in that stabbing? Brothers, apparently.'

'So Luna told me. But there must be more to it than that, otherwise why would Lenny be trying to convince me I didn't see anything? Why would he be trying to bump me off?'

'And you know, I looked through your notebook and saw nothing like you've described.'

'Code,' says Ralph. 'But they might cotton on to that.'

'Right.'

'It's a mystery,' says Beth. 'That's for sure.'

'Yes,' we all say, while Ralph chews.

'Fab house,' he says when he's finished.

'Thanks.'

'I've got a house. In Lincoln. Nice little thirties semi. Well, *had* a house, that is. My wife's probably got the deeds transferred into her name by now, aided by one of her creepy lawyer friends. Another long story. Want to hear it?'

'No,' says Beth, forcefully. 'One long story at a time, I think.'

When he's gone, Beth and I sit in the garden going over what Ralph told us. The guys who are after him sound as though they mean business, but we decide Ralph might be a bit confused about why they're out to get him.

'I wish I'd looked through his notebook more carefully,' I say. 'It just seemed like short descriptions of people and places. "Raging mongrels. Teeth like portcullises." Stuff like that.'

'Well,' says Beth, 'I think it's good that we offered to help him look for Lenny and Dog.'

'*You* offered.'

'Someone needs to help him resolve this, and Luna seems a bit useless, sleeping through his attack and only waking up when he hit the water. Talking of sleeping...' Beth yawns and stretches her arms above her head. 'Feel like going to bed for a bit?'

'OK.'

We pass Dad in the kitchen, one hand making a cup of tea, the other holding a sheet of calculations. 'Morning,' he says.

'Evening,' I say back.

'Ah.' He drips the teabag to the bin and sips straight from the boiling hot mug without flinching. '*Tempus fugit,*' he says with a shake of the head, then leaves the room in the clothes he's worn for days.

'Oh dear,' says Beth.

'No, he's all right, really.'

250

SEVENTEEN

Daniel I've extended my stay to take in my mother's seventieth birthday. She has her long-time neighbours, Pat and Kitty, helping her concoct a punch out on the porch. 'A touch more vodka, don't you think, dear?' I've heard more than once.

In the house, my sister and niece are fussing over salads to accompany the barbequed steaks. My brother-in-law, Don, is in charge of the barbeque, which he's trying to get going now with a good deal of cursing. In these God-fearing, church-attending circles, that stretches to a 'Darn!' and no more. The first guests will be arriving soon and the coals are nowhere nearing glowing. When he turns down my offer of help, I go fiddle with chairs and tables in the garden, just to look as though I'm contributing. I want the whole thing to be over, so I can head off to New York City and mix with folk who've never voted Republican or made a patchwork crib set.

There's clearly nothing to do, so I take my holiday reading (a biography of Dylan Thomas) to a chair in the shade, where I stay until the guests begin arriving. Most are elderly, although several younger family members seem to be in tow. I'm in no doubt that someone will bring along a spare, single, young-but-not-too-young woman for June's unfortunate son (me) to cast his eye over.

They all know about Lauren. Mom still won't say the name. Only 'her', 'she', 'that dreadful woman'. For my mother, the lack of a marriage certificate was at the root of our troubles, believing, as she does, that Lauren would not have become the unprincipled whore she did if we'd had that piece of paper.

Ten minutes in, I'm greeting a couple I've known forever – '*My*, Daniel, you're sounding so English!' – when I think I spot the spare single woman, walking slightly behind the Harrisons toward the door.

And this is Bobbie,' Ann Harrison tells me, after we've shaken hands. 'The latest addition to our library, here in town.'

'Hi,' I say. She's an attractive blonde woman in her mid-to-late thirties. She's in blue jeans and a white sleeveless blouse that shows off her slim tanned arms.

'Hello, Daniel,' she says in what sounds like a husky smoker's voice. If she lights up in front of my mother, there'll be trouble – my father having died of smoking-related heart problems. It's an appealing voice, though.

'Would you like punch?' I ask the three of

them. The women say yes, while Ken Harrison declines.

'Better not, since I'm the driver,' he tells me.

The Harrisons live just one block down, 'but perhaps he's giving Bobbie the librarian a ride home.

'Maybe one beer,' he adds with a wink. 'So, how's little old Britain treating you? Understand cricket yet?'

'No,' I say, 'but then neither, it seems, do most Brits.' The four of us chortle our way to the drinks table, where my mother's face lights up at both the gift she's proffered and the sight of Bobbie.

'How splendid that you could come, Bobbie.' She hands her a glass of punch, then pours one for Ann Harrison. 'And here's some for you, Daniel.' My mother winks at me. 'Now, why don't you show our newcomer the rose garden? Punch, Ken?'

'Just a beer, June.'

I take my time walking us across the lengthy lawn, because being with Bobbie saves me from hearing how the other guests' children, contemporaries of mine I can barely remember, are faring. I've been at several gatherings such as these over the years, the last being my father's funeral, and have noticed that family news is always good. 'Gerry's just made deputy chief, and has a charming wife and three darling and *very* clever daughters.' Bad news doesn't generally get a look in. Which, on the whole, I feel to be a good thing. For example, they all know of my academic success, and usually enquire as to how that's going, but they carefully never mention the Lauren business.

'So, how long have you worked in the library?' I ask Bobbie.

'Since May. Before that I lived in Boston and worked as a librarian in the university.'

'This is quite a change, then?'

'Yeah,' she says with a short husky laugh.

When we reach my mother's vast and intricate rose display, I want to tell Bobbie that this would be the best place for a smoke, if she needs one. But I don't, because she goes into raptures about the flowers, sniffing and swooning and moving on to the next.

'Tell me about you,' she says between sniffs.

'You mean my mother hasn't?'

She laughs again. I like her laugh, and am realising that she's even prettier than on first acquaintance. 'A little,' she says.

We sit on the neat lawn with our drinks and I talk about my job, about living in London and some of the places I've visited in the UK. She asks questions about my field of research. Intelligent questions. The kind you'd expect from a former university librarian. I'm warming to her, I realise, and for the first time in weeks, have gone fifteen minutes without thinking of Caitlin. In spite of my determination not to think of her, she pops into my head with annoying regularity.

'It must take some getting use to,' I say, wanting to find out more about Bobbie. 'Small-town life.'

'Sure, but I was raised in a small town. Sort of feel I've come home, if only for a short while. And the townsfolk have made me so welcome.'

There's a bit of a breeze going today, and Bobbie's fine pale hair is blowing playfully across her face. She keeps tilting her head and brushing it from her eyes. Gorgeous dark blue eyes, I notice. I don't know if it's the vodka-heavy punch I've just gotten through, but I'm suddenly realising there are a lot of lovely, smart women in the world, and that I'm lucky enough to be sitting beside one on this beautiful summer's day. My spirits are higher than at any point since leaving Wales, and I intend to make the most of this fateful, if slightly engineered meeting. Starting by showing what an interested and sensitive guy I am.

'You don't have to tell me,' I say, 'but was there a reason for leaving Boston?'

Bobbie moves hair from her cheek and tucks it behind her ear again. 'Well, yeah. There was this guy.'

'Ah. As I say, you don't have—'

'I loved Shelby with all my heart. We were engaged and planning to marry this fall. My mom was making my bridal gown, the honeymoon was all arranged. Hawaii.'

'Uh-huh?'

'Then...' Bobbie breathes in deeply, 'then I caught him cheating on me. Well, a good friend told me he was.'

'Oh, how terrible.' It must be hard to love a man called Shelby in the first place, but then to discover he's a love rat.

'I've kind of heard you went through a similar experience?' Jesus, who doesn't know? 'Yep,' I say. 'And it was devastating. I can imagine how terrible you're feeling, what with it being so recent.'

I wonder what would make a guy cheat on someone as nice as Bobbie. Or Caitlin. Could be a lot of men don't want 'nice'. I'm pretty sure I do. Bobbie may be nice but she's also flirtatious. Something she's doing with her eyes, her mouth. I notice she too has finished her punch, which might explain these come-on looks. Something is stirring in me. It's a long time since I've gotten physical with a woman, not counting Faiza. Could Bobbie become an interesting and intense mid-vacation fling? Might she even leave her new job and fly back to London with me? I'm being ridiculous, but romances can strike up in a flash and last for ever. My parents' did. Christ, what am I thinking? The punch must be lethal, I decide.

'You know...' Bobbie takes my hand in her wonderfully soft one, and leans toward me so I can peek down her blouse. I'm not sure how deliberate that is, maybe not at all. 'It could be,' she says in her sexy gravelly voice, 'that the Good Lord, in all his wisdom, has brought us together on this auspicious day ... your mother's birthday.'

'Well...' I say. I'm about to move my hand, when her other one lands on top and I find myself firmly sandwiched.

'Perhaps we could offer him a short prayer?' she says. 'Dear Lord and everlasting Father to us all, may we give thanks...'

I look at the top of Bobbie's bowed head as she continues, and try to work out an exit strategy. When she's done and I've joined in the 'Amen', and she's lifted her face and blinked her eyes open in the strong sunlight, I leap to my feet. 'Hey,' I say, 'completely forgot I was supposed to help Don barbeque the steaks!' I look at my watch and tut. 'Here, let me help you up. No, no, we can leave our glasses.'

I introduce Bobbie to my divorced cousin on my father's side, Joey. He has Hispanic dark good looks that might contrast nicely with Bobbie's fairness, and I leave them to it in the belief that she goes for dark men, and because Joey is wearing a crucifix. I have no idea if it's merely an accessory, since Joey's always been a snappy dresser. But I'm sure Bobbie will soon find out.

I take the stairs two at a time, enter my room and fall on the bed. 'Oh, Caitlin,' I say, eyes closed, hands clasped on my chest – almost as though in prayer, oddly enough.

Caitlin 'For you, Cait!' shouts Zac, and my heart stops. 'It's Joe.'

'Oh.' I go into my workroom, or more accurately Zac's workroom, and take the phone. 'Hi,' I say, wandering out and down the stairs. 'How's things?'

'OK. Really good, in fact. Beth's still here.'

'So I heard.'

'And you?' Joe asks.

'Oh, er ... fine.'

'You sound a bit down. And why's Zac answering the phone with "Cait's Kiddie Clobber"? Is he your secretary, or something?'

'Actually, he's my everything. Does all the sewing now.'

'Very funny.'

'No, it's true. Didn't he tell you?'

'He said he was too busy to talk.' Joe laughs. 'Since when has Zac sewn?'

'I'm not sure, but he's good. And I felt like a breather. How's the café?'

'Great. I took some time off too, to be with Beth. Now we're both working there.'

258

'Oh, yes? It's serious, then?'

'Hopefully. But listen, the main reason I'm ringing is Ralph.'

'Fallen off a college roof?'

'No, no more accidents. But he keeps coming to the café and talking about finding these guys he says are after him. Lenny mostly. Wants to give him that notebook because it's full of incriminating stuff, which I don't think it is.'

'But doesn't he know that stabbing was just an accident between two young brothers?'

'We've tried telling him, but he says Lenny and Dog pushed him off that ledge on Snowdon, then tried to drown him in the canal.'

I fall on the sofa and roll my eyes. 'It was *a* dog, not a person called Dog, pushed him off the mountain path. I know, because he nearly did the same to me. Stupid great thing.' I explain about Ralph the dog, and his owner's confession.

'So,' says Joe, 'he probably didn't get chucked in the canal either.'

'I'd guess not.'

'He's dead convincing, though. You should hear him.'

'Hmm...' I say, stretching out and putting my feet on the arm of the sofa. 'You know, maybe I will.'

'What?'

'Come and hear him. I'm bored and

restless and I'm not doing anything here.'
I'd also been thinking of getting Daniel's
London address from Val and checking it
out. Not that he'll be there. I'd just like to
see where he lives. 'I have to go to London,'
I tell Joe, 'so I could come via Oxford. Bring
Ralph's case with me.'

'Great. Stay here, if you need to. Dad's on
a work binge, so it's quiet.'

'Um, I don't know. Have you told Beth
about us?'

'Yeah, I have, but she knew anyway. I think
she'd be cool. So, what, are you going to
leave Zac in charge of your business? Jesus,
I still can't believe he's sewing.'

'Kind of obsessively,' I whisper, then we
both laugh. 'He'll be fine. Listen, I'll try and
find a B & B, Joe. But if I get stuck...'

'OK. When's this trip to London, then?'

'Maybe tomorrow,' I say, uplifted at the
thought of going somewhere, doing something. I tell Joe I'll ring him when I arrive,
then I hang up and go and drag Ralph's
luggage back up the cellar steps. I lock it in
the boot of my old car, which I pray will get
me all the way to London, and even back
again. Then I go to the computer and look
up Val's number.

'Oxford Singles' Weeks,' she sings.

'Hi, Val, it's Caitlin. Remember me?' She
says of course she does and we chat about
the weather and how our respective busi-

260

nesses are going.

'Whilst I remember,' Val say, 'I'm offering a ten per cent discount for last-minute bookings, and another ten per cent for return customers.'

'Great. I'll spread the word amongst my single friends.'

'*Male* friends,' she says, 'preferably. One's constantly oversubscribed with ladies.'

'Right.' All the single men of a certain age I know are single for a reason. Except Daniel. 'Talking of males,' I say, 'I, er, was wondering if you might have Daniel Sanchez's home address in London?' I pull a face, waiting to be told it's confidential information.

'Oh dear, Cait. I'd have thought you'd know it. Does this mean there's been something of a rift?'

'No, no, no. He gave me his address but I lost it. Now he's in America and not contactable and I ... need to send him something, for when he gets back.'

'Golly, one wouldn't have thought crossing the Atlantic meant being incommunicado, these days. Just a tick, I'll go and look him up.'

'Thank you,' I say, although she's already gone.

She's quickly back and reading out the address, then says, 'You must have his home phone number?'

'Er, lost that too.'

Val reels off the number and I scribble it down. 'Must dash,' she says. 'I've some under-forty-fives waiting to punt.'

When we've said our goodbyes I come over all nostalgic for Oxford, then run upstairs and tell Zac my plan.

'Cool,' he says. 'Only if it carries on like this we'll have to be Zac's Kiddie Clobber.' He titters to himself and does a quick sleeve seam on the machine. 'I might drop the Kiddie, though. Branch out into adult clothes. Zac's Clobber. I might employ you as my like creative director. What do you think?'

'Sure,' I say, heading out the room and only half listening. I'm going to Oxford and London – how exciting. 'Listen, do you know where Frankie is?'

'At his girlfriend's, I think.'

I stop dead. 'Frankie's got a girlfriend?'

'Oops.' Zac's slapped a hand over his mouth. He turns and looks at me. 'I wasn't meant to tell you. He thinks you might not approve.'

'Why wouldn't I approve?'

'Er, something about her age, but don't tell him I told you, because he might be seventeen but he's way bigger than me.'

'Age?' I ask.

'Look, man, I'm not saying any more.' Zac gets back to work and I leave the room, thinking *Please no*, my son can't be having

262

relations with an under-age girl. Where would I start with that one? I'll phone his father, I decide. Get Steven to agree to come and have a man-to-man word. It's the least he can do.

While I pack a medium-sized case with one hand, I try getting hold of my ex-husband, but with no luck. On some exotic holiday, I decide. He used to tell us what he was doing, but that stopped a year or so back. I think Steven considers Frankie grown up now, and off his hands. Practically, if not financially.

I chuck a cardigan in, just in case. It's still hot, but you never know. I'm trying hard to look forward to my trip, but my head's all over the place now. If Frankie got this girl pregnant, could he be jailed? Could he be jailed for just having sex with her? I remember the wine stain on my quilt. Should I stay and sort this out? What could I do, anyway? Frankie's a strong-minded and stubborn child at the best of times.

I go to shove a handful of knickers in one of my suitcase pockets, when I come across something solid in there. I pull it out and see it's the sandalwood soap Daniel bought me. I feel a pang of guilt that I didn't use it while he was here. That I'd forgotten about it, really. It smells so lovely through the wrapper. I picture Daniel handing it over, a bit awkwardly, and I'm suddenly crying.

'Oh, Daniel,' I say. I look round my room and realise he'd never once come in it. 'Where are you?'

'Cait!' comes a strange, strangled cry from across the landing. 'Cait!'

I drop the soap and hurry to the work-room, imagining a fire. What I see when I get there is Zac with his head on the sewing machine, a horrified expression on his face.

'Hair!' he says in a kind of quiet screech, pointing in the direction of the needle.

'Hang on,' I say, while I go to leave the room. 'Not that you've got any choice!'

Zac's pointing frantically at the cutting-out table. 'Scissors. There.'

'Yeah, I know,' I say, almost crying again, but this time with laughter. 'I just need to get my camera.'

Daniel With all the guests gone and the house back the way my mother likes it, I announce that I'll definitely be going to New York tomorrow. I counter her protests with claims that there are plants to be tended in the apartment I'm renting, and I'm already three days overdue. She knows all this, but it's a widowed mother's prerogative to pile guilt on her departing offspring.

I'm touched and a little surprised that she still wants my company, since I've been lethargic and untalkative, often bordering on morose, during my stay. 'Are you OK, dear?'

I've had at least once each day. Just reading/
thinking/resting I'd reply, with a wan smile.
I'd decline another root beer and go on
being the dullest house guest imaginable.

Being in the city will no doubt buck me
up. With so many distractions to drag my
thoughts away from Caitlin, I'm bound to
feel perkier. There'll be friends to dine out
with, go to the movie theatre with. And just
the general and constant buzz that is New
York. On top of everything, I'll have a PC
and the internet back in my life. Some work
to do too. How will I possibly find time to
dwell on a lovely woman in the Welsh mountains?

Caitlin I check the laptop for messages one
more time before going to bed. Nothing
from Daniel, of course. How good it will be
to get away from all this waiting. To see
people and be busy, and not dwell on
someone who's clearly never going to reply
to my email, or the email I sent this afternoon, asking if he'd received my first email.
By my reckoning, he must be in New York
and have access to modern technology. It's
early evening there now, so I'd have
expected some sort of response.

But then, anything could have happened.
If, for some reason he didn't receive my first
message ... and say he's been out all day and
not yet received my second message... Yes,

that would be it. Either that, or he's found a new woman. One who has time for him and doesn't screw much younger men. I'll check my emails before I leave in the morning. If there's nothing then, I'll give up on the whole Daniel idea. Although I might still check out his place in London.

EIGHTEEN

Ralph It's a bit ironic, really. Now I've got hold of the blinking notebook, Lenny and Dog are taking a break from trying to do me in. I keep it on my person all the time, just in case they make an appearance. Got it all planned. 'Here, take the thing,' I'll say. 'And leave me in peace.' Lenny will look pleasantly surprised, make me promise I won't grass to the police about the stabbing, and that will be that. We might even shake hands.

While I wait for him to find me again – I'm on Luna's boat, so how hard can that be? – I occasionally go looking for him. Or Dog, or any of the others. Just sort of roaming the streets. Sometimes not the most salubrious of streets, which isn't that much fun. Especially as I'm still drawing attention to myself with the arm plaster.

Until I resolve things with Lenny, I can't

relax and get on with my life. Which is basically enjoying the rest of the summer holidays and not being anywhere near Hilary. Oh God. Hilary. The other day I thought about her, and my stake in our house, and I was actually sick in the boat's little toilet. Luna made me tea, which was the PG Tips I now insist on, and gave me a massage and did a little spell thing, and I felt so calm and safe. As she massaged, Luna kept telling me, over and over, in her new gentle hypnotist's voice, that I wasn't afraid of anybody. Not Hilary, not anyone. Also, that no attempts had been made on my life at all. That I'd just imagined them. It's incredible how persuasive she can be, because for a full five minutes, maybe ten, I actually believed none of it had happened. Only then I could feel Dog grabbing me on the mountain again, clear as anything.

Luna's teaching herself hypnosis from a book, and is using me and a few neighbours as guinea pigs. She thinks she'll get more clients as a hypnotist, as there's no 'Witch' section, white or otherwise, in the *Yellow Pages*. In all the time I've been here, she's only had two white witch sessions with people, and one of those was me. That explains why she can't afford another mobile, and why she has to go and sign every fortnight, and maybe why we eat a lot of pulses. I think I'll start paying her rent, and also buy her a phone. I'd get one for myself if I didn't think Hilary would track me down on it. Oh God. Hilary.

Joe Beth and I clock off around seven, then get home to find Cait reading on the sofa.

'How did you get in?' I ask after giving her a hug. No kiss because Beth might not like it. I nod towards Dad's study, where the zippy noise of a printer can be heard.

'I had to bang like mad on the window,' she says. Cait looks quite tired and stressed. There are dark circles under her eyes and her mouth turns down at the corners. She definitely looks older.

'Can I get you anything?' asks Beth.

'Just a bed for the night, if you still have one. No vacancies anywhere. Sorry.'

I tell Cait she can stay as long as she likes. She looks as though she could do with a bed right now, but when Beth suggests we all go for a drink, Cait jumps at the idea.

'Give me five minutes,' she says, getting up and grabbing hold of a big red bag. 'Same room?'

'Yeah, same room.'

While she's upstairs, Beth whispers, 'I'm not sure I like this.' So, once again, I tell her that Cait and I have completely gone off each other, and not to worry.

'She's looking a bit rough,' I add, just for a bit more reassurance. 'Don't you think?'

'No. I think she looks great, and so slim too. Admit it, Joe, you prefer skinny women, don't you?'

I love these rare times when Beth gets all insecure. People say it's awful having a jealous partner but I think I'd love it. 'No,' I say, even though I've always gone for skinny in the past. 'I don't.'

We have a snog while we wait, then when Cait comes back down the stairs, she looks amazing. She's changed into a sleeveless top and tight jeans. She's wearing earrings, and has lovely black shiny hair and no dark rings under her eyes. And yes, she's gorgeously slim. I realise I'm staring when Beth nudges my arm quite painfully.

In the pub, Cait tells us all about Zac and what a brilliant asset he's turned out to be, apart from getting his hair sewn into a trouser leg. She shows us a photo and the three of us are in hysterics for a while, practically crying into our beers. But then I say, 'And how's Daniel?' and Cait's whole face changes and the atmosphere goes weird and she suddenly has to go to the loo.

'Oops,' I say, when she's gone.

'Might be best not to enquire,' Beth whispers.

'No.'

For the rest of our quite heavy drinking session, we talk about Ralph, the weather,

Wales, Oxford, the Italian Job ... basically, everything except Daniel, who I suppose is now history. At one point, I look over at Beth and realise how lucky I am. Maybe I should just marry her, I'm thinking, in my slightly pissed state.

'So, what are you doing tomorrow?' Cait's asking. 'I was wondering if we could get together with Ralph. Maybe take his case to him on the boat.'

'We're working all day,' says Beth. 'But maybe in the evening? We knock off at seven, don't we, Joe?'

'Er, ish. Yeah.' I don't want to commit because sometimes I stay on if it's busy.

'Oh, I'll go to Luna's boat on my own,' says Cait. 'With or without the suitcase. Ralph can always come and get it later.'

'Sure?' I ask, trying not to show my relief.

'You know it was Luna got Joe and me together?' says Beth.

'I thought I did that?' asks Cait, jokily.

Beth tells the story of Luna and the text message and the spell she cast, only it takes her a while, what with being quite pissed.

'Must make sure I don't leave my mobile on the boat!' says Cait. Then, with a bit of a faraway look, she says, 'Or maybe I should.'

'Not that you'll have it with you,' I say, and Cait and I laugh at our little in-joke.

Beth frowns at me. 'What do you mean?' She puts her hand in my lap and squeezes my leg.

'Oh, nothing,' I say, giving her a kiss.

Daniel I hit the city late afternoon, get a cab to the apartment, water the flaccid plants, stare out the window whilst drinking an ice-cold beer, and feel ... nothing very much. Being here isn't exciting me the way it normally does. I wonder why that is – tired, perhaps – then go to the phone, look up Dean and Carolyn's number and give them a call. Talking to like-minded urbanites might give me a boost, but I get Carolyn's voicemail. I leave a message saying I'm in town and to call me back some time.

I watch some CNN, which depresses the hell out of me, then go to the study I know well, having rented this place twice before. I leave the computer to boot up and get another beer, hoping this isn't going to be my life for the next ten days. Beer, TV, PC, beer. While I'm at it, I take milk, bread and a pizza out to defrost. I'd imagined eating in one of my favourite restaurants this evening, but have lost all inclination to call other friends, and don't want to dine out alone. The pizza doesn't need to defrost, I decide, so put it in the oven at the stated temperature.

Back at the screen – a new flat one since I was last here – I log into my email account to discover I have only fifteen messages. I suspect Fiona, bless her, has weeded out the dross. I swig at beer again, longing for one of the cigarettes I gave up two years ago, and run my eyes down the inbox list. Third email down, I see the first 'cait' in 'cait@caitskiddieclobber.co.uk.' and my heart stops. I click on it and hold my breath while I read. 'Did you get my other email?' it says. 'Hope all's well. Caitlin.'

Another swig, then I scroll down to the next 'cait@ caitskiddieclobber' and open it. As I read, I feel this wonderful warmth surge through me, but then when I look at the date it was sent, I go cold. Fiona was supposed to call me if anything important came up. My fault. I should have said that included Caitlin.

I bound to the kitchen, grab a third beer, open it, go to the bathroom because I'm drinking on an empty stomach, and return to the computer – all the while with a stupid grin on my face. Caitlin's been missing me. Wishes I were still in Wales, and deeply regrets that she hadn't found time to do more things with me. Or 'regerts', as she put it. There were a couple of other typos, but I guess that can happen when you pour your heart out in a message and quickly click on 'Send'. Either that, or she can't spell. Not that it would matter.

'Oh, Caitlin,' I say, while I look up her website for her number. It's in my cellphone, but I deliberately left that in London. After finding the number, I go fetch the phone and dial it, forgetting in my haste to add the international code. I try again and it rings three times before being picked up.

'Cait's Kiddie Clobber,' says a familiar voice. 'Zac speaking.' Zac? Huh, so he made it there after all. I picture him taking it easy and eating for three. 'Hi, Zac,' I say.

'Hey, Daniel. How's things? Cait said you're in the States now. Lucky you.'

'Er, yeah. I guess. How are you? How long have you been there?'

'Dunno. I've been so busy, man. Sort of lost track of the days. Anyway, I'm running the business for Cait now, while she's away.'

Cait's away? Damn. 'You don't mean sewing?'

'Sewing, taking orders, ordering materials and stuff.'

'Actual *sewing?*' I ask again.

'There's nothing says blokes can't make clothes. Look at all the top designers.'

'Yeah,' I say, 'I just didn't know you had that skill.' Or any, I could add. I take a deep breath and ask where Caitlin is. Perhaps she took the brat on holiday, after all.

'In Oxford.'

'Oh?'

'I got a text earlier, saying she's arrived. She's staying with Joe. You could call her there, or like try her mobile?'

'Right,' I say, slumping back in the plush

office chair. 'Joe.' I'm finding this hard to digest, but write down the phone numbers Zac's reeling off. 'Right,' I say again, when he's finished. 'Thanks.'

'So, when are you back?' asks Zac.

Caitlin's staying with Joe. Why? Did it all go wrong with Beth, and now he and Cait are...? And all because she didn't hear from me?

'You still there, Daniel?'

'Yeah.'

'Shall I like pass on a message, if I–'

'No, no message. Look, gotta go. Sorry.' I hang up, realising I should have said good-bye. I shut down the computer, get out of the plush office chair and make my way to the smell of burning pizza.

Caitlin I'm feeling a lot happier. Could be the booze, but so what. It's been good for me to relax, unwind, have a bit of fun. I really like Beth, I decide. Joan's been a regular presence in our lives over the years, being Frankie's best friend, but I've never got to see much of Beth, the older sister. She's definitely good for Joe. When he goes quiet, which he often does, Beth's quite oblivious and just rattles on in a jolly way, until he feels confident enough to say something again. I can't imagine her being moody, which Joe said was his big problem with Charlotte.

He's made us all coffee, and it's sobering me up enough to think about my business, and whether everything's OK. Since it's only eleven, I excuse myself – 'Long day' – then go to my room and call home.

The phone rings for a while, then I hear, 'Cait's Kiddie Clobber. Zac speaking.'

'Zac, I don't think you need to say that at this time of night.'

'Well, you never know.'

'Anyway, just phoning to see everything's all right.'

'Yeah, yeah.'

Zac tells me about the things he's done today, which included milking the goats and seeing to the hens, on account of Frankie's not yet returning. I managed to block thoughts of my son and his underage woman out, but now I start worrying again. I'll call him on his mobile and see what he's up to, deserting his duties like that. Mind you, I suppose I'm doing the same.

'Oh, and Mrs Turnbull in York wants another one of those, what do you call them ... pinafore dresses. For her other grand-daughter.'

'Great. Do you think you'll be able to manage that?'

'No problem.'

I'm still thinking that Zac's going to lose this weird talent he has for running up children's clothes. That it's some kind of 'automatic sewing' thing, coming via a mischievous spirit. 'Hey, man, I could do it yesterday. What's like happened?'

'Anything else?' I ask.

'No, not really. Oh, Daniel's just called.'

'Daniel who?' I ask, more to give me time to register the news.

'American Daniel.'

Suddenly, my heart's thumping in my ribcage. I feel a bit sick. All those beers, perhaps. 'Oh?' I say casually.

'Yeah.'

'Well? What did he say? What did you say? Did he get my emails? Did he leave a contact number?'

'Er ... no. No number. I said you were away ... and, then he went, I dunno, a bit funny.'

I'm not liking the sound of this. I fall back on the bed and stare at the ceiling, still gripping the phone at my left ear. 'Now listen, Zac. This is quite important. Please, if you remember, could you tell me how the conversation went.'

'OK, well. I said, "Cait's Kiddie Clobber. Zac speaking," like I usually do, then he seemed surprised to hear me, then I explained that I was running your business while you're away, and he wanted to know where you were and I told him.'

'Told him what?'

'That you were in Oxford. I gave him Joe's number, so he could give you a call ... and then he like didn't say much and hung up.'

276

I carry on staring at the ceiling, carry on gripping the phone.

'Hello?' Zac's saying.

I hear myself swallowing hard. 'I don't suppose you mentioned Beth? That she's here too, and that Joe and Beth are still an item?'

'Not that I remember. Oh, I see what you're saying. Daniel might think...'

'Yes, he might.'

'Well, if he phones again, I'll put him straight, yeah?' He laughs. 'Least I can do. Anyway, is there like anything else you want to discuss? It's just that I was in the middle of eating.'

Only that I'd like to kill him. 'Not really,' I say. 'Good night, Zac.'

This is terrible. Wonderful that he's been in touch, but terrible that he thinks I'm screwing my toyboy again. Maybe. I have to talk to him, but how? Email again? I jump from the bed, find Joe and ask if I can use his computer. He tells me to help myself, that it just needs switching on, and asks if I'm OK. I'm looking pale, apparently.

'Fine,' I say. 'Well, not really. Tell you later.'

Up in Joe's bedroom, I drum fingers while the laptop starts up, and pray to a God I desperately want to believe in, for a message from Daniel. But there isn't one.

'Bugger,' I say. I find his address and start

typing out a message. Once again, I'm a bit under the influence as I write. I tell him I've brought Ralph's luggage to Oxford, and am staying with Joe and Beth – it's tempting to put 'Beth' in capitals – for a couple of nights, before going to London for a short break. That I've caught up on the backlog of CKC orders, and have left things in Zac's capable hands. Exclamation mark. I say I was sorry to have missed his call, and ask if there's a number I can phone him on. I sign off with a 'love' but no kisses, and carry out two spellchecks.

NINETEEN

Joe It's decided over breakfast that I'll take the morning off to help Cait. Since Ralph hasn't got a phone, we'll take the suitcase to him, rather than wait for him to turn up. The main reason for going to the boat, though, is for Cait to talk to him about the Lenny stuff. To tell him what happened to her with Ralph the dog, and talk him out of this quest of his, to get the notebook to Lenny. Talk him into going back to Lincoln and his wife, even. Before he has another accident.

'Sure you don't want to come?' I ask Beth.

Beth looks at me, then at Cait, then at me again. 'No. I'd rather go clothes shopping, thanks.'

'Me too!' says Cait. 'I can't see dragging this case down the towpath is going to be fun.'

Luckily, Ralph's bag is a wheelie type. I extend the handle and we set off on foot for town. On the way, Cait asks me about Beth and how it's going, and I tell her it's good, in fact very good. And that I'm even beginning to feel a bit secure for a change.

'I think she's perfect for you,' says Cait. 'Not that I'm an expert on relationships.'

I laugh. 'You sound like my dad.'

'It seems to get harder as you get older. I don't know why.'

'You and Daniel,' I say. 'Did it not–'

'Just think how many famous people must have gone through those doors,' she says, pointing over the road at the Examination Schools. Either she didn't hear me in the roar of buses, or she's changing the subject.

'Yeah,' I say, as though such thoughts are always occurring to me. I think you just get a bit blasé about the city's history when you've grown up here.

'Oscar Wilde, Gladstone, Indira Gandhi.'

'Amazing. Shall we stop for a coffee? There's a good place just up here.'

'OK,' says Cait, but then we get to it, she hesitates before following me in.

'Don't you like it?'

'No, it's fine,' she says, finally stepping through the door. 'It's just that I came here with ... someone. Here, let me help with that.' She holds the door open wide and gives Ralph's case a shove through the limited space. 'God knows how people with wheelchairs manage.'

Cait goes quiet over our coffees, just staring out of the window most of the time. Every now and then flicking through a newspaper, then closing it with a sigh. She seems to be very up and down at the moment, not just emotionally but physically. Last night in the pub, she'd been happy and youthful one minute, then miserable-looking, and hunched up and chewing her nails the next. I'd mentioned this to Beth in bed, but she said she hadn't really noticed. 'I was probably talking so much,' she said. I like the fact that Beth's a chatterbox, and sometimes, like last night, it's quite strange when she finally falls asleep and has nothing more to say.

Then suddenly, there in the café, Cait starts pouring it out to me. All about her and Daniel, and how she'd messed up big time, and how I'd come into the equation too.

'Sorry,' I say. 'Only I–'

'No, no. You're hardly to blame for what happened, Joe. Sorry, I shouldn't have... Anyway, then, after Daniel left, Frankie tells me what a top-rate bloke he thinks he is, and starts fantasising about having him as a stepfather. I mean, honestly! And now, because Zac didn't paint the full picture, Daniel thinks I'm back with you, and I don't have a phone number for him and it's all a big horrible mess.' Cait blows her nose into a napkin, takes some deep breaths and knocks back the rest of her latte. 'Anyway, I emailed him again last night and filled him in, and hopefully he'll give me a call at your house, or just email me back. Oh God, this is ridiculous, Joe. I'm forty-five, not fifteen. Look at me.'

She blows her nose again and leans back in her seat, looking very tired.

'If you want my opinion,' I say a bit nervously, because I can never imagine that people do want it, 'you're blowing this up out of proportion.'

She sits upright again. 'Really?'

'Mm. It's easy to let your imagination run away with you when you're miles apart and communication goes haywire. I did that with Beth, but now look at us. Daniel will be back in London soon, and you can sort things out then.'

'Unless he's met someone in the meantime.'

I nod. 'Unless he's met someone in the meantime.'

Ralph is home. He's sunning himself on a fold-up chair beside the towpath, and I see his arm's no longer in plaster.

'How are you?' Cait asks him.

'Fine,' he says, standing and kissing her cheek. 'And you've brought my suitcase, so even better. Thank you.' He bends and shouts into the boat. 'Hey, Luna. Got my clothes at last. I can stop wearing yours.'

Luna pops her big red hair through the little door and says hello, tells Ralph to open up more chairs and asks if we want tea.

'Real tea,' Ralph reassures us and we say yes, even though we've just had coffee.

While Luna brews up, Ralph unfolds two more chairs. 'And what brings you to Oxford, Cait? Not just my suitcase?'

'Oh ... having a bit of a break again. You know what it's like, the summer can be over before you've taken advantage of it.'

'That's true. Listen, I don't suppose you've heard from the wife?'

'Hilary?'

Ralph gives a bit of a shudder. 'Yes. That one.'

'No, I haven't. But why don't you just go home and sort it out?'

Ralph looks up at us. 'Can't face it. Plus, as you know, Joe, I have to find Lenny. Give him the notebook.'

I roll my eyes. 'Listen, Ralph. You didn't get pushed off the mountain by a man called Dog. It was an actual dog. Cait will explain, won't you, Cait?'

Cait explains, at length, but it's obvious Ralph can't accept this version of what happened. 'Come with me,' he says, when she's finished and Luna's stepped on to the towpath with a tray of mugs. 'Help me find Lenny. Please?'

Cait takes one of the mugs and thanks Luna. 'OK,' she says to Ralph, which takes me by surprise. 'We'll help, won't we, Joe?'

'Er, I suppose. Only, I've got the business ... you know.'

'Well maybe Beth, then. The sooner Ralph resolves his problems with Lenny, the sooner he can move on. Isn't that right, Ralph?'

'Spot on.'

'Anyone for a rice cake?' asks Luna, waving a bland-looking packet at us. Only she takes one.

When I get up to go, thanking Luna for the tea and saying I'm expected at the café, I wait for Cait to jump up too, but she doesn't.

'See you later, Joe,' she says.

I can't make out why she wants to stay here, but decide to leave her to it, waving as I walk off. 'Come into the Italian Job,' I call out to her. 'Have something to eat on the house.'

'Gosh, that's very kind,' says Luna with a wave back. 'Isn't it, Ralph?'

Caitlin I want to get Luna on her own, but Ralph's rabbiting on about Lenny and showing me a list of areas we could try searching. I agree to go with him to one of them today, but can't work out how to get shot of him now, just for ten minutes, or however long it will take Luna to do some white witch business for me. Eventually, I just say, 'Luna, I don't suppose I could have a consultation with you? Like now? I'll pay.'

'Yes, of course, dear.' She gathers up mugs and things. 'Ralph, why don't you go and hunt out some more dandelion leaves?'

'Do I have to?'

'Well, just sit quietly where you are, then. I'll need to concentrate, so no popping in to fetch something. Come along, Cait.'

Once inside and perched on the sofa, Luna opposite me on a stool in her big floaty frock, I'm asked what kind of spell I'd like.

I say, 'Love, please,' and for the second time in one morning, find myself telling the Daniel story.

I wonder why I'm doing this. Why I'm sitting on a hot bus with a person I hardly know, looking for someone who may or may not exist, to hand over a notebook which may or may not be important. Ralph won't let me look at it. Says the less I know the

284

better. We've set off from town heading for a place called Barton, which the driver said was just beyond the ringroad, and Ralph is talking to me about his house in Lincoln, the size of the mortgage, the house's last valuation, the amount of capital he put in personally, and Hilary's friends in the legal world.

Actually, I do know why I'm doing this. It's to keep my mind off Daniel. Also, by helping Ralph, I might build up some sort of credit with God, or the gods, or whoever, and he, she or they might look favourably upon me and make things right with Daniel. Because, I can't honestly say I have much faith in Luna, who'd really dented my confidence after I described Daniel to her.

'Right, we'd better make this quick,' she said. 'A man like that's going to get snapped up.'

'Hilary seems like a nice person to me,' I say to Ralph. 'So surely the worst-case scenario is that you end up with half the house. You must be entitled to that as a spouse?'

'I don't know. You see, since I became a student ... actually, since before that because I had a spell out of work ... well, Hilary's been paying the mortgage.'

'Oh.'

'And the council tax, house insurance, all repairs and maintenance. She had the garage converted to a bedroom for her mother.'

'I see.' Not being an expert on property law, or on Hilary, I go quiet and look out of the window. We go up a hill with parks on either side of the road, then at the top sit idling at traffic lights. The bus picks up more passengers, then idles again at another set of traffic lights. It'll take us forever to get to the ringroad, let alone this Barton place. But I don't mind. What else would I be doing? Miserably staring at Daniel's place in London? A huge house, he'd said, converted into a dozen tiny studio flats. Perhaps it hadn't been such a good idea. Since I haven't arranged accommodation in London, I may as well sit on this bus with a slightly unhinged man.

After a while, we reach a more commercial area with shops either side of the road – a supermarket, travel agent, Boots – and again the bus grinds to a halt in a row of traffic.

'Headington,' says Ralph, who's opened a map of Oxford on his lap. 'Not much further,' he adds, smiling at me. He then does a double take at something in the street and leans right across me, peering intensely out of the window. He's actually squashing my arm, and I'm about to say something when he shouts, 'Lenny!'

'Where?' I ask, but Ralph jumps from his seat and runs to the front of the bus, just as the driver gets moving again, in that jerky way they do. I look in the direction Ralph had been looking and see a bald tattooed man with quite a tummy. He's with what look like twin boys and between them they're carrying lots of shopping.

'Stop!' Ralph's saying, grabbing a rail to steady himself. 'I've got to get off!'

'At the next stop, mate,' the driver shouts back, while Ralph bends his long body and looks past a worried woman towards Lenny. 'Hurry up! Hurry up!' When the driver pulls into a lay-by, then comes to a faltering halt, Ralph's out of the bus the moment the doors open.

I leap up and exit through the central door just as he's passing. 'Ralph!' I say, because I think he's forgotten I'm there.

He turns briefly to look at me. 'It's Lenny,' he says, 'over the road.' He then strides on at a pace I can't possibly keep up with, rounds the end of the bus and breaks into a run. 'Lenny! Lenny!' he's shouting, darting between the cars and waving his canvas bag. 'Lenny!' he shouts one last time before the screech of brakes, the thud of someone being hit and the sound of a woman screaming all reach my ears.

'Oh Jesus,' I whisper. 'Not again.'

The bald man gets to Ralph first and is gently slapping his face. He's got studs and rings piercing his face and tattoos every-where. It's almost more stomach-churning than the accident.

'Ralph,' he's saying. 'You all right? Come on, Ralphy, open your eyes. Say something, mate.'

A woman gets out of the car Ralph's half under and come to inspect. She's visibly shaken. 'Oh my God, is he...?'

'Ralph!' I shout, and miraculously his eyes open.

'Someone call an ambulance,' shouts a distant male voice.

'My husband's just doing that,' says the driver of the car.

'It's in my bag, Lenny,' Ralph's saying weakly.

'What is, mate?'

'The notebook.'

Lenny snorts and puts a hand on Ralph's forehead. 'What you on about, you silly old bugger. Now tell us where it hurts.'

Lenny's boys have joined us. They are twins, I can see now. 'Dad, is that the bloke what slept on our floor?' asks one.

'Yeah, it's him,' says Lenny. 'Now git your arses back on that pavement, will you?'

'He just ran in front of the car,' says the woman. The initial shock seems to have worn off and now she's crying. 'There was no way I could have stopped in time.'

'The notebook you wanted so desperately,' Ralph's telling Lenny. 'You know, the one with all the ... information in. It's in my bag. Take it. Just take it, please.'

Lenny feels Ralph's forehead again. 'I reckon he's suffered a bit of brain damage. Where's that bleeding ambulance?'

'Not another hospital,' groans Ralph. 'Look, I'm OK really. See, I can sit up. *Ouch.*'

'You mustn't move,' I say, helping him lower his neck and head. 'Just lie still.'

'Take it, Lenny,' he says. 'And I promise I won't say a word about that ... unfortunate incident with the knife. Not to the police, not to anyone. And, what's more, I won't press charges against you for pushing me off the mountain, or into the canal. Tell him, Cait.'

Lenny takes his hand away and shuffles back a few paces on his knees. He folds his arms defensively, but doesn't stand up. 'Poor old sod's lost it, hasn't he?'

'Mm,' I say. Slowly and carefully, I unwrap Ralph's bag from his wrist. He yelps when I lift his hand, and I wonder if his arm's broken again. Or was it the other arm?

The only thing in the bag is the notebook, since the map is still on the bus. I tug the thing out and hand it to a bewildered Lenny. 'Just take the damn thing, would you? He won't be happy till you have.'

'Whatever,' says Lenny with a shrug, making a tattooed rat jump alarmingly.

TWENTY

Ralph They say things happen in threes, so fingers crossed this will be my last hospital stay for a while. Not that I *can* cross my fingers. Two broken digits, apparently, one on each hand, from when I tried to stop the car. Still, at least my nose isn't in plaster. They're keeping an eye on me and have done some tests, but think I can go home soon. Trouble is, I might have become institutionalised, because I'd quite like to stay here a bit longer, eating dollops of jelly with a little square of melting ice cream, which is what I'm doing now with the help of a rather lovely nurse. It makes me feel seven or eight again, and safe. It's a dangerous world out there.

Much better in here, where everyone's being so nice, including Lenny and even Dog. The first time Dog walked into the ward, I almost choked on a grape. 'Long time no see,' he said, and I said, 'It wasn't that long ago you chucked me in the canal,' and he said, 'You what?' Then yesterday, they sat one either side of my bed and told me that they hadn't ever been to North Wales. 'Me, up a friggin' mountain?' asked Lenny. 'Or me?' said the even more overweight Dog. They shook their heads and told me I've got an effing brilliant imagination, and had I ever thought about writing thrillers.

They were taking it in turns to speak and my neck started aching from swivelling back and forth. Then Lenny pulled the blanket up because he thought I might be cold, and Dog asked if I wanted my pillows plumped, and ever so slowly ... it just sort of crept up on me, really ... I began to wonder if any of it had happened. Apart from the couple of days I'd spent with them, hanging out, sleeping in the field, staying in Lenny's grotty house. I lowered my voice and said, 'But that stabbing business. Didn't you put "Have you seen this man?" posters in shop windows?'

'Oh, that was us,' said Cait, who was approaching my bed, with another bag of grapes. 'Didn't anyone tell you? I thought Joe might have done. Sorry.'

They'd all started laughing then – all of them round my bed – until I shouted, 'It's not funny!' and they shut up.

I was glad when they left. Now I just want to be alone for a while. Well, alone with this young nurse feeding me dessert and telling me about her holiday in Greece. I say, 'But I thought nurses were poor and couldn't even afford to get their worn-down shoes re-heeled,' and she tells me it was a last-minute bargain. 'Do you know anything about LSD?' I ask, and she says only a bit. 'Call

291

yourself a nurse?' I chuckle, and she says actually she's just an auxiliary and that's why she's feeding me jelly and ice cream, and not sticking needles in my bum. I say, 'I just wondered if you can have hallucinations and, well, severe anxiety after you've taken it and it's worn off. Perhaps days or weeks after.'

She tells me yes, she thinks so. That someone she knows knows someone who went a bit psycho after he'd tried it, only he was always a bit odd. Then she lets me lick the bowl, holding it to my face and giggling away. Her blue eyes and blonde hair and sweet nineteen-year-old, or whatever, lips so close that I could kiss her, if I wanted to. If she wouldn't mind me getting ice cream on her.

I look at her face as I lick and lick the little plastic bowl, and compare it to Hilary's, which I visualise really clearly, just beyond the nurse's shoulder. It's almost as if she's in the room. Then I hear Hilary's voice. 'Ralph?' it's saying. 'Why are you licking the bowl like that? Didn't your parents teach you table manners?'

Then Hilary laughs and comes and kisses my forehead, because she *is* actually in the room, and the nurse lowers the plastic bowl, wipes my face with a tissue and disappears. 'I've brought you some grapes,' says Hilary and I try to act pleased. 'Also, something to sign. But, looking at your hands, that might be tricky.' She laughs again and kisses me again, while I thank God for my broken fingers. Sign over the deeds to our home? No way. Hilary says, 'Since Mum's given me the proceeds of the sale of her house, I thought we could use it to pay off the mortgage. Seems only fair, since you put all your equity in. Apparently, I can't just pay off our joint mortgage without your say so. What do you think? Here, let me feed you some grapes. Open your mouth.'

I do as I'm told and, in fact, the grapes taste delicious. Could be I'm developing an addiction. And the way Hilary lets each one dangle provocatively, just above my mouth, reminds me of what a little sexpot she can be. Could be ... before her job and her mother made her crawl into bed at nine every night in my old frayed Marc Bolan T-shirt. 'I think I took LSD,' I admit between grapes ... because, thinking about it, Hilary's always been the one person I could talk to about things, the person I probably trust most in the world. 'It made me see things and imagine all sorts of crazy stuff.'

'Honestly, Ralph,' she says, shaking her head and smiling and dangling another grape. 'The things you get up to.'

TWENTY-ONE

Daniel I'm waiting for my flight, wondering if this is such a good idea. Not everyone likes surprises. One time, I'd left the university early to surprise Lauren with flowers and chocolates on her work-at-home day. I'd crept into the apartment slowly and quietly, only to find her lying on the bed, talking on the phone in what was clearly an intimate manner. When I'd let my presence be known and asked who the hell she was talking to, she'd gotten really mad at me for spying on her like that, and the flowers never were put in water. It was an awkward incident – the first of several to come – and had, I thought, put me off surprising people for ever.

But I must have recovered, because now I find the idea of arriving unexpectedly far more romantic than emailing Caitlin my movements. Or, worse still, would be a phone conversation that goes wrong: 'Oh no, you mustn't, Daniel. I'm just off to Paris with a new, er, friend. We just met last night.' Either way it's a risk. Romantic, foolhardy … whatever I'm being, it's too late to change my mind, at least when it comes to travel. For we're now filing on to the airplane in that quiet way that people always do. Something about the enormity of what's about to happen, perhaps. That this fairly small metal box we're stepping into will soon be several miles above the Atlantic, with us in it.

I have a sudden feeling of regret for the things I didn't get round to doing in New York. The people I'd have liked to hook up with, the plays and concerts I wouldn't get to. However, if it still doesn't work out with Caitlin, friends will be drifting back to London soon. It won't be so bad. It's summer, and I'll be able to leave my studio flat and sit in parks, or work on my laptop outside cafés. I'll meet a beautiful stranger, who'll have me over Caitlin in no time. But then I remember Caitlin's friendly and explanatory email. She's as keen to see me as I am her. All being well, I'll be spending the rest of the summer in Wales. And then what?

No, I decide, finding my window seat and settling myself in, best not to think beyond the end of the vacation. I give a curt nod to the young guy now seating himself beside me, then open the legal thriller I'd just bought in the bookstore. I always try to indicate, from the outset, that I don't intend to make idle chitchat for the duration of the flight. When my neighbour lowers his seat, clasps fingers on his chest and closes his eyes, I suspect he has the same policy.

I awake after a short doze, three and a half hours into the flight, and instantly think of Caitlin. Where she might be now, who she's with, how she's feeling. It occurs to me that she might be anxious or upset because she hasn't heard from me. Of course I should have sent a quick email, made a quick call, left a message with Zac, even. I curse myself for this impetuous journey, stranded mid-air as I am now. Unable to get in touch with her... Or am I? The guy beside me had been online on his laptop earlier. You pay a fortune for your short-notice ticket, but you do get broadband.

'Excuse me,' I say and he goes to stand up. 'No, sorry. I was wondering if I might use your internet to send a quick message?'

'Oh,' he says, frowning. I think I woke him. 'Er, yeah.'

From those three syllables I can tell he's British. 'Thanks,' I say, while he starts it up and hands it over. I search for Caitlin's website, click on the email link and write a simple and to-the-point, 'I'm on my way, but where are you? Daniel xx' – then send it quickly and hand the machine back, before I decide to stick to the surprise approach. Closer to the UK, I may ask for the computer again, to see if she's replied.

'Good book?' my neighbour asks, while he checks his own emails. He nods towards my lap.

'Yes,' I tell him, raising it to my face and finding my place before he asks what I do, how long I've been doing it, and then starts telling me what he does. 'Very.'

TWENTY-TWO

Joe Beth's late. Only five days late, but she tells me she's had a twenty-eight-day cycle, give or take a day, for twelve years. We've only known each other a few weeks and you'd think we'd both be in a major panic. But when Beth woke up this morning and still nothing had happened, and her boobs were sore and she felt sick, she'd just sat up and said, 'Well, if they burst, they burst.' She was talking about condoms. 'Fate, I expect.' She'd looked upwards when she said that. Sometimes I think Beth's more religious than she makes out.

Personally, I'm a bit dazed and can't quite believe it – maybe because it hasn't been confirmed yet – but I'm not distraught or anything. In a couple of weeks I'll be thirty, which isn't a bad age to become a parent. Some of the people I was at school with have got two or three kids. They're a bit wiped out, but happy. And tied down, obviously. But then, I'm not sure being tied down doesn't suit me. Over the past couple of days, the thing that's been pleasing me the most is that, if it turns out Beth is pregnant, I'm not likely to get the 'Look, Joe...' speech.

Do I love her? Yeah, I think so. Maybe. I wouldn't say I'm head over heels and all that, but I do really like her, and I feel comfortable with her. And, although she's not stunning in the way Charlotte is, Beth's definitely got inner beauty. Two days ago, for the first time in ages, I got my cameras out. I took loads of shots of Beth, and I could almost see that beauty more in the photos than in the flesh.

I think we'll be fine, me and Beth. There's been no arguing, no sulking since we met. That could come later, I suppose, when Beth's hormones go berserk. I think I've heard that happens. Or if I suddenly get cold feet. You never know.

Anyway, we're in town now buying a testing kit, and also, maybe a bit prematurely, a book on pregnancy. The book was my idea, because I want to know what I'm in for. Much more, it seems, than Beth does. 'It's like finding out all about the place you're going on holiday to,' she said, 'then having no surprises when you get there.' I think she's more worried about having to give up her sports. 'How will I fit in a canoe?' was one of the first things she'd come out with, panic in her eyes. One good thing is that there's this unspoken agreement that we're definitely having the baby. If it's there.

I can't believe how expensive the kit is, but we buy it anyway. When we get home, we read the instructions together, then Beth disappears to the loo, and within a minute of her coming back with the little stick thing, we know she's pregnant from the blue line that's appeared. We're sitting there at the kitchen table, the blue line between us, saying, 'Wow,' over and over, when Dad walks in.

Having just come out of a work binge, he's looking better than he has for a while. This is mainly because he's eating and showering and wearing proper outfits again. This morning his hair's wet and combed back off his face, giving him a bit of a teddy boy look.

He says, 'What consistently clement weather we're enjoying. Brunch, anyone? Thought I'd rustle up a chicken and asparagus omelette. What do you say, Beth?'

Beth's face goes odd and she excuses herself. Then she practically runs from the room and I think I hear her retch.

'Might be best not to talk food in the mornings,' I tell Dad, nodding Beth's way.

'Oh?' He opens a cupboard and takes out hot pepper sauce, Worcester sauce, *herbes de Provence* and a garlic bulb. 'Let's give it a bit of zing, eh?'

'Um, Dad.'

'Yes, Joe.' He turns towards me, his arms full of jars and garlic. 'Everything OK?'

'That depends on what you mean by OK. Er, do you think you could put those jars down? I don't want you dropping them.'

He does as I ask, then spots the plastic container on the table. 'Specimen bottle?'

'Pregnancy test.'

'Ah. Not something I've had first-hand experience of, ha ha. We left it to the experts to tell us.' He reaches into the fridge for eggs and leftover chicken, which he places on the counter before turning round again. 'Are you going to put me out of my misery?' he asks, a lock of hair flopping forward now, in a young Elvis way. Sometimes I see how good-looking he is. How it might not be just his way with words that lights women up.

I fiddle with the evidence and pull a face. 'I don't know if I should say, but since Beth's more or less living here and is probably going to be throwing up every morning, then ... yeah, it's positive.'

I don't know what I was expecting his reaction to be, but I really wasn't ready for bear hugs and tears. I've never seen him so emotional. Never seen him emotional, really. 'A grandchild,' he says, once he's let me go. 'How extraordinary. How utterly staggering.' He reverses in the direction of his ingredients, then suddenly stops. 'Tell me Beth's going to keep it?'

300

'Yeah, yeah. *We're* going to keep it. I'm just not sure where.'

'Oh,' says Dad. 'Not Wales, surely? Such a trek.'

'We haven't talked about it.'

'And we have all this space here, Joe.' He waves an arm, as though I hadn't noticed our space before.

'Yeah, I know. But we'll see. Listen, I'm just going to check on Beth. She's feeling queasy. The omelette, I think.'

'Ah.' He starts putting things away again. 'Well, we can't have that. Shall I conjure up some celebratory white toast?'

'Good idea.'

'I told Dad,' I tell Beth. She's lying on the bed looking lovely. I join her – the mother of my child to be. 'Hope you don't mind. He's really pleased and he's doing you white toast.'

'How sweet,' says Beth, rolling towards me. 'He'd make someone a wonderful husband, you know.'

'I keep telling him that but he doesn't believe me. He, er, said he'd like us to live here.'

Beth's face changes, as though she might be feeling pukey again. 'I was thinking we'd go back to Wales.'

'*Were* you?' I say, hearing a hint of something I don't like in my voice.

'Yes.'

'Oh.' I roll on to my back and fold my arms.

Beth does the same and we both stare at the ceiling. I'm wondering if we're on the verge of our first argument, when Dad shouts, 'Toast up!' and we make our way downstairs in silence.

Caitlin I give up on trying to get hold of Zac. Each time I phone I get me, asking me to leave a message. I've been trying since last night and have left so many messages, I've run my mobile down. How stupid of me not to bring my charger. Would they charge it up for me in a shop somewhere? You'd think you'd be able to find someone to do that in London. But then I'd have to leave the phone with them, and it might get nicked.

I decide I'll phone home from a call box next time, tell Zac my mobile's dead. It's a drag, and it's also worrying, not being able to get hold of him. Frankie's not answering his phone to me either. Perhaps Zac told him he'd let slip about the under-age girlfriend. Is anyone taking care of the animals? That's my biggest worry. I'd also like to be told Daniel has phoned or emailed. I could go to an internet café, I know, but there's a big part of me doesn't want to find no message from him. And even if there's no email, I still won't know if there's been a call from him. Talk about frustrating.

I'm feeling more and more cross as I take the tube to Camden, the piece of paper with Daniel's address on scrunched up in a pocket. The last-minute decision to come to London, after all, was turning out to be a mistake, but now I'm here I may as well go and see this flat. The building, anyway. I'm booked into a hotel that was offering a good deal, and had planned to take in some exhibitions and just generally wander around soaking up the city for two days. But now, once I've got this quest out the way, I'll have to go straight back to Oxford, pick up my car and drive home. Unless someone answers my home phone, that is. I have visions of Zac all tangled up in the machine again, or electrocuted by my old and frayed iron flex. Zac would never iron his own things, but I'd shown him how to neaten out the children's clothes, once they're finished. How many times have I almost bought another iron? And where the hell is Frankie?

I get off at Camden Town, step out into a hot and busy street and follow the *A–Z* I'd picked up at Paddington. Down Camden Road, turn right, left, right. I'm in Daniel's street now. Huge old houses, trees. Everything's neat, which I wasn't expecting. I find his building, then walk up the path and steps to see if his name is by the doorbells.

But it's all numbers you have to punch in, and no names. His is Flat 16. It's tempting to press one and six, but what's the point when he's not here? Instead, I go across the street and look at the four storeys, wondering if he has one of the big bay windows, or one of the flat windows to the left – or if he's tucked away somewhere at the back of the house.

As I stare, I visualise coming and visiting Daniel. The two of us strolling up the path and steps, hand in hand, after a lovely night out. They say if you picture something strongly enough it will happen. But then I come back to my senses and shake my head. What am I doing here?

Daniel Following a remarkably good night's sleep in my own bed, I'd had strong coffee and a light breakfast before taking a deep breath and dialling Caitlin's number. I'd gotten her voicemail and gone a little weak at the knees. Being unprepared, I didn't leave a message. Maybe later. I'd then tried her cellphone but wasn't able to connect. After the build-up, it had been a little disappointing not to get to talk to her. Perhaps she's still in Oxford, I'd thought, or feeding the chickens, or ... please, no ... in Paris with a new friend.

Feeling at a loose end, I'd vacuumed the flat, then gone to the local store for fresh food. After both the vacuuming and the outing, I'd tried Caitlin's numbers again. If I've had no luck by this evening, I decided, I'd call Joe's place.

Now, having spent a good hour catching up on email correspondence (nothing from Caitlin – I'd checked last night) and online news, I'm shutting down the computer and considering just heading for North Wales, come what may.

I stand up and rub at a twinge in my back, then drink the last dregs of cold coffee. Should I make another pot and a sandwich, or simply go out for lunch? Already, I'm suffering cabin fever in my tiny London home. And the day looks good. I bend a little and peer through the window at the sky. There are one or two clouds, but the forecast is for constant sunshine. Whoever said British weather is miserable had obviously never been here. Even in Wales it had been pretty good. Wales ... shall I just go? Hope she's there and pleased to see me? Lovely Caitlin, with her dark shiny hair and trim figure. In fact, just like the woman I'm watching in the street below, tugging a large red bag further up her shoulder, then turning and walking away. I stick my head out the raised sash window and screw my eyes up against the sunshine. The woman is so much like Caitlin, it's remarkable.

'Huh,' I say, pulling back into the room

and shaking my head. Now I'm imagining I'm seeing her. I must have it bad.

After an early sandwich-bar lunch and a stroll around the market – all the while thinking about what to do – I return to the flat and try Caitlin again. I should leave a message, but would that complicate things if I'm just going to shoot up there? I click the phone off with a thumb, then the tone tells me I have a message. It's from Warren, a work colleague I'd emailed a reply to earlier.

Finally, I take out the number Zac had given me for Joe and tap it out. It rings several times, then I hear Julian's upper-crust voice telling me that unfortunately they're unable to answer my call, but would be 'delighted' to receive a message from me. I hang up and decide it's just one of those days. The whole world's busy and doesn't want to talk to me. Apart from Warren, the industrial revolution expert, who seems a little too desperate to 'go for a few jars and catch up' this evening.

I could maybe go to Oxford, see if Caitlin's still there. And if not, stay over-night somewhere, then head for Bangor on the train tomorrow. This feels like a good plan, and before long I've ordered a cab and repacked the smaller of my two cases, remembering to throw in the perfume I'd bought at the airport. This may go awry, but

306

anything's better than sitting around dialling Caitlin's number and going for a few
jars with Warren, as nice as he is.

Joe I'm surprised when Cait walks in the
Italian Job with her overnight bag on her
shoulder, since she only left for London this
morning.
'Change your mind about going?' I ask.
'Er, no. I went and came back. Now I need
to go home because I can't get hold of anyone there and I'm worried about the
animals. Zac may have gone off somewhere
thinking Frankie's around, and Frankie
might have done the same thinking Zac's
around, and I'm really too anxious to enjoy
exhibitions. Anyway, I just thought I'd call
in to say goodbye and thanks for putting me
up. And also to have a bite to eat. It's a long
old journey.'
'I know.'
'Of course you do.'
'Take a seat,' I say, 'and I'll get a menu.'
'Thanks. But I don't suppose I could use
your phone first?
'Sure.' I point to where it is behind the
counter, and while I set a place for one and
stand a menu on the smallest of our tables,
I watch Cait bite her lip as she waits for
someone to pick up at the other end.
'No,' she says, coming and sitting down.
'No answer still.'

'There's probably some reasonable explanation,' I say, although I can't think of one. I'm dying to tell Cait my news, our news, but Beth and I have decided all prospective grandparents should be informed first. We're planning to go up and see Beth's parents this weekend, not that Carlo knows that yet. He's not happy that Beth's off sick today, since the second of the new waiters has now left. Beth said she couldn't face the smell of tomatoes and herbs, not even in the afternoon. I'd thought morning sickness meant just that, but apparently not.

Cait rushes through her pasta dish, then tips too generously and goes to catch a bus to my house and her car. I'd told her it wouldn't be much fun in rush hour with a big bag, but she was keen to get off and didn't want to hang around for a taxi.

'See you in Wales at the weekend!' I call after her, then kick myself when I see Carlo's wild eyes staring my way. Suddenly, living in another country seems a good idea.

At six, I take a two-hour break and go home. I'd expected to find Dad feeding Beth those plain crackers she likes now and trying to talk her into living with him. But, instead, to my astonishment, there's Daniel in the reclining leather chair. He's talking to Beth, who's stretched out on the sofa and looking pale. My first thought is that if she's like this early on in the pregnancy, what will she be like at eight months? It seems a bit odd, considering how robust she is.

'How are you?' I say to Daniel. 'Aren't you in the States?' I go and give Beth a kiss and she makes room for me.

'Cut it short to come back and do some work,' says Daniel. 'And to try and track down Caitlin. No one's answering the phone in Wales. I'd heard she was here, but now Beth tells me she's in London.'

'Not any longer,' I tell him. 'She's on her way back to Wales. Didn't she call in here when she picked up her car?' I ask Beth.

'Maybe. Your dad and I were out.'

'You were?'

Beth grins. 'He took me up to the mat– er, hospital. Said it was one of the best.'

'Yeah, it is.' Dad will get Beth to change her mind, even if I can't. 'And so close by. Not like up in–'

'Yeah, yeah, I know,' says Beth, rolling her eyes but still smiling at me. We hear Daniel cough.

'Caitlin,' he says. 'I must have just missed her, dammit. Is she driving?'

'Yeah,' I say. 'Listen, she might stop some-where and pick up messages. Why not try her mobile?'

'I have,' he says. 'Several times today. No luck.'

I look over at the TV corner, where Cait

309

used to charge up her phone. There's the charger, still plugged in. 'She's hopeless with that phone,' I tell him.

'So I'm discovering.'

'Daniel wondered if he could stay here tonight,' says Beth. She's propped herself up and is looking a bit brighter. I think this nausea thing comes and goes. 'I said of course he could.'

'Yep, that's great. I'd suggest all going out for something to eat if I wasn't working and if Beth wasn't suffering from–'

'A bug,' she says quickly.

'That's OK,' Daniel says. 'I'm still a little jet-lagged. Might go for an early night, then take a train to Bangor tomorrow. Or rent a car.'

'I'll go and change the sheets,' I say. 'Cait was sleeping there.'

'No need,' says Daniel. 'Honestly.'

We all jump when the front door bangs open. There's another bang, then Dad shouts, 'Come and give me a hand, someone? Not you, Beth!'

Daniel and I get up and go to the hallway, where Dad's holding an enormous brown box that looks as though it might hold flat-pack furniture.

A cot,' he puffs. 'For the baby.'

'Baby?' asks Daniel.

TWENTY-THREE

Caitlin I'm in a B & B near Shrewsbury, having given up on the driving yesterday, on account of being knackered and a danger to other drivers. I don't know why I was so tired. Emotional exhaustion or something. I'd stopped around eight, got my room for the night, tried calling home again and fallen asleep early. Now, refreshed, I'm wading through everything on the breakfast menu, expecting empty cupboards and fridge at home. It's good and I take my time.

I pay up and hit the road around eleven, with ten times the vitality I'd had last night, and about twice the anxiety. Still no luck with the phones. I can tell from my slow speed that I'm no longer that keen to see my house, my livestock, my business. Different scenarios drift through my head, one after the other. Then they repeat themselves. It's like a never-ending horror slide show. Listening to the radio or my old cassettes doesn't help, and neither does the fact that the day is ominously dark and threatening rain. Increasingly so. It had been nice and sunny in Shropshire.

By the time I reach Bethesda, I'm certain

311

my entire place has burned down, and that the charred remains of bodies are being bagged up by policemen who can't get hold of me because my mobile's dead. But then, ten minutes on, I spot my pretty flinty house in the distance, and as I drive up the lane can see that the chickens and tethered goats are still alive and not eating each other. The vegetables look healthy – so many runner beans! – as does Merlin, bounding out of the house at the sound of my car.

After turning off the engine, I sit for a while and just stare at the dog doing his usual contortions. Everything's fine, after all. How annoying. I could be back in London, doing cultured things, spending money I haven't got. But then, there is still the business of the phone not being answered. And ... well, so far, no actual humans have come to greet me.

I get out of the car, play at cuddles with Merlin, then follow him into the house, holding my breath as I step into the hall. 'Hello?' I call out. It feels chilly and unlived in. 'Hello?'

In the kitchen, Merlin goes straight to his dried food and water. Someone's been feeding him, then. 'Hello?' I call out again, back in the hall and approaching the sitting room. 'Anyone home?'

Everything's relatively tidy and there's even a vase of fresh flowers in the fireplace.

Frankie wouldn't have done that. Maybe Zac's into flowers as well as sewing now. Or perhaps some house-proud squatter has done everyone in and taken over.

Merlin's at my heels all the time, even when I go up the stairs. If only dogs could talk, he'd be able to fill me in. 'Well, this man with a gun came and...' I push at my work-room door and it squeaks in a way that I'm sure it didn't used to. There's a half-made garment dangling from the machine, but nothing unusual in that. There's also a musty air, so I go and open a window. Through it I see a white car approach and my heart immediately starts thumping. A white car? I don't know anyone with a white car. Who could it be? The squatter?

Don't be ridiculous, I tell myself. I ruffle Merlin's ears and say, 'Come on. Let's go and see who it is.'

Out on the landing, the spare-room door is open a little, so I give it a gentle push in passing. What I see sends a chill through my every bone. There, lying on the bed, perfectly still and as white as the sheet beneath him, is Zac. Merlin barks twice and Zac still doesn't move. I think he's dead. The car's beside the house now and I hear a door slam.

'Oh, Zac,' I whisper. 'I'm so sorry.' I look down at Merlin and say, 'Go! Attack!', pointing in the direction of the stairs. But either Merlin doesn't get it or he hasn't

313

greeted me enough yet. There are noises downstairs and I begin shaking. Zac still hasn't moved. I don't know what to do but think I should hide. I hear steps on the stairs and can't see anywhere to go but under the bed. The bed with a body on it. After three strides on tiptoe I'm there and crouching, then flattening myself and sliding under the old cast-iron frame of my grandmother's. But there are books and other accumulated things and I can't get that far back.

Footsteps creak nearer. One door squeaks open, then another. Now Merlin's barking again and trying to squeeze under the bed with me. I see shoes coming nearer, then a voice saying, 'Hey, what's the matter, buster?' in an American accent. Then Daniel's face is sideways near the floor and looking at mine. I'm not sure who's the most shocked, but I think it's him.

'*Jesus*, Caitlin. What are you doing under there?'

'I think Zac's dead,' I whisper.

'No, man,' comes a ghostly voice from above. 'It's like *really* bad flu.'

Daniel While Caitlin's showering off the dust she'd gathered under the bed, I heat up some canned soup for Zac, who claims he hasn't eaten for days. I take it to him and he manages a spoonful before falling horizontal again. Beside the bed are boxes of different

314

painkillers – aspirin, Co-codamol, ibuprofen – and I wonder if he's been overdoing the drug-taking. When his eyes close, I scoop them up and exit with the soup bowl, still warm and full.

My timing is perfect, for I catch Caitlin leaving the bathroom in only a short towel. Her hair is dripping on to her shoulders and down her face, and she gives me an embarrassed smile. It's a lovely sight, and if I were a different type of man I'd ask if she'd like help drying off. I say, 'No appetite yet,' and nod at the bowl in my hand.

'Oh dear,' she says, padding along the hall and to her room. Will she stop, look over her shoulder and invite me in? And am I, in fact, ready for her to do that? 'Smells good,' she adds, not turning. 'If there's any left, I'll have some.'

Sure.

I return to the kitchen a little relieved. No point in rushing things, just because we've missed each other. We'd hugged for a full minute beside the not-dead Zac, but Caitlin had been conscious of the dust and cobwebs, and goodness knows what, in her hair and on her clothes.

When I sneezed, Caitlin laughed and pulled away, and Zac groaned, 'That's how this starts, man. One sneeze.'

Caitlin emerges looking fresh and lovely,

315

and wearing earrings and a touch of lipstick. I feel flattered, and also hopeful, as we sit sipping at soup and laughing over our recent communications problems.

'I just checked my emails,' says Caitlin. 'Zac deleted your last message for some reason. The one saying, "On my way." So, even if I'd checked, I wouldn't have found it.'

'Perhaps it was flu delirium.'

'Mm. Anyway, you're here now and I'm ... well, it's great that you're are.'

'Yeah?' I ask. We're still a bit wary, I can tell. Still shy with each other.

'Yes,' she says, smiling prettily at me again. 'Now, tell me about your trip.'

'It was boring as hell.'

'Really? I'm glad I didn't take you up on that offer, then.'

'But it wouldn't have been boring with you there.'

She laughs and I can see I fell into a bit of a trap. 'Thank you,' she says.

We talk about Frankie for a while. Caitlin is worried that he's got himself another very young girlfriend. 'Last year, when he was sixteen, he was hanging out with a fourteen-year-old girl. I saw it as innocent, but I couldn't be sure.'

'Some people think it's a grey area. You know, fourteen-to-sixteen-year-olds.'

I look over at the half-emptied red bag, sitting by the door and suddenly recall a woman with a red bag. 'So, what did you do in London?' I ask, partly to change the subject from underage sex. 'Joe said you went for the day.'

'Oh, this and that,' she says with a dismissive wave.

'Only, I thought I saw you.'

Caitlin stops sipping at her soup, looks up at me and blushes. 'Where?'

'Camden.'

'Er, yeah ... yeah, I was there for a while.'

She came to my street. Came to check out where I lived. That's so sweet, I want to get up and hug her again. I want to tell her that she should have buzzed my buzzer. Instead, I reach across the table and lay my hand on hers. 'I know it's not the best of weather, but how about a walk after lunch? Unless you have work to do?'

Caitlin's face slowly goes back to pale. 'Bugger the work,' she says.

We finish our lunch and begin clearing the table, when we hear the sound of a car. Caitlin raises her eyebrows at me, and I follow her through two doors and out to where an old Citroën is pulling up beside my rented car. First Frankie gets out, then from the driver's side appears a woman, who bends and collapses her seat to unbuckle a child of around two and help it jump the short distance to the ground.

'Hi, Frankie,' says Caitlin.

Frankie's clearly surprised to see us and shoves his hands in his trouser pockets. 'Er, this is Delia,' he says. 'My er...' He's nodding at a woman who might just remember being fourteen, and who actually looks a bit like Caitlin, only younger. But perhaps not that much. 'And this is her daughter, Olivia.' He introduces Caitlin and me to his whatever she is, and we all make our way back into the house, because it's not only miserable out now, but raining too.

'We've been coming over twice a day to see to things,' Frankie's telling his mom, 'since Zac's been faking flu.'

Caitlin, meanwhile, still has her furrowed brow. Once everyone's seated and I've put the kettle on for tea, I hear her say, 'I'm sorry, Frankie, I don't quite understand. Are you and ... and...' I wander back into the sitting room.

'Delia,' says Delia.

'Delia, sorry. Are you ... an item?'

'Er, yeah,' says Frankie, an arm slung around his woman on the sofa. 'Been together five weeks and two days.'

'Only five weeks?' asks Delia. 'It feels longer.'

I think she's giving me the eye, so don't see this relationship lasting. But long enough to give Caitlin and me some time, I hope.

While little Olivia takes lumps of coal from the scuttle, the aroma of diaper is filling the room. This is a far cry from the reunion I'd dreamed of on the airplane. 'Anyone for sugar?' I ask.

Caitlin My son's girlfriend is Welsh, wears vaguely hippy clothes and works in a nursery. The type that sells plants. Her daughter is adorable, if wilful, and seems to like Frankie a lot, even though he gently pushes her away when she comes to him, and cuddles her mother instead. At an opportune moment, I ask Frankie to come and help me with something in the vegetable patch, but once we're outside and out of earshot, I say, 'What on earth are you up to, Frankie? Or should I say, what's she up to?'

'What?'

'The age gap, of course. It's not on, Frankie and it has to end. Why is that women going out with someone so young?'

'Er, pots and kettles, Mum,' he says before turning back towards the house. And, anyway, she's only twenty-six.' Olivia runs towards him with her arms wide open, obviously wanting to be picked up. 'Where's your mum?' he says, and the toddler follows him through the door.

I want to shout, 'At least Joe wasn't a schoolboy!' but Frankie's gone. He'll never get his A levels now. He'll get ribbed by his friends all the time, then cradle-snatching Delia will have him childminding and

DIYing and giving her another baby before he knows it. I'm standing there, hands on my hips, wondering where I've gone wrong, when Daniel comes out of the house and my insides do a little spin at the sight of him. At the same time, a face pops out of an upstairs window.

'Have you got the drugs, Daniel?' asks Zac.

I feel my expression turn back to a scowl. Has Daniel brought cannabis, or worse, to my house? I may adore him, but how dare he?

'It's bad to take too many painkillers,' Daniel calls up to Zac. 'I've hidden them.'

'Oh, man,' says Zac, his head disappearing.

Daniel and I are discussing the weather, when Frankie and his new family emerge and head for the Citroën.

'Cheers for the tea,' says Frankie. 'Does this mean I don't have to come and do everything tomorrow?'

'Yes, it does,' says Daniel, quicker than I can.

It occurs to me that I don't know where they're going. 'Hang on,' I say and rush into the house for pen and paper. I'm going to pay her off, I'll need this woman's contact details.

I'd been wrong on three counts. I'd thought

Zac was dead, Daniel was in America and Frankie was dating a pubescent. I'd never been so pleased to see someone as I had Daniel, or less pleased to see someone as I had Delia. Hearing Zac talk had come about halfway.

Now, as Daniel and I quietly clear away the dinner things, all alone – Zac having recovered enough to slouch down the stairs and aim for the pub – I'm beginning to think I might have been wrong on a fourth count. That there's some simmering grand-passion thing going on between me and Daniel. Because, so far, we've had one cuddle and two pecks on cheeks. He's attractive and warm and kind and easy to talk to, so why don't I just jump on him? He's cut his holiday short and come all this way, so why hasn't he jumped on me? It's my house, I suppose, so he might be holding back out of politeness.

We've talked about all sorts of things, and we've laughed and given each other affectionate looks, and we've downed enough wine to throw all inhibitions aside. So, what is it? Could it be we've reverted to the relationship we had when he was staying here, and don't know how to move it on?

'Anything on TV?' he asks as he fills the dishwasher.

'Ooh, *déjà vu*,' I say, hand on my chest.

Daniel stops and looks at me, a dirty plate

321

in either hand.

'Yeah,' he says with a sigh. I get the impression he's as disappointed or baffled, or whatever, as I am.

'There might be something on Film Four,' I say. I give him a big smile and he smiles back. Maybe it'll be all right, after all, although I can't stop thinking about where he's going to sleep. When he'd gone for a shower before dinner, I'd quickly changed Frankie's sheets and semi-tidied his room. Just in case. I'd felt that putting Daniel back out in the guest accommodation would be the death of us. If we don't fall into my bed together, better to have him near enough to creep to my room in the night. Or vice versa.

'I'll go and check it out,' he says, slotting the plates in the rack, then squeezing past me without touching.

We're where we were a month ago. Daniel in the armchair, me on the sofa. I'm saying things like, 'Is it too loud for you?' He's saying things like, 'He's never been my favourite director, but this isn't bad.' There's a bowl of cashew nuts on the coffee table, which we take it in turns to dip into, so our fingers don't touch. When he goes to the bathroom during an ad break, my shoulders relax for the first time since dinner. After weeks of regret and angst and frustration, this shouldn't be happening. I'm close to crying but know I mustn't. Perhaps more wine would help.

'Do you really want to watch TV?' Daniel asks, when he comes back and sits in the worn-out chair with its threadbare cover.

'Not if you don't,' I say, and begin to feel even more tense. What would we do instead? A board game? I find the remote and switch the film I haven't been following off. Then Daniel comes and sits beside me on the sofa and takes my hand.

'Hi,' he says.

'Hi.'

'It all feels kinda strange, doesn't it?'

'Yes,' I say. 'But I don't know why.' He's caressing my skin lightly with his fingers. It's nice and it's comforting, and I feel relief flood through me.

'Perhaps the transition from friends to ... more than friends, gets harder the longer you've known each other.'

'Mm,' I say. 'Perhaps.'

'We could just give it a little more time. The adjustment, I mean.'

'We could,' I say. 'Or ... it's just an idea I had. Earlier this evening. That we could...'

'Yes?'

'Well ... start from the beginning.'

'Oh?' says Daniel.

TWENTY-FOUR

Joe The trouble is, there are so many plusses. The air is good, the way of life is more relaxed and the property is still reasonably priced. If I sold my half of the business, we could buy a little house outright. Beth would take maternity leave, then go back to teaching. I'd try and make something of my photography, and maybe find something else to do too. Nothing in the catering line, though. Beth and her family are trying hard to sell the idea to me, and it's more and more tempting.

'We could keep chickens and grow vegetables,' Beth's saying now. 'Like Cait.'

'Are you calling Cait a vegetable?' I ask, and Beth hits me. I'd rather she didn't hit me on such a steep incline, but the man in me won't mention it. One good thing about the pregnancy is that it's bound to slow Beth down. Eventually. Having found a homeopathic cure for morning sickness, she's back to her old energetic self. The one that doubles in energy when she's back in the mountains. It's an effort to keep up and my thighs ache, but we'll soon get to the hill fort and burial chambers that Beth's aiming for. It's becoming more and more windy as we reach the craggy moorland, where people a lot hardier than me once built their settlement. I don't know how much fun I'm having, but it's good to see Beth full of life again. I'm worried that her pace might induce a miscarriage, but if I say that she'll think I'm just flagging and want to slow down.

We reach the remains of the hill fort and I make all the right noises about how interesting and amazing it is, all the while wanting to get back to the cosy tea shop I'd spotted, next to where we'd parked. Beth might make an outdoorsy type of me, but it'll take time.

'Won't it be great bringing the baby up here?' she shouts against the wind. 'He or she will love it. You know, when it's aged two or something.'

I look down at the steep rocky path and wonder if you'd get a pushchair over it. Because no way am I carrying a dead-weight toddler up here.

We arrive back at the house as dinner's being prepared. Beth's family is great, even if they do keep breaking into Welsh. Her mother, Annie, is a teacher too. She's about to go part time and has said more than once how useful she'll make herself once the baby's come. No one here's commented on how quickly all this has happened. That was the first thing my mother said on the phone: Are you sure about this, Joe? So soon. What if you're not right for each other?' I said even if you're with someone for years, they might not be right for you. 'Like you and Dad.' She sort of came round then, and asked when I was going to bring Beth to Ireland, and if I wanted her to start knitting.

We sit down to a lamb casserole and there's talk of playing cards later. It's very cosy and comforting in this ramshackle family home, where nothing ever gets put away and the conservatory's full of guinea pigs and recycling boxes, and you trip over shoes, leaflets and brollies every time you come in the house. Well, I do. Beth's younger sisters, both in their early twenties, have left home, so it's just the four of them now.

I don't know how good I'll be at cards, but I can't see anyone making fun of me if I'm crap. They're all so nice, even the seventeen-year-old Ioan, but especially Tom, Beth's father. Tom is thoughtful and hospitable and very interested in me, but in a way that's never overbearing. He laughs a lot and cracks terrible jokes, but maybe you have to when you spend your days trying to rehabilitate drug addicts. It's all very reassuring, I decide, when it comes to the baby's genes. My dad's brains and Beth's dad's nature would be a perfect mix.

I'm avoiding thinking about Dad. He'd be

gutted if he knew what plans we were hatching up here. We'll have to break it to him gently, or wait till he's busy working on something and forgotten all about the baby. But then, we haven't made a final decision. Although Beth looks as though she might have, sitting across the table from me with a healthy happy glow, surrounded by her nice family. She gives me a big beautiful smile and I realise for the first time... properly realise, that is... that I do love her. Which is a bit of a relief.

'Did you get plenty of lamb, Joe?' asks Tom, peering over at my plate.

'Yes, thanks.' I notice I've got a bigger portion of stew than anyone else. I think they like me.

Ralph Lenny and Dog drove me to Lincoln. They didn't have to. Hilary would have come and got me, but not till the weekend. It might have meant Hilary meeting Luna too, and that could have been strained, even though nothing carnal had gone on with Luna. She cried when I left the boat with Lenny and Dog, both of them carrying my stuff, on account of my fingers.

At the first service station stop, I told Lenny and Dog how good it was of them to do this, and Lenny said anything was better than spending the day in his shithole of a home with his ugly wife and screaming kids,

327

and Dog had been laid off and only had a room in a shared house where someone had nicked his telly. So, basically, I was doing them a favour, which made me feel better.

I introduced them to Hilary, who brought us all coffee and Hobnobs, and then to my very ill mother-in-law in the converted garage. I thought Marjorie was going to have a seizure or pass away on the spot when she saw Dog, who isn't what you'd call pretty. Her mouth dropped open unattractively and her grey rheumy eyes flickered in a sort of terrified way, until Dog said, 'Pleased to meet you, and may I say what a lovely nightie you're wearing. Just your colour.' She held her hand out for him to shake or kiss, then couldn't take her eyes off Lenny's studs and tattoos. It's not something you see in our cul-de-sac. They left after dinner, or 'tea' as they called it, and then there I was, back in my home, which Hilary is pumping a lump sum into and which I hadn't realised I liked so much.

At the moment, despite my finger problem, I'm trying to make the rotary washing line stand up straight, instead of at forty-five degrees. I take rocks (a bit awkwardly) from the rockery behind the pond and place them at the bottom of the washing-line pole. I'm going back for rock number four, when one of the small slabs edging the pond wobbles beneath my right foot, which leads to me doing a kind of tightrope, arms-out type balancing thing. I calculate there's a fifty-fifty chance that I'll end up in the four-foot-three-inch-deep pond. I know it's that depth because I made it. 'Ralph!' I hear, then the sound of heavy footsteps and the familiar feel of Dog's arm round me and his breath in my ear. What will they do? Push me in just for the hell of it, or hold my head under the water till I go limp? Someone's tugging at my T-shirt and suddenly I'm on the lawn, flat on my back.

'For goodness' sake, Ralph,' says Hilary. She's kneeling beside me, panting. 'I can see I'll have to follow you everywhere you go.'

I lift myself up on to my elbows and look into her kind eyes. 'If you wouldn't mind,' I say.

TWENTY-FIVE

Caitlin I find my room without any help and draw the curtains against the blazing sun. After a long traffic-jammed drive, I'd had to leave the car at Joe's place, since there's no free parking in town, and catch a bus. It's hot and I'm exhausted, so I go and lie on the single bed, hoping to grab a nap before 'Afternoon Tea and Introductions'.

This will be followed by dinner in college and outdoor Shakespeare in another college. The leaflet doesn't tell me which play, but I'm hoping for nothing taxing.

I wake, remember where I am and feel pleasantly jittery. After showering and dressing – simple white top, cream skirt, expensive flip-flops – I dry my hair, put lipstick, mascara and a dash of blusher on, then make my way over to the hall.

Val greets me with a handshake, a wink and a, 'Welcome back. You're a little late, but never mind.' She ushers me towards a group of ten or twelve people, already standing in a circle. 'Now,' she says, 'when the ball comes your way, say your name and tell us, briefly if you please, something about yourself. Here goes!' She lobs the ball towards a small woman in sensible sandals.

'I'm Lorraine,' the woman tells us. 'And I come from Durham.'

She goes to throw the ball, but Val says, 'No, no, dear. Not that brief.'

'Oh, sorry.' Lorraine blushes and adds that she's divorced and a chiropractor. 'Is that enough?' she asks nervously.

'Yes,' says Val with a charming smile. 'Thank you. Now, throw the ball, there's a good girl.'

It sort of comes my way and I snatch it before the man next to me has a chance. 'Hi,

I'm Caitlin,' I tell them. 'I'm from North Wales, where I work at home making children's clothes and running a very small small-holding. In fact, my son calls it a tinyholding, ha ha.' There are some polite chuckles, while I think of the newly single Frankie, asking if he could come with me. 'Don't they do a week for the under-eighteens?' I'd told him I'd suggest it to Val, who's now sighing and saying, 'Caitlin, dear. The ball?'

I apologise and throw it to the man directly opposite. 'I'm Daniel,' he says, 'from New England, but currently working in London. I so enjoyed my first stay on one of Val's weeks, I've come back for another.' There's more laughter, then Daniel throws the ball on. Who to, I don't know. Or care. Daniel and I just stand smiling at one another, while the others give their potted stories.

'Hi, I'm Liz,' I hear and my head spins to the left. Liz? 'I too have been on one of these weeks before. I came with a friend, who's recently met someone on the internet, lucky devil.' More chuckles. Anyway, I'm a retired palaeontologist, although I still keep my hand in part time. Oh, and I live in Suffolk.' She throws the ball to the tall man opposite, who misses it because his eyes are on Liz's breasts.

He retrieves the ball from beneath a table and returns to the circle not looking the least embarrassed. 'Hello,' he says. 'I'm Julian, and an academic for my sins. Worse still, a mathematician. I've lived in Oxford most of my very long adult life, and would be pleased to show those interested some of the city's delightful hidden treasures.'

'Ooh, yes, please,' says Lorraine from Durham.

But as he continues, Julian's gaze is still on Liz. Just as hers is very firmly on him. 'I have a large, vastly modernised, soon to be empty house,' he says, 'and would very much like to find an ideal partner to share it with. Someone with limitless patience, who understands the foibles of a slightly nutty professor.'

I sense several women are wanting to put their hands up, but Val says, 'Would you like to throw the ball now, Julian?' and we're suddenly listening to Peter from Andover, who's between jobs but keeps himself busy with model aeroplanes.

We're among the last to pin our tags on. Daniel says, 'Pretty name.'

'Thank you.'

'Welsh?'

'Yes. And did I hear you're from New England?'

'Uh-huh.'

'I've always wanted to go–' My eyes land on the one remaining name tag. It says 'Derek'.

332

I put a hand on Daniel to steady myself.

'What?' he asks, just as a guy in long shorts bounds into the hall and apologises to Val for being late. He's short and grey and not a bit like Ralph. I breathe easy again and let go of Daniel.

'Nothing,' I say.

'Not another headache?'

I laugh. 'No.'

'Looking forward to the Shakespeare, Cait?' asks Val, rather pointedly, I feel.

'Yes,' I lie. 'What is it, by the way?'

'*A Comedy of Errors,*' says Derek, who seems to know a lot for a latecomer.

I laugh and say, 'Perfect!'

'The story of our summer,' agrees Daniel.

Val tuts. 'No, no, dears. That's at Worcester, but we're going to Trinity. *All's Well that Ends Well.*' She gives us a nice wrinkly wink and says, 'Much more apt!'

'So,' says Daniel, beaming at me. 'Are you coming this time?'

'Oh, yes.'

'Let's hope the heavens don't open,' says Val, before striding away and tapping a spoon on a cup for silence. 'Now, everyone make your way to the refreshments, if you wouldn't mind. Then take your tea and sandwiches to the table on the left.'

We queue and pile our plates and take a cup of tea each, then head for the table. Lorraine from Durham smiles sweetly and pats the seat beside her, just as Daniel is passing. I stop dead and give her a look. I don't think she'll be doing that again.

This Large Print Book, for people
who cannot read normal print,
is published under the auspices of

THE ULVERSCROFT FOUNDATION

... we hope you have enjoyed this book.
Please think for a moment about those
who have worse eyesight than you ...
and are unable to even read or enjoy
Large Print without great difficulty.

You can help them by sending a
donation, large or small, to:

**The Ulverscroft Foundation,
1, The Green, Bradgate Road,
Anstey, Leicestershire, LE7 7FU,
England.**
or request a copy of our brochure for
more details.

The Foundation will use all donations
to assist those people who are visually
impaired and need special attention
with medical research, diagnosis
and treatment.

Thank you very much for your help.